TAMZIN ATKINS

Published by: Flame Light Book Publishing, Cape
Town, South Africa
Editing: Hannah Dinklemann
Interior Design: Amy Hoffmann, Amy Hoffmann
Designs, Cape Town
Cover Design: Amy Hoffmann, Amy Hoffmann
Designs, Cape Town

ISBN: 978-0-6399459-0-3 (print)
ISBN: 978-0-6399459-1-0 (epub)

Dedication

I dedicate this book to God. When I wanted to give up on writing, He gave me this story. I finally realised I had a choice to make, and that it was to write.

To my friends who help: Amy, Hannah, and Bjorn for their support and all of their hard work, and to Stacey Underwood and Chane Keese for reading this and following me on the journey of writing.

I also want to give thanks to Grant Ross and Melissa Haiden for being the voice of my characters in my videos and bringing them off the pages into something more real.

Prologue

The trees were blowing in the wind as colourful leaves dropped off branches and floated to the ground all around them. A small hand reached out and caught a bright orange leaf floating to the ground. The cool breeze around them was blowing her auburn locks in her face.

"Did you catch it, Bella?"

Bella smiled a toothless smile and looked up at her father standing behind her. He had a smile plastered on his normally serious face, one just for her. She showed him her orange leaf and placed it the pile with the others they had already collected.

"Daddy, why do the leaves fall off the tree?" asked Bella.

Her father knelt down in front of her and touched her chilly red nose. "Because everything needs a new beginning and we can't start our new begin- ning with the old things holding us back."

She scrunched up her nose in confusion.

"I don't get it. When I grow up I want to be smart like you."

Her father chuckled and pulled her into a hug, Bella giggled in return and wrapped her small arms around his neck.

Arabella McCullen opened her eyes in confusion, her heart beating fast as the constant ringing in her ears woke her up. Her sleep-muddled brain tried to figure out what the noise was before realising that the phone was ringing next to her. She peered out of her cocoon of blankets at the room, still bathed in darkness. Bella stretched out her hand and fumbled for the phone lying on the bedside table. She let out a tired yawn and answered the phone, trying to stay awake to listen to the voice on the other end.

"Hello, is this the McCullen Residence?" repeated the dark husky Irish voice on the other end.

"Yes, it is," mumbled Bella, confused and drowsy.

Bella blinked open her eyes and shifted slightly so that she was leaning against the headboard. The alarm clock next to her bed was blinking 5: 45. She focused back on the caller, trying to understand what he had just been telling her.

"I am sorry to tell you this over the phone Miss, but it is an urgent matter at hand. Mrs. Cathella McCullen has passed away the early hours of yester- day morning and I'm calling you because I have this residency listed under family."

Bella took the phone away from her ear and looked at the unfamiliar num- ber. It had to be some kind of mistake or some kid playing a prank on her.

"I'm sorry, who did you say was calling?" asked Bella.

The person on the other end sounded increasingly frustrated as he replied again.

"Aye, I didn't say, lass. I am Cathella's solicitor. I am calling from the Mc- Cullen residence in Cork Ireland, and I have the name Scott McCullen under 'son.' Is this the right number?" questioned the man.

"Yes, that was my father. He passed away last year. You say his mother died?" asked Bella.

"Aye, she did. I'm sorry for your loss, lassie.

I am calling in connection with her castle here in Ireland. We need someone to come and sort out all her belongings."

"I'll need to speak to my mother about all of this and then I'll get back to you," replied Bella.

"Aye, thank you for your time, lass. Cheers, and you can call me anytime on this number."

Bella sighed in confusion, listening to the droning dial tone before putting the phone down. She switched on the bedside lamp; her mind a whirlwind of thoughts. Her grandmother has just died and they needed someone to go to Ireland. Bella knew she should feel something like sadness or loss, but her grandmother was a stranger to her. Her mother would not take this news well. Bella was trying hard to help her mother, but she felt just as lost and alone. She was currently unemployed and living back at home, trying to help her mother through her grief while she herself still felt the heavy loss every day. Bella looked around her room. This was the room she had grown up in…this was her safe haven from feeling unwanted. This room was filled with memories, photos on the wall of her and her father doing the many adventurous things they had done together. Her walls were painted white because any colour was unacceptable and her teenage posters were still stuck behind the door where no one would find them.

This very room had made her feel safe at times. It was the only messy place in the house. Her mother never approved - she always pulled a disgusted face when she entered the room. A lady never made a mess! If anyone found out that she was anything less than a proper lady it would bring embarrassment to the family name.

She was only 27 but she felt much older than that, especially when receiving news like she had just received for the second time in just over the span of a year. This was not meant to be her life! She was not meant to be fatherless at 27. She had a plan and it had been going exactly as she had wanted it to, until that one call she had picked up last year that had shattered her world. Now her plans didn't make sense.

The whole world didn't make sense anymore. She tried to remember the grandmother that she had only met once in her life as a child, but the memory was hazy. She did remember an old, friendly lady with soft hands and kind eyes that always looked sad. At the time she had wondered why anyone would want to be that sad. But Bella understood now. Only genuine loss could bring on such immense sadness. Bella switched the lamp off and snuggled back under her blankets. The light of day wasn't far off, and with it came another world shift.

Bella woke up with a start, realising she must have dozed off again. Her mind was buzzing, thinking she had dreamt last night's phone call. She rolled over and saw the scribbled number on a piece of torn paper next to the phone with it came the harsh reality that the conversation was, in fact, reality. Bella groaned and threw her arms and legs up and down in frustration repeatedly. The blankets flew off the bed in a mess on the floor. She blew a strand of hair out of her eyes and stared up at the white ceiling. A thought occurred to her: maybe her mother wouldn't care about the news about her grandmother. With that hope in mind, she got out of bed and opened her wardrobe. All the clothes hanging up were matching suit pants in dull colours.

Bella pulled a face and opened the drawer below. She pulled out a comfortable pair of worn jeans and a long-sleeved beige jersey. She walked out of her room barefoot and followed the smell of bacon towards the kitchen.

Rosaline, their cook for the last 20 years stood at the stove cooking break- fast. The kitchen had always been her and her father's favourite spot in the whole house. Her father could always be found here eating ice cream, and would silently hand her a spoon when she discovered him. The kitchen had an island in the middle, and across from it a large, informal dining table. Bella walked towards Rosie and kissed her on the cheek before sitting at the table across from her mother, Bethany. They had assigned seats at the table. The table was always neat and set to dine for the rich and famous, even when it was just the two of them.

"Oh my, dear. What did I tell you about wearing those pants? You have perfect outfits in your wardrobe," cried Bethany.

"Mother, we spoke about this."

Her mother waved her hand dismissively and sipped on her morning tea.

Bella took the cup of coffee Rosie held out to her and took a small sip.

"Kyle was asking about you at the banquet last night."

"Mother, I told you I am not interested in dating yet," said Bella, pulling a face when her mother looked away.

They sat in silence for a few minutes, the only sounds coming from their forks hitting the plates.

"Did I hear the phone ring this morning?" asked Bethany, cutting her egg up into tiny slices.

"Yes," mumbled Bella as she stuffed egg into her mouth.

"Oh? And who would be calling at such an ungodly time?

People can really be so inconsiderate," Bethany sighed with a shake of her head.

Bella swallowed the egg and washed it down with a mouthful of coffee. "I don't know how to tell you this, Mom…But I got a call from Cork, Ireland."

"Really?" questioned Bethany, staring at Bella.

"It was some solicitor…he told me that Cathella McCullen had passed away" mumbled Bella, staring at her plate.

She heard her mother's cup hit the table with abrupt force and looked up.

Her mother rarely displayed anything but perfect manners. "Are you sure?" whispered Bethany shakily.

"Yes, Mother, and there's more. He needs us to go there to sort out her stuff…something about a castle?" replied Bella.

"Ireland? No! No, this just won't do! I can't go!" cried Bethany, smoothing out her already neat hair.

"I'll call him and tell him to do what ever he wants with the stuff, we don't need it."

"Don't you dare! Your father might not have spoken about his mother, but he loved her dearly and when I asked him to leave Ireland for me, he did it. Your father would want one of us to say goodbye," declared Bethany, standing up.

"Okay…so we are going?" asked Bella, putting her empty plate in the sink. "No," said her mother, suddenly turning to Bella, "You are, my dear."

Bella turned to face her mother, her mouth hanging open in shock as she stumbled for words.

"Close your mouth. It's not lady-like. You aren't in college anymore, nor are you working, and it would be good for you to learn about your heritage and where you came from," answered Bethany with a forced smile.

"No, Mother, you need me here and I can't go alone!" cried Bella.

"Now listen here, dear. I am 60 years old and I know how to care for my- self. You're young and don't need to care for your mother. Someone needs to go, and it should be you."

"Mother, why? I don't even remember my grandmother and I've only been to Ireland once when I was little," cried Bella, knowing she sounded like a whiny child.

"I love you, Arabella McCullen, I really do. But you are so much like your father that it hurts at times. You are strong and determined, and you will

do this for me. Maybe you'll find what you want in life while you're there," answered Bethany as she left the kitchen as gracefully as she had entered. Bella slumped against the counter. How was this happening? She felt a soft hand touch her shoulder and turned to look at Rosie.

"It'll be good for you to get away, Bella. I'll watch the missus for you. You have a good heart and you'll do what's right."

"Rosie, I don't want to go to Ireland," whispered Bella. "What would your Papa say about this?" asked Rosie.

Bella wiped the tears away and watched Rosie clean the kitchen. Could she just get on a plane and fly to Ireland? It sounded crazy, but then again, her father would say, "It's not crazy until you've done it."

She pulled out her phone and dialed the number on the piece of paper in her other pocket. Bella didn't know it yet, but this was the beginning of something more. This was the time for new leaves to appear.

Chapter

1

Ireland 2000

When you get scared next time, Bella, come and tell me, and I will keep you safe from all the scary things," whispered her father into her little ear.

"But what if you aren't around anymore?" asked Bella.

"I will always be around, and when I am not, I will be in your heart, Bella."

Bella wrapped her arms around her father's neck, snuggling on his lap in front of the fire.

"Do you think the trees are scared that they won't get any new leaves?" asked Bella as she yawned, drawing closer to sleep.

"The trees will always get new leaves. Without it they would look boring and die of sadness," answered her father.

"Why do you have a funny accent when you speak?" questioned Bella as her eyes began to flutter closed.

"I was born in another country...where everything is beautiful and green." "Can we go there some day?" Bella mumbled, falling asleep in her father's arms.

"Lass, wake up. We're here," said a rich Irish accent.

Bella opened her eyes, realising that they had stopped moving. She looked out of the window of the taxi to see that they were parked in front of a large dock. There was a large ferry in the docks behind her. She got out and held the handle of her bag tightly, watching the taxi drive away. She turned to stare at the beautiful town of Cork, Ireland. It was like something out of a fairy tale, with cobblestone walkways and stone buildings. The laughter of children running around filled the busy streets as people gaftered outside of coffee shops and sheep crossed the road ahead. Bella stood staring in awe at the simple beauty before her. Bella crossed the road and walked up to the coffee shop, then stopped a waiter on his way back from a table to show him her tourist map.

"Sorry to bother you, Sir, but do you know how to get to this town?" asked Bella, pointing towards a small town on the map.

"You have to take the ferry there," answered the man, pointing towards the ferry behind her that was just beginning to pull away from the dock.

Bella groaned in frustration and thanked the man before walking back across the road. She grabbed her long red coat by the lapels and pulled it tight with her free hand as a cool breeze blew by. Bella buttoned up her coat and slowly walked across the jetty in her black stilettos. She looked around the empty dock, spotting an elderly man tying off his boat.

"Excuse me, Sir, but do you know when the next ferry arrives?" yelled Bella, hoping he could hear her.

The man dropped a crate of fish by her feet. Bella let out a shriek and jumped back as the man chuckled and wiped his hands on an old rag. He looked her up and down cautiously. Bella tried not to stare at the stranger in front of her, attempting not to notice the large scar across his left cheek.

"You seem a little lost lassie, a foreigner too. The last ferry just left, you can catch the next one tomorrow," he said, taking his hat off and running a hand through his thick black curls.

"Tomorrow!" squeaked Bella. "But I have to get across tonight. Is there no other way across?"

"You're in some luck…I happen to be going across right now, if you want you can catch a ride with me?"

Bella looked at the old boat rocking in the water. The paint was peeling off and it looked rusted on one side. The boat's name, Lochness, was missing a few letters, but she couldn't see any other options in the immediate area. He reached out his hand towards Bella.

"Name's Fergus McDonald. I've been captain of this ol' ship for 20 years now."

Bella stepped forward and shook his hand in return.

"Bella McCullen. Pleased to meet you."

The man chuckled and lifted her luggage onto the boat.

"A real English greeting if I ever heard one. What's a lass like you doing all the way out here alone? You do have an Irish surname - are you visiting relatives?"

Fergus helped her up onto the boat.

"I have some family business to clear up here."

Fergus showed her to a seat.

"You might want to hold on," said Fergus ominously as he started the engine.

Thee boat lurched forward and Bella grabbed onto the railing, barely stop- ping herself from falling forward.

⸻⁂⸻

Bella waved goodbye one last time to Fergus as he tipped his hat off towards her in a friendly gesture, the boat leaving the dock. Bella looked around the small town. It was even smaller than the last one.

Evening was approaching quickly and everything seems to be closed up for the night, Bella looked around for ay signs of a taxi. She spotted a woman with two small children exiting a candy store and hurried after them.

"Hello Ma'am, sorry to interrupt you, but could you please show me where to find a taxi?" called Bella, breathlessly.

The woman gave her a strange look before she laughed, her children joining in. Bella looked at them, confused and exhausted. She just wanted to find this place and sleep. Seeing Bella's crestfallen face, the lady stopped laughing and put a hand on Bella's arm.

"There are no taxis here - what you see is what you get," said the lady as she waved her hand around the small town.

"Well, then…do you know where the Scarlett Manor is?" asked Bella.

The woman smiled sadly before pointing straight down the main road.

Bella stared down the empty road.

"Follow the road. You'll eventually find it. It's the only place out there."

Bella thanked the lady and grabbed her bag. She walked for what seemed like hours with nothing in sight but green grassy fields on either side of her. Bella groaned in frustration and dropped her suitcase onto the dusty road, sitting down on it. She looked up at the darkened skies and pulled her jacket tighter around her body. Her feet were killing her – she would definitely have blisters by tomorrow. Bella finally stood up, grabbed her bag handle and began walking as fast as she could. She heard a loud crackling sound in the sky and saw a flash of blue in the distance before a large raindrop landed on her nose. She looked around the deserted road as rain suddenly poured down in torrents around her.

The ground rapidly turned to wet mud and her shoes started slipping as she rushed forward. She tripped over a small rock, losing her balance and landing in a small mud puddle that had just formed. She knew her knees would be sporting bruises and the stinging sensation in her hands was becoming increasingly intense. Bella swiped her tangled hair out of her face and took off her stilettos. She stood up, knowing she must look a terrible mess, and carried on. The road ahead of her was misty, making it harder to see. She realised suddenly that this was a huge mistake showing up in a foreign country all by herself. She tripped again, stubbing her big toe and biting her lip in pain. She grabbed onto an old sign post and tried to figure out what to do next. Suddenly realising what the words on the sign post said, she could have kissed it in relief. The letters were mostly faded but she could read the word manor clearly. How many other manor houses could there be in this place?

Bella marched down the gravel road with as much dignity as she could muster despite her soaked and muddy appearance. There were more trees around here, but once she reached the top of the hill, everything changed. She stared up at the large, ancient-looking stone castle at the end of the road. Even through the rain she could see that it was magnificent, like something from a movie or a fairy-tale. It had large wooden windows on either side of the wide front steps that led to a magnificent hand-carved door. Bella pushed forward with renewed energy for those last few steps as she approached the castle. She ran up the steps, trying not to slip, and started banging on the door. After a few moments of relentless knocking on the door until her knuckles hurt, the door let out a loud groan and slowly swung open. Bella stumbled forward into the open doorway, grabbing onto the wall for support. She looked up and felt like her heart had stopped for a second. The man in front of her was, there were no other words for it - beautiful. He had thick black hair that curled at the collar of his blue button-down shirt, and deep blue eyes that matched the sharp angles of his face. His muscles stood out firmly through the shirt that he wore. Bella's mouth went dry, knowing she must look like an idiot for staring. She looked back at his face to find that the man was scowling at her.

"Is this the McCullen residence?" asked Bella, her teeth chattering as she tried to compose herself.

"Yes," answered the man; crossing his arms in irritation.

Bella sighed with frustration and shoved past him, dragging her bag with her into the dry foyer. She dropped her bag and looked around the room in amazement, shivering slightly.

"I am Cathella's granddaughter, Bella McCullen," said Bella, rubbing up and down her arms in hopes of warming up.

"Right, I know who you are. We weren't expecting you for another two days. I'm Wylie McIntosh, Caretaker of this castle."

He stared at her like he was trying to see through all of her secrets; search- ing to find an imposter. After a few seconds of awkward silence he closed the front door and turned to face her.

"Do all you English lassie's have such short names?" asked Wylie.

"Funny guy. Just my luck," sighed Bella. "My name is Arabella, but I prefer to be called Bella."

Bella looked around the large empty hallway, hoping to find anyone friendlier than this guy.

She glanced up at the stairs, seeing no one above, and wiggled her cold toes on the plush carpet.

"An Irish name? You have such a beautiful name. Why not be proud of it?"

Bella stared at him, why was he asking this now? She wasn't in the mood for this, even if he was possibly the finest looking man she had come across in a long time.

"Because I'm not Irish, and never will be. Besides, if they're all are as ill-mannered as you then I'm thankful that I'm not Irish," replied Bella, sarcastically.

"So it is true: the English are cold," stated Wylie with a shrug.

Bella's eyes widened in surprise. How dare he insult her?

"If you don't mind…I'm cold and wet, and I would like to change, since this conversation is clearly over."

"Of course. My sincere apologies. Your room is this way," Wylie replied shortly, walking past her to head down a long, dark passage.

Bella grabbed her bag with an irritated huff and followed him.

Wylie pushed opened the last door along the dimly lit corridor and wait- ed for Bella to step inside. The room looked like the inside of a fancy hotel room, with a small chandelier hanging from the centre of the room. The cur- tains and bedding were a rich red that blended well with the dark mahogany queen size bed. Bella stood clutching her bag, dripping water onto the wood- en floor as her mouth hung open. The small wooden side tables each held an elegant looking lamp, and in the corner of the room was a luxurious black sofa - perfect for reading. She let go of the handle of her bag and walked over to the window. Bella pulled the curtain to look outside. All she could see was mist and rain.

She shivered and dropped the curtain closed before turning to face Wylie.

"The room is beautiful," said Bella.

"Your grandmother had good taste. She always said this was your room."

Bella smiled weakly and approached her bag. She turned it on its side and zipped it open. Water poured out of the bag and onto the floor. Bella groaned and looked up as Wylie stared back at her with a look of sheer irritation.

"Do you perhaps have something dry that I can borrow?" asked Bella hopefully, gesturing toward her wet clothing. Wylie walked out of the room without another word.

"Or not," mumbled Bella, walking through the door that lead into the adjoining bathroom.

She nearly cried in relief. She never wanted to leave this room. Bella stared at the large white claw-foot bathtub and the clear glass shower with multiple showerheads. A small whimper escaped her cold lips. She turned the taps in the bath on fully and shivered in relief. Bella left the water running and went back to her room, then took out her wet clothing and hung them up in front of the fireplace. Wylie knocked on the still-open door and stepped into the room, after she acknowledged his presence. He dropped a bundle of clothes onto the bed and knelt in front of the fire to light it. Bella picked up the clothes hesitantly; he had given her a dark blue long shirt and black sweatpants with drawstrings so that she could tie it.

"There's food in the kitchen when you're done," said Wylie as he turned to leave the room.

Bella clutched the dry clothing to her chest and walked back into the bath- room. She pulled off her wet muddy clothes and climbed into the bath. Bella sighed in relief at the sensation of the heat soaking through to her cold bones.

She dipped under the water, soaking her hair through before coming up. The water felt so wonderful that she nearly fell asleep in the tub. Eventually, Bella yawned and got out the bath, finally feeling a little more human. She put on the clothes from Wylie. The top hung on her small frame and she had to roll up the pants. Bella slipped on the black woolly socks he had left her and clipped up her wet hair. Her stomach grumbled loudly in the empty room, reminding her that she hadn't eaten all day.

She left her room and walked down the passage in search of the kitch- en. The space was dimly lit with wall lights that gave it a cosy feeling. One of the doors on the side was open. Curiously, Bella peered inside. It was a large library filled with floor to roof shelves of books with a soft cosy reading chair in the middle and a small table next to it that held a beautiful lamp.

She stepped into the room and did a full-body twirl of the room. Her emer- ald green eyes searched the space before stopping and landing on a large oil painting, a portrait of Cathella and her grandfather almost 80 years ago. She heard footsteps approach from behind her but her eyes never left the painting.

"Fiorghrá," said Wylie directly behind her, his voice whispering down her neck, eliciting a shiver.

"What does that mean?"

"True love," answered Wylie.

"I look just like her," whispered Bella, staring at the younger version of her grandmother.

"Yes, you do. You both have those auburn thick curls that are common to us Irish, and emerald green eyes," answered Wylie, thinking her more beautiful than anything he had ever seen.

Bella swallowed and drew her eyes away from the painting to look at Wylie. He was staring at her instead of the painting.

"Dad looked like his father…he had the same colour hair and the same eyes. Mother said he wasn't very handsome, but I always thought he looked like a knight in shining armour," said Bella softly, looking back at the painting.

"Are you hungry? Mama has made a good Irish stew, it will warm you up after that cold weather," said Wylie.

He left the room without waiting for her reply. Bella sighed and took one last look at her grandparents; love and happiness captured in their expression. She left the room and followed after Wylie's retreating form. He walked through a swinging door to the left of the entryway. They walked through a large formal dining room that put her one back home to shame. Bella shivered at thoughts of sitting there eating alone like she had done so oThen in her own home throughout her childhood. Bella felt relieved when Wylie led her through another door and into the kitchen. Upon entry she was hit with the tantalising aromas of a home-cooked meal wafting through the air, causing her mouth to water instantly.

She was surprised to find two women in the kitchen, having assumed that Wylie lived alone here at the castle. They both stopped their conversation and turned to stare at her. The older lady standing in front of a large black stove smiled warmly. Her thick black hair was tied back in a severe-looking bun, but her soft blue eyes showed warmth and love. this woman was nothing like her mother, even down to her larger than average size, but she somehow made Bella feel like she was at home for the first time in ages.

Oh my, she looks like Cathella herself at that age!" cried the woman, wiping her hands on her apron.

"Hello, I'm Bella McCullen," said Bella nervously.

"Her name is Arabella, but it's too Irish for her," Wylie piped in, taking a seat at the small wooden table in the centre of the room. Bella gazed around, taking the space in. The walls were the same cobble- stone that the rest of the house was made from, with a door that seemed to lead to the pantry on one side of the fridge, as well as a stove and a small wooden table in the middle of the room. There was a door that led outside from what she could see and another next to it. Her curiosity was getting the better of her. She blushed suddenly, realising how rude it was for her to be ignoring the people in the room.

"Wylie! You stop that, you're embarrassing our guest," cried the woman flustered.

"Bella is a beautiful name. My name is Catriona, like 'Ka-treena.' I'm Wylie's mother."

"Mamai look, she's drowning in his clothes," giggled the other woman, who seemed to be much closer to Bella in age than Catriona.

"My clothes got wet on the walk over here," admitted Bella, embarrassed at her state of dress.

"It's alright, we understand. Maybe my clothes will fit you better, I'm Fiona, Wylie's younger sister," replied the girl as she rose up from the table.

"I don't want to be a bother...these clothes fit fine," mumbled Bella, staring at the old wooden table in front of her.

An awkward silence followed. Bella heard movement and looked up to find Fiona standing in front of her. The woman had the same colour hair as her brother and chocolate brown, doe-like eyes.

"Nonsense, child. My Fiona is such a dear and doesn't mind sharing her clothing at all," smiled Catriona.

"Thank you," replied Bella, following Fiona out through the other closed door.

She found herself in the underground area of the castle that seemed to have been turned into some sort of miniature home. She assumed that Wylie's family lived here. Bella felt more comfortable changing into a pair of jeans and top her own size. Not only did Fiona wear the same clothing size as Bella, but they were the same age. This brought a slight feeling of peace into her confused mixture of emotions and thoughts.

Bella followed Fiona back to the kitchen and took a seat next to her, across from Wylie who sat with his arms crossed as he stared at her. Catriona handed her a full bowl of steaming stew. She looked around to see that Fiona also had a bowl and had already picked up her spoon. Bella dug into the bowl with full gusto, her stomach protesting at the sudden intake of food. She barely came up for a breath, wanting to lick the bowl clean. Bella looked up and found everyone staring at her. She blushed and noticed for the first time that an older man had joined them at the head of the table.

"My wife makes good stew, does she not?" asked the man with a grin.

Bella nodded her head and wiped her mouth on the serviette in front of her.

"I believe we haven't met. I'm Clancy McIntosh, father of these two."

Bella stared at him. He reminded her of Father Christmas, if he really existed. He had thick grey hair that curled all over his head and brown eyes like his daughter, as well as a long grey beard and a round belly.

"Hello, I'm Bella, Cathella's granddaughter," replied Bella.

"Her name is Arabella," mumbled Wylie.

"It's Bella. I can tell people my own name, you know. It is polite to introduce yourself," answered Bella, irritated by his behaviour towards her.

"You call that polite?" scoffed Wylie, arching a brow in a gesture that looked like a dare if she ever saw one.

"Yes I do, and I call you rude with no manners," cried Bella, her temper flaring despite her best intentions.

"Wylie, hush! Where are your manners? The poor lassie is alone in this country," shouted Clancy, banging his fist firmly onto the table to get his point across.

"She could make an effort," replied Wylie, sounding like a sulking child. "Like you have," scolded Fiona as she kicked him under the table.

Bella felt exhausted and was in no mood to argue with anyone. She looked around at everyone and stood up politely.

"Thank you for your hospitality and clothes, Fiona, but I'm going to go to bed now."

"Don't go, Wylie is always like this," cried Fiona, grabbing Bella's wrist.

No, it's okay. I'm just exhausted. The whole jet lag thing is catching up with me," answered Bella as she left. The kitchen without a backward glance.

She found her way back to her room and got into the large bed, not bothering with the light as she fell asleep with her clothing on.

2

Bella opened her eyes to the sun shining through a gap in the curtain onto her face. She rolled over and buried her head under the blankets. The whole evening before came flooding back, embarrassment and all.

Why am I here?" yelled Bella, kicking her legs in the air in aggravation.

A knock on the door startled her and stopped her mid-rant, all anger draining away. Bella sat up abruptly, trying to neaten her messy curls that always reminded her of a bird's nest.

"Who is it?" called Bella nervously.

"It's Fiona," replied the soft, feminine voice.

"Come in," called Bella.

Fiona opened the door and ran towards the bed. She sat down next to Bella smiling shyly.

"Did you have a good sleep?" asked Fiona, tying her black hair into a sleek ponytail.

"Yes I did, thank you," smiled Bella.

"Good! Don't let Wylie ruin your mood. Now get dressed and I'll show you around before work," Fiona said warmly.

"Where do you work?"

"At the library," answered Fiona, getting up to leave.

She waited for Fiona to leave, then got out of bed and found a dry pair of jeans and a blue silk blouse to wear. Bella dressed quickly as the morning chill caused her to shiver, then tried to tame her wild hair as much as she could. She pulled it into a ponytail and put on some light makeup to complete the outfit. She then made her way to the kitchen in search of everyone else and something to eat.

Morning lass! Fiona says you slept well," Clancy said without looking up from his morning paper.

"Yes, I did," Bella replied, sitting down next to Fiona.

"Are you ever going to look at Cathella's things?" questioned Wylie from across the table, looking at home in a worn pair of jeans and a grey sweater as he typed away on his sleek black laptop.

"First I'm going on a tour of the property with Fiona."

"Wylie, will you go with them?" asked Catriona.

"No Mamai, we'll be fine. I am 27 and not four, you know!" exclaimed Fiona, putting down her cellphone to glare at her brother.

"And I'm a grown man of 33, and I'm busy. I don't need to babysit them. It isn't dangerous – we have no other neighbours close by," replied Wylie, irritation written all over his face at the thought of hav'ing to babysit two grown women.

"You two. Show some manners in front of our guest," scolded Clancy.

"It's alright, I'm sure Fiona and I will be fine on our own," replied Bella.

"Arabella, it's not her we're worried about," grinned Wylie with an arrogant arch of his eyebrow.

"Why do you insist on calling me Arabella? I am not Irish and I never will be."

Only her mother ever called her that, and that was when she disapproved of something Bella was doing or wasn't getting her own way.

"Ain't that a blessing!" laughed Wylie, leaning back and crossing his arms. "Come Bella, lets go for that walk before I hurt my brother accidentally,"

cried Fiona, pulling Bella up with her.

"Sure you won't need me?" teased Wyle with a grin

"Need you? Ha! That is laughable. Please!" answered Bella pointing her nose down at him.

She watched him mask his irritation and anger, knowing the look she gave him had sent lower men to their knees.

They left the room after that and made their way out the front door. It was still cold outside, but the sky was clear after yesterday's rain. Bella stopped on the bottom step and looked around the property. She had barely seen a thing yesterday. She held her breath for a moment at the beauty of it all. To the left of the castle was a steep cliff with what looked like a forty-foot drop, and on her right were pathways that led to the side of the castle.

"I know this place well...been here as long as I can remember," said Fiona.

"How do you know Cathella?" questioned Bella, jumping off the last step.

"Your grandma was a good lady to us. She took us all in and helped us with work when we needed it."

"She sounds wonderful. I wish I knew her."

They slowly made their way across the wet grass towards the cliff, stopping a few feet away. Bella sat down on a flat rock overlooking the edge. A light breeze blew her curls across her face as the waves were crashing loudly against the rocks below.

"And my Grandpa?" asked Bella pocketing her phone.

"Aye, your Grandpa loved your Grandma with all his heart. I wish I had known him," answered Fiona as she sat down next to Bella.

"My dad spoke about him dying in the war...and something about a scarlett penny?" replied Bella, pulling up her knees and wrapping her arms around them.

"It's a beautiful story, the scarlett penny, that is," sighed Fiona with a tone of girlish longing as if she were imaging true fairy-tale love.

"So, what's the story?" asked Bella, resting her chin on her propped up knees.

"That's a story only told by Cathella herself." said a male voice that had become quite familiar to her over the last 24 hours.

"Well, she's dead so she can't tell me," replied Bella bluntly, refusing to look at him.

"It's bad luck to speak ill of the dead!" cried Fiona, shocked.

"Some stories are just not meant to be heard. If you were meant to know, you would."

"A philosopher at heart," stated Bella sarcastically.

"I don't know how you'll ever find anyone with that attitude."

"Arabella, lots of woman are into me, but you certainly won't find an Irish man that'll put up with your prissy attitude. Although you sure act Irish with that temper of yours," chuckled Wylie.

"You two barely know each other and you already hate each other," Fiona said bluntly, standing up and brushing the grass from her clothes.

"Besides, I don't want an Irish man. I want a real man" answered Bella.

"Oh and us Irish aren't real men?" questioned Wylie, his accent growing thicker as his temper rose.

Bella stood up and faced Wylie. His sunglasses were hiding his eyes from her. She swiped the curls from out of her face and placed her hands on her hips.

"If they all act like you, a know-it-all alpha male that thinks woman belong under a man's thumb, then no," said Bella with a roll of her eyes.

His posture stiffened with every word she said.

"Wylie, stop being so arrogant," scolded Fiona, gently pushing them apart.

Bella looked at the space between them, realising that they had stood inches apart.

"I don't know what I did to offend you, but I'm sorry," replied Bella with a sigh.

She was being petty and she knew it, but something about him just got on her nerves. He stared back at her with an unreadable, guarded expression. Bella threw up her hands in defeat and turned to face Fiona.

"Fiona, if you don't mind, I am going to start sorting out Cathella's things."

—✽—

Bella walked off towards the castle, ignoring the other two arguing in the background. She would not look back. He stirred up emotions in her that she didn't understand. She would never like or love a man like Wylie. She would rather be alone for the rest of her life. She stepped back into the castle and climbed the first step.

Bella slid her hand along the cold metal railing along the stair case that led to the upper floor. She walked along the passage. All the doors were closed except one. Bella peeked inside and smiled in triumph- this was definitely Cathella's room. The air still smelt faintly of lavender and roses blended together; this room looked well lived in. The large four-poster wooden bed took up most of the space in the room with a faded pink duvet over it that matched the curtain hanging from the bed posts. Bella sat down on the comfy bed and took a deep breath. The realisation dawned on her that this really was Cathella's room…the grandmother she had barely known. She wondered once more what type of person she had been. What type of life had she lived? Bella sighed and looked over at the old writing desk in the corner of the room, and noticed an open book on it. this was the last thing that Cathella had read!

Bella went over to the desk and picked the book up. She realised right away that this was no ordinary book. It was an old, thick, handwritten journal. The last entry was dated the day of her death. She flipped through the pages quickly. This book looked like it had been to war and back. It smelled like lavender and the pages were soft from being touched so frequently. She closed the journal, noticing the cover had the words The Scarlett Penny engraved upon it. Could this be the key to the whole story? She really wanted to know what made this scarlett penny so special. She opened the first page and found a photo inside. Bella picked it up and smiled. Her grandmother stood next to her grandfather and in their arms was a small baby. It must have been her dad, she imagined. She turned it over, but the date marked on the photo made little sense. The date was 1918, so who is the little girl her grandfather is holding. So…who was the baby in their arms?

And why hadn't her father ever told her about it? She put the journal back on the desk and left the room feeling strangely cold and uncomfortable. She made her way to the kitchen where the air smelled of fresh baked biscuits. Catriona sat at the table sewing a button back onto a shirt. Bella sat down across from her.

"Did you know Cathella kept a journal?" questioned Bella.

"Your grandmother wasn't one to talk much. If anyone would know it would be Wylie. They spoke for hours in that garden," replied Catriona, not looking up from her sewing.

"Do you think it would be wrong for me to read it?"

"Your grandmother would have wanted you to read it," answered Catriona.

"Really? Why do you say that?" asked Bella, picking up a second shirt and helping to sew a button on.

"You don't need to work, dear!" cried Catriona.

"I need to keep busy. Besides, my nanny taught me how to sew."

They sat in silence sewing together for a few minutes. Catriona put down the shirt she was sewing and poured them a cup of black tea.

"Your grandmother spoke of an Arabella all the time, like you were her own child," smiled Catriona as she added cream to her tea.

"I wish I had known her," answered Bella, taking the cream for her own tea.

"Maybe the journal will tell you about her. You could learn a lot from someone's journal," said Catriona.

The door opened behind them and Wylie walked in.

"Mamai, have you seen Dadai?"

He stopped mid-sentence and stared at them sewing, his face a mass of unreadable emotions.

Bella picked up her tea cup, ignoring him completely.

"I should go," mumbled Bella, taking her cup with her.

She saw the stern look of disapproval that Catriona gave Wylie.

Bella walked aimlessly around the castle, exploring the bottom rooms. She wanted to go home, to go back to her house. Maybe if she sorted her grandmother's belongings out then she could go home sooner. She went back to the room and opened the wardrobe, staring at all the clothing hang- ing up. Bella looked over at the desk with the journal lying there innocently and turned back to the cupboard angrily. She grabbed handfuls of clothing and threw it out to the floor. Her anger and frustration, fear and hurt began building up inside of her. All of her energy draining with the last piece of clothing landing on the floor.

She wanted to feel something for her grandmother, but she felt nothing for this woman. So how was she supposed to do this? Hot tears pooled in her eyes as she blinked them back and turned to leave. Wylie stood leaning against the door frame with his ankle crossed over his booted foot and his arms across his chest. Her cheeks flared with embarrassment. How long had he been standing there? He held himself with a stance that appeared relaxed, but she sensed the control he exuded.

"What do you want? Can't you leave me alone?" yelled Bella, crossing her arms in defence.

He smiled a slow, sexy smile that causing her blood to boil.

"Cathella's solicitor is in the study. He wants to have a word with you," answered Wylie.

Bella walked past him, pushing him out the way as she went.

He chuckled and, infuriatingly, gained his balance back instantly. They made their way to the study - the only room that had been locked downstairs.

An old man stood with his hand behind his back as he scanned the book shelves. A large desk and computer were the only other items in the room. He turned to see her and his face lit up with a smile. He walked towards them with a black cane and removed his brown cap.

"Hello, I am Arabella McCullen," said Bella.

"Now she uses her name," mumbled Wylie from behind her.

Bella shoved her elbow into his stomach, grinning as he grunted in pain.

"I am Martin McDonald, your grandmother's lawyer and dear friend for many years," replied the man.

"Do you want to do this alone?" questioned Martin, looking past her at Wylie.

Bella peered over her shoulder at Wylie. She didn't expect anything and didn't care less if he was here. She shrugged her shoulders, seeing Wylie relax a fraction.

"Your grandmother was a lovely woman with a good heart. She was in her right mind, you know. Some said she was long gone, but I knew her and she was herself till the end. She had this castle your grandfather built for her."

"Okay, so what is going to happen to this place?" asked Bella, jumping right to the point.

"It's all yours," stated Martin with a smile.

Bella's eyes widened in shock as she slumped back in the chair.

"M..me..." stuttered Bella nervously, "What? No! There must be a mistake! I only met her once in my life and I just can't..."

"Says it right here in the will, 'I leave all my worldly possessions including my castle, to my granddaughter, Arabella McCullen! I hope she will love it as much as I do.'"

"But what am I supposed to do with it? I live in another country, and I'm not Irish at all!" yelled Bella, throwing her arms in the air.

She felt a headache coming on and put her head in her hands with a groan.

"That's up to you, lass, it's all yours. Now you could sell it, not that I would want you to. Also, I see you are acquainted with your grandmother's business already," answered Martin.

"Business?"

"Aye, that shirt you are wearing. My granddaughter has the same. Didn't you know? It's your grandmother's fashion line," said Martin with confusion in his voice.

Bella slumped back into the chair. She heard Wylie snicker behind her.

"Pennies is my grandmother's creations?" questioned Bella, her mouth hanging open.

"Aye! She started it after her husband died. It started out just her and her daughter-in-law. But word of mouth spread and it became internationally known. It all belongs to you now, and it's managed by people all over the world. You'll need to go to certain meetings, but you'll never have to work again," answered Martin.

"A company! Are you sure she meant me?" said Bella, her mind spinning, "I don't know what to say."

"Aye. She loved you very much and left you everything."

"What were you saying about selling?" asked Bella.

"Your grandmother loved this place, many tried to buy her out. Some tried to get her institutionalised. But she died in this castle where she belonged.

You're sure you want to get rid of it?" questioned Martin.

"Yes, I just want to go home."

For the first time since they had entered the room, Wylie spoke up; his voice laced with emotion.

"No, don't! You can't sell it - Cathella loved this place more than life itself!" shouted Wylie, stepping towards her.

"This is not your choice, Wylie, it's mine. I don't know why she left it to me and I don't care," replied Bella.

She turned back to Martin.

"How long will it take?"

"Could be a month to three months…you'll have to be here until it gets sold. As for the company, you can do that from anywhere," answered Martin standing up slowly, his movement suddenly showing his age.

"I'll look into it. My mother will be thrilled."

"Arabella, please don't do this!" cried Wylie.

Bella stood up and faced Wylie.

He had a pained expression on his face. He barely looked at Martin as the man left the room with a promise to call.

"Oh, so now you want to be nice to me? I told you - my name is Bella and I am not Irish," said Bella, heading towards the door.

Wylie grabbed her arm, pulling her towards him. She lost her footing and she stumbled into his hard chest. Bella looked up into his blue eyes, her mouth opening in shock at the raw emotions displayed on his face.

"I am begging you, don't be so heartless," whispered Wylie.

Her heart stuttered at his cruel words. She gave him a hard shove. "Get your hands off me," growled Bella.

Bella glared at him once more and walked away. She felt tears prick her eyes but held them back.

He could hate her, for all she cared.

Bella went to her room and got into bed, then took out her laptop and started it up. Why would Cathella leave her this castle if it meant so much to her? Why did she have to die before Arabella could have known her? The thought that bothered her most, she had to admit, was the question of just how wealthy she was now. She heard the door open but refused to acknowledge the person. The bed dipped and a cold hand touched her on her arm. Bella took her earphones out and looked up at Fiona.

"He doesn't really think you're heartless," said Fiona.

"What else can I do, Fiona? I don't live here and I didn't know her. She made a mistake leaving it to me," exclaimed Bella, moving her laptop off her lap.

"Cathella never made mistakes. She loved you. Your grandmother would be proud no matter what you do," replied Fiona as she gave Bella's hand a squeeze.

"I hope so."

"You know what's best for you," answered Fiona, giving her a smile before leaving the room.

Bella put her movie back on, trying to drown out all unwanted thoughts.

Once the movie ended, she made her way to the kitchen for lunch. Bella sat in her now usual spot next to Fiona and accepted her lunch from Catriona. She was told it was corned beef and cabbage as her stomach let out a growl in hunger. The food didn't look bad and now was not the time to be picky. They ate in silence for the first few minutes.

"Fiona tells me you are selling!" stated Clancy, suddenly.

"Yes," mumbled Bella, feeling uncomfortable.

"Good for you, this place needs some life in it," smiled Clancy.

"Thank you. this is a hard decision, but I don't belong here. Martin said it could take a few months, so I'm here until then." replied Bella.

"Finally! Another girl my age," smiled Fiona.

"I always wanted a sister," replied Bella.

"So did I, but I got Wylie," joked Fiona.

Bella finished eating and then went outside. She sat down with her legs hanging over the side of the cliff and took a deep breath. Bella sat staring at the view in front of her before opening a photo of her father.

"Dad, I miss you…" whispered Bella.

"How did he die?" asked Wylie from directly behind her.

Bella held in a scream, jumping slightly. She glared at him over her shoul- der. He held his hands up in surrender with a small laugh. Bella turned back to stare at the blue sky.

"A heart attack," replied Bella.

"I'm sorry. You loved him a lot. I can see that," said Wylie, sitting down next to her.

"Yes…as cheesy as it sounds, we were best friends. One day we were sitting and talking as usual, then he told me he was tired and went to bed, and I never saw him alive again. I lost a part of me that day."

"You can get it back, you know? You just need to let go of all the anger," replied Wylie.

Bella turned to face him, her eyes blazing with fury.

"How would you know, Wylie? He was my dad and I lost him. Now I'm left to make these big decisions about a person I never knew but who just happened to mean the world to him," shouted Bella.

He gave her a sad look, shaking his head.

"Arabella just look at you - you are so much like Cathella," answered Wylie.

"Well then she must not be as nice as everyone says," growled Bella in frustration, standing up.

"I meant it as a compliment!" Wylie called to her retreating back.

But it was too late. Bella was halfway back to the castle. She went up to Cathella's room and picked up the journal. She was frustrated, angry, and homesick. So, she would see how alike they were. What was the big fuss was about an old lady, anyway? She got comfortable on the floor with her back leaning against the bed and opened the journal. It was written in English and the first entry was many years ago. Bella sucked in a breath. She realised that this was a powerful book, filled with knowledge and more secrets than a soap opera. She scanned through the first page, instantly becoming enthralled by the teenager's words. In no time, Bella was deep in the story; a story that was the true, hidden life of Cathella.

One life had started all of this, had set all this in motion. A journey that, once read, would change a person forever. It started long before her time. But here was a story told through the eyes of a remarkable woman who had begun her new life when barely a teen.

—Chapter—
3

1912 South Africa

Mama, please don't make me go!" cried 17-year-old Cathella.

"Cathella, you know your papa won't change his mind, lass. Your aunt and uncle are nice people and they're excited to meet you.," Agnes replied with her Irish lilt, still there after all these years.

Cathella grabbed onto her mother's arm, tears welling in her desperate green eyes.

"Mama, I don't know them and Ireland is big and scary. Please, come with me!" pleaded Cathella.

"You know I would if I could," soothed Agnes as she cradled Cathella's soft cheek in her calloused hand.

"I hate Papa! He doesn't love me!" screamed Cathella before fleeing to her room.

Her father wanted her move to Ireland to live with an aunt and uncle that she had never met. Cathella threw herself on her bed, crying hysterically into her soft pillow. Life was so unfair.

She loved her home and her family; why was her father doing this to her?

—⁊—

Her door opened and Cathellas peaked through her thick mass of auburn curls to see her father, Thomas, standing there looking devastated with dark rings under his eyes.

"Don't be sad my Cathella... I love you so much," said Thomas, sitting on her bed.

"How can you say that and still send me away? this is my home!" sobbed Cathella, rolling away from him.

"One day you will understand that I have to do this. So hate me now, but know that I was thinking of you when I made this decision," replied Thomas as he stood up.

Cathella refused to look at him, twirling a curl around her finger. After a moment she lifted her head up and looked up at him through tear-stained eyes.

"I don't really hate you papa... I'm scared," whispered Cathella so softly that he almost didn't hear.

"Did I just hear my Cathella say she was scared? The girl that had the boys running and girls screaming in fear?" smiled Thomas, breaking the tension in the room.

"Oh! Papa! I will miss you so much," cried Cathella before jumping off the bed and wrapping her arms around his waist.

She felt her strong Papa's body tremble with emotion and heard the slight tremble in his voice when he replied.

"I will miss you so much, my girl. Your mother will miss you. We love you so much - always remember that...and maybe we can come visit soon," croaked Thomas.

"Papa, I won't fit in with them," sobbed Cathella.

"You look Irish! No one will know you're English until you open that mouth of yours and speak," replied Thomas, kissing her on the head.

Cathella pulled back and kissed him on the cheek as their eyes both filled with tears. As if coming to his senses, Papa cleared his throat and left the room. Cathella picked up her old worn teddy bear, the one with a missing ear, and hugged it close. She placed it in her open bag along with all here meagre possessions. It looked out of place in her square brown suitcase filled with dresses. She took it out and placed it back onto her bed. No matter how hard it would be, her time had come to be a woman. After that she wandered around the house that had always been her safe haven when nothing made sense in her world, and found her mother ironing a dress. Cathella snuck up behind her mother and slipped her arms around her waist. Her mother jumped slightly before wrapping her free hand around Cathella's.

"Mama, I love you," whispered Cathella into her mother's shoulder blades.

"Lass, I will miss you with all of my heart. My dear, sweet child," sobbed Agnes, her large body trembling with emotion.

"Mama, I will always be in the one place no one can take me from," answered Cathella.

"Ireland can be taken in a second!" cried Agnes.

"Not Ireland - your heart, Mama. Every time we miss each other we just have to touch our chest and know that we are right here," said Cathella moving her hand up to her mother's chest.

"You're going to make me cry," scolded Agnes, lovingly.

"Good then you will know what a bad idea this is," Cathella teased, wishing she could change their minds.

"Child, this is the hardest decision I have ever had to make. You're my little girl and I have to say goodbye to you. I raised you and cared for you, and I wanted to hold my grandchildren one day. But life tells a different story and we have to go along with it."

"I know, Mama, and maybe soon you can come visit me?" smiled Cathella weakly.

"No matter what happens, Cathella, I love you and your Papa loves you.

We are doing this for you," Agne said in a firm tone.

"But why can't you come?"

"Your Papa had to use all of our money just to send you," Agnes replied, truthfully.

"It's not because you want me to learn my heritage, is it Mama?" questioned Cathella, stepping back from her mother.

"Go finish packing before Papa gets back," demanded Agnes as tears ran down her cheeks. Her strong mother was crying. As she fought back her own tears, Cathella wanted to argue, to make them see her side, but it was pointless. She was leaving.

Ireland

Cathella stood with her back to the docks and her large case hanging from her hand. She felt butterflies in her stomach and the remnants of nausea from the journey. Her palms were sweaty with nerves. People walked past her, barely noticing her as they carried on with their lives. One old man stopped to tie his shoe and Cathella took the chance to approach him.

"Excuse me sir, do you know where the McPhersons live?" asked Cathella.

The gentlemen stood up and stared at her.

"Lass, there are four McPhersons in this town," laughed the man before shaking his head and walking away.

Cathella looked around the small town feeling lost and scared. She placed her trunk on the side of the road and sat down on it.

It would be dark soon and she was getting cold and hungry. Tears leaked from her eyes despite her best efforts to hold herself together. She wiped her eyes before anyone could see and pulled her cardigan closer around her body as a cool breeze blew through her. She looked up and suddenly let out a shocked gasp at sudden appearance of a large young man in front of her.

"Lass, are you alright?" asked the deep Irish voice.

He had short black hair combed neatly to the side and soft brown eyes filled with concern. He was tall, and admittedly not very handsome, but he had a kind face in that moment, he was the most beautiful person Cathella had ever seen.

"I'm lost!" cried Cathella.

"A pretty lassie like you, it won't do," smiled the boy, or was he a man?

She wasn't quite sure.

"I'm looking for my Aunt Athole and Uncle Riley McPherson," replied Cathella dejectedly.

"The Reverend is your uncle? Father Riley?" questioned the man as his eyes lit up.

"Yes, I'm Cathella Smith and Uncle Riley is my mother's brother. She was born here and moved away when she married my father. They're expecting me..." replied Cathella.

"Well then! We better not keep them waiting," said the man, holding out his hand for her trunk.

"I'm Finnigan, by the way. Most call me Fin."

He took her trunk from her hand and marched off down the road. Cathella hurried along behind him, trying to keep up with his long legs. She hoped she could trust this fella because it was too late to back out now. He looked back at her half-jogging behind him and slowed his pace.

"Are they nice?" asked Cathella, finally walking in step with him.

"Your uncle has saved many lives, including mine," stated the man.

He led her though a white wooden gate and pointed to the church at the top of the hill. Cathella stopped to stare at the magnificent church in front of her. It was an old wooden building with glass windows that reflected the sun.

"It's beautiful," breathed Cathella with sincerity.

"Aye, it is. Your family lives behind the church," he replied, pointing to a small wooden house at the bottom of the hill.

They finally arrived at the little house and he walked up to the door and lifted his fist to knock. Cathella held her breath nervously, standing as close to him as possible. The door suddenly opened and an old man stepped into view with a warm smile on his face.

"Finnigan McCullen! What brings you here?"

"Father Riley, I've brought you someone."

"Aye and who might this lass be?" asked Riley, looking her up and down.

Cathella stepped forward so that he could have a better look.

"It's me, Uncle...Cathella Smith," answered Cathella nervously.

His green eyes lit up with recognition as a large smile dawned on his weathered fac "Dear child! You look just like your mother - how did I not see it?" cried Riley.

"Finnigan showed me the way," said Cathella, giving Finnigan a shy smile.

"Thank you, brother Finnigan, you are blessed. Come in, child, before you catch your death," said Riley, pulling her into the house.

"Are you coming?" asked Cathella, looking back at Fin standing rather awkwardly on the porch.

"No…I'd better go. Cheers, Cathella, I'll see you on Sunday for church," said Fin, grinning like a schoolboy on Christmas Day.

Riley closed the door and led Cathella through the quant sitting room that had just two small benches and a coffee table.

"Love! Look who Finnigan brought," called Riley, putting down her trunk next to a rocking chair.

A large woman stepped out of the kitchen with an apron on.

"Oh my! Cathella - look at you! So much like your mother. Oh how I miss her so terribly," cried Athole pulling Cathella into a bone-crunching hug.

Cathella hugged her in return. She had heard so much about the short fiery redhead that had been her mother's best friend all those years ago. Every- one was surprised to find her accepting Riley's proposal, as the shy quiet man had taken loud Athole as his wife.

"Hello, Aunty Athole." Cathella politely replied.

"So formal, lass! Call me Attie," smiled Athole, pulling her into the warm kitchen. "I'll show you the Irish way of cooking, get some meat on them bones," laughed Attie.

"Let her be Attie, she must be tired," scolded Riley playfully.

"All you think of is sleep. Us women think of food, isn't that right, Cathella? Are you hungry?"

"Yes" answered Cathella - her empty stomach growling on cue, making itself known in the quiet room.

She felt slightly overwhelmed by their quick kindness and effortless acceptance of her in their home.

Attie grinned as she placed a bowl of hot thick pea soup with a slice of home-baked soda bread in front of her before sitting down at the other side of the table.

"Attie is one of the best cooks in Ireland," smiled Riley with pride as he put an arm around his wife's shoulder.

"Stop it Riley, you're embarrassing me…Don't let Cathella think us proud people."

"I don't think you're proud," replied Cathella, dipping her bread into her soup.

She finished off her food while talking, gradually opening up about her family back home. When she was done she was shown to her new room. The room was smaller than the one she'd known back home, with a metal framed bed in it and a small chest of drawers in a corner. She was blessed with a long mirror hanging from the wall and a small window that faced a beautiful gar- den. Cathella sat on her new bed and opened her bag. She took out her teddy bear and placed it on her pillow.

⁓ℬ⁓

"Cathella, hurry up or we will be late for church!" yelled Attie from the next room.

Cathella moved her hands through her thick Auburn curls once more and smoothed out her favourite blue dress. She wanted to look her best for her first day at church. She was hoping to see Finnigan today. He had said he would be there. It had been a week since she had first met him and she was keen to get to know him better. She followed Attie out of the house and up the hill into the church that was filling up with people at a rapid pace.

Cathella sat in the front pew and picked up the service programme to read the hymn lyrics, all written in English and Gaelic.

"Looking to learn something? I didn't know you understood our songs," said a husky male voice.

Cathella nearly dropped the paper in fright, looking over her shoulder to see Finnigan standing there in his Sunday best.

"Finnigan! So nice to see you again," cried Cathella, unable to conceal the excitement in her voice. She quickly put the hymn notes away with a blush creeping over her embarrassed cheeks.

"Aye, I've been counting the days 'til I see you again. You can call me Fin, everyone else does," smiled Finnigan.

"Fin it is. Thank you for saving me the other day."

He smiled before sitting down next to her. Attie was seated on her other side. The service started, but Cathella barely paid attention to the sermon. Every once in a while she would sneak a peek at Fin, only to find him look- ing right back at her. Cathella would blush and face forward, pretending to listen to her uncle's sermon.

Once the service had ended, people stood up and approached her aunt and uncle. Cathella wasn't in the mood to be the centre of attention and hurried outside for some fresh air while no one was looking. She stood out on the grass near an old tree, watching families walk towards their cars or amble back to their homes nearby.

"Where are you running to?" called Fin from behind her.

Cathella spun around with her hands on her hips. Fin stood at the bottom of the steps facing her.

"It's was hot in there," answered Cathella, fanning herself with her hand.

They stood staring at each other until another younger voice interrupted them.

"Fin! Fin! Where you going?"

Cathella stepped sideways and stared past Fin towards the front of the church. She saw a small boy standing on the church steps. He had black hair and brown eyes, just like Fin.

"Patrick, go back inside," Fin barked as he turned to face the boy.

"Mamai said you must take me home," called Patrick, placing his hands on his hips in defiance.

Cathella put her hand over her mouth to smother a laugh. Fin looked ready to kill his little brother. Fin shook his head and turned to face Cathella again.

"Cathella, this is my little brother, Patrick," replied Fin with a tone of aggravation.

"Little? I am 10!" wailed Patrick, jumping down the stairs.

"Hello Patrick, I'm Cathella," Cathella said, waving kindly.

"You are an Englisher!" shouted Patrick, excitedly.

"I am?" said Cathella with feigned shock, "Oh my! Fin, why you didn't tell me I was English?"

Patrick looked at them both, clearly confused.

"Patrick, you could have warned me." added Fin, playing along with Cathella's game.

Patrick stood with his mouth gaping like a fish. Cathella couldn't keep her laughter in anymore, giving it all away. Patrick smiled and Fin joined in, laughing aloud. Once they had all stopped giggling, they stood on the grass staring at each other. Fin gave his brother a pointed look, which Patrick blatantly ignored.

"Cathella, my brother was just leaving," told Fin, giving his brother a push.

Patrick stuck his tongue out at Fin, who lunged for his younger brother in return. The little boy let out a loud yelp before running back into the church.

"He is so cute," smiled Cathella with a small chuckle.

"I would never use that word to describe him," answered Fin, rolling his eyes.

They heard a throat clear and turned to find Attie standing in the doorway watching them.

"Cathella, there are a few people who would like to meet you," called Attie.

"I'd better get going," sighed Cathella.

Fin nodded his head in agreement and then touched her arm gently as she passed. Cathella stopped and turned to look up at him.

"Can I see you again?" asked Fin, hope shining in his eyes Cathella gave him a smile, then ran towards her aunt. "I'll take that as a yes!" called Fin happily.

Chapter

4

Cathella opened the front door to stop the persistent knocking. She had been living here two weeks now and missed her family more than anything, but had come to realise that this place was now home. She looked to find Patrick standing in front of her as he grinned ear to ear.

"Hello Patrick," said Cathella, looking around for Fin.

"Good Morning, Miss Smith. I am here to invite you to a picnic at the church with Mr. Finnigan McCullen," Patrick chanted in his Irish lilt.

His speech was clearly rehearsed with great care. Cathella giggled and took the hand he held out to her. Her aunt and uncle were up at the church sorting out flowers and other things for the next service on Sunday. She was home alone and a picnic sounded wonderful. . She was extremely lonely, with no other friends to speak of. Patrick pulled her up the hill, talking non-stop the whole way about school and how nervous Fin had been this morning. She followed him up the hill toward the church.

Cathella looked around and spotted Fin lying under a tree near the gate.

"Hello, Fin," called Cathella as she made her way to the blossoming tree.

"You look beautiful," replied Fin straight away, sitting up and using his hand as a shield against the glaring sun.

Patrick laughed at the two of them and ran off to play in the tree. Cathella sat down across from Fin, suddenly shy and nervous. He sat staring at her for a while before finally asking a question

"How old are you, Cathella?" asked Fin.

"I'm 17–years-old," beamed Cathella, proudly. "So you think you are old?" teased Fin.

"Don't laugh at me! How old are you?" asked Cathella as an unwanted blush made its way across her cheeks.

"Me? I am 19 years old and a man already," smiled Fin, throwing his red apple up into the air and catching it.

"So…that makes you smarter than me?"

"No! But noticing a pretty woman does," replied Fin, biting into his juicy red apple.

Cathella smiled and took the other apple he offered her. Patrick jumped down from the tree and sat down cross-legged next to Cathella.

"Fin! Fin! Can we go swimming?" begged Patrick.

"Swim where? I miss my bathing pool back home!" cried Cathella excitedly.

"Bathing pool? What is that?" questioned Patrick.

"It's a big tub built in the ground with water in it."

"We don't have anything like that, but we have a little river by our house!"

"Patrick, it won't be proper for a lass like Cathella to be alone with us," said Fin throwing his apple core away.

"But she's alone with us right now," stated Patrick,confused.

"Look behind you," answered Fin.

They both turned around to find Attie sitting on a chair by the church steps, watching them while she knitted a sweater.

"Doesn't she trust us?" asked Cathella.

"It's me she doesn't trust," chuckled Fin, "Now eat your food, Cathella. My Mamai made it especially for you."

"Mamai hardly ever cooks no more…she's sick a lot and has to care for all the little ones," replied Patrick, grabbing a sandwich for himself.

"How many of you are there?"

"There's Fin, he's the oldest and then me, and you know how old I am. Then there's Sean who's eight and Brennan is turning five," Patrick listed carefully, counting on his fingers.

"Don't forget Johanna who is three, and Mamai is expecting any day now."

Cathella nearly choked on her food as she counted the children in her head.

"There's only me back home. I never knew people had so many children!" cried Cathella.

"Dadai believes it's a woman's duty to have children, Mamai is getting old now and life isn't always easy for us. We lost Gordon three years ago when he was 12 to the fever," answered Fin with a sombre tone that she hadn't heard in his voice up until now.

"Gordie was a good older brother, like Fin is," said Patrick, suddenly very serious for such a small boy.

"What about school?" Cathella asked, shocked.

"Sean and I go to school," beamed Patrick proudly.

"What if I were to help?" questioned Cathella.

Fin stopped eating mid-bite and stared at her in confusion. "What do you mean 'help?'" replied Fin.

"I would have to ask my aunt, but since I don't have anything to do and love children, I could come help care for them," replied Cathella, over- whelmed by a sudden urge to help this over-burdened family.

"That would be nice!" cried Patrick, excitedly.

"Aye, that it would, but I would need to be speaking to Mamai and we won't be able to pay you," answered Fin, frankly.

"I don't need money."

Fin gave her an honest smile, her heart doing somersaults as she returned it.

"You are something special," smiled Fin.

"Cathella I like you a lot. No other Englisher is as nice as you," said Patrick hugging Cathella.

"You don't know any other Englishers," replied Fin, smacking his brother on the side of his head playfully.

Patrick glared at Fin while rubbing his head. They all started laughing and finished the rest of the food in good humour.

Once they were done, they packed up and said their goodbyes. Cathella went up to the church and linked arms with her aunt. They made their way back home and Attie put a pot of water on the stove for tea.

"You must be careful…Fin is a good man, but he is still a man," said Attie with motherly warmth. Cathella pulled her Aunt into a hug,

just as Riley walked in behind them.

"What's this all about?" asked Riley looking at them.

"Uncle, I am going to help Fin take care of his siblings," said Cathella.

Riley's eyebrows rose in confusion as he looked at his wife. She touched his arm lovingly.

"Attie, what do you say about all this?" questioned Riley.

"She's smiling for the first time since being her - how can we deny her this?"

"Then what else can I say. Just be careful, lass. Mr. McCullen can be a bit much at times," warned Riley.

"Yes, Uncle, I will be careful. I promise."

"Now go to your room, so your aunt and I can talk."

Cathella nodded her head and kissed him on the cheek before running off.

Two days later, Fin came to fetch her in the early morning to take her to his house. He had walked Sean and Patrick to school before coming to meet her. Cathella followed him out of the church gate and across the dusty main road. They walked through the town and down an alleyway.

"Fin, slow down!" called Cathella, running to keep up with his long strides.

He stopped and looked at her apologetically, running a hand through his hair.

"Sorry Cathella, I don't want to be late for work," replied Fin, his anxiety clear in his voice.

"But if you were just a little late today then you could show me the way then I can walk by myself everyday and you won't be late again," answered Cathella.

"Hmm, I never thought of that. Do you know how we got here this far?" asked Fin.

"Yes, I do," smiled Cathella.

"Now we're going to cut across the meadow, jump over the river, and walk up the hill to my house."

Cathella nodded and followed Fin through the meadow.

It was stunning, with rich green grass that had water droplets still clinging to it from the morning dew. Her dress grew heavier as the dew wet the bottom. Cathella held the hem in her hands to stop the damage from spreading any further. Fin jumped over the river and held out his hand for her to take. Cathella took his hand and let him help her across the small stream. She stood on the other side, finally catching sight of the small wooden cottage at the top of the hill. She surveyed it with concern in her eyes. It looked old and neglected, with smoke puffing out of the chimney. The door flew open suddenly and a small boy came bustling down the hill towards them.

"Fin! Fin!" shouted the boy eagerly.

Fin smiled and caught the boy in his arms before throwing him in the air playfully. He settled the boy on his hip and turned to face Cathella.

"Cathella, I would like you to meet my youngest brother, Brennan. Brennan, this is Cathella," said Fin.

"I am not little, Fin, I five and bigger than Johanna. She's only three!" scolded Brennan, crossing his small arms.

"You are so right! I don't know why Fin would think of you as little. Especially if you have a little sister to care for," answered Cathella.

Brennan nodded his head in agreement, his black locks falling in his face. Fin carried Brennan into the house. Cathella followed after them, unsure of what to expect. She stepped inside and looked around. It was one large open plan, wooden structure. In one corner was a small black stove and little table with many chairs around it. On the other end of the room were three tattered chairs and a fireplace with doors leading to rooms. Cathella turned to look at the wisp of a woman standing by the stove.

"Hello lass, you must be Cathella? You are a real blessing to us, deary, and I appreciate you being so willing to help," cried the woman.

"Hello, it's so nice to meet you," said Cathella approaching the heavily pregnant lady.

She had long strawberry blonde hair and blue eye. Despite the curve of her pregnant stomach, she looked frail and unwell.

"Mamai, Cathella will do whatever you need her to do, but I must go," said Fin, putting Brennan down and leaving the house in a rush.

Cathella noticed a little girl clinging to her mother's dress and saw the weary look of fatigue on the mothers face.

"Hello, you must be Johanna. I'm Cathella," Cathella said softly as she crouched down on her haunches in front of the girl.

"Hello," mumbled the girl before sticking her thumb in her mouth.

Her stringy red hair hung limp around her small doll-like face, making her look younger than three.

"She don't talk much," declared Brennan standing next to Cathella. "I hope you can handle them," smiled the lady, wearily.

"Of cousre I can, Mrs. McCullen. You go relax now - maybe take a nap," smiled Cathella.

"Call me Susanna, but there is so much to do around here," replied Susanna, her voice brimming with fatigue.

"Now I'm in charge, and I say go lie down," demanded Cathella, taking control of the situation quickly as she sensed Susanna's desperate need for rest.

"No, Mamai! Don't go," sobbed Johanna, clinging tighter to her mother's dress.

"Johanna, I think I saw a frog down at the river when I crossed it. I was wondering if you would want to come see it with me?" asked Cathella, hold- ing out her hand.

"A frog! I love frogs! Please can we go?" shouted Brennan, hopping around excitedly with the unbridled energy that only a five-year-old has.

"Only if Johanna comes with us," laughed Cathella.

"Jo-Jo, please come! I'll carry you and I won't let it hurt you," begged Brennan.

Johanna looked at her brother and let go of her mother's dress. She took Cathella's hand. Internally, Cathella let out of a sigh of relief. Brennan took her other hand and together they walked back down the hill towards the river. Johanna slowed them down considerably, so Cathella lifted her into her arms. As Cathella decended the girl wrapped herself around Cathella like a monkey, she realised that the toddler was thinner than usual for a girl her age. When they got to the river, Brennan took off his socks and shoes and rolled up his trousers.

"Are you coming?" asked Brennan, looking over at Cathella.

"No, we can watch from here. Are you sure it's safe?" replied Cathella, sitting down on the drying grass with Johanna on her lap.

"Sean taught me what to do," stated Brennan, getting in the water without any sign of fear.

They sat watching him as he walked easily into the water and in no time Brennan was letting out a loud shout and climbing out of the river, running towards them.

"I got it, Cathella, I really did!" squealed Brennan, holding his hands together.

Johanna got up and walked over to Brennan to see the frog.

"No, Jo-Jo! You'll scare it!" shouted Brennan, turning his back on her.

Johanna took one wide-eyed look at her brother and then collapsed onto the grass in a fit of sobs. Cathella jumped up quickly, trying to think of what to do to calm down the screaming child.

"Brennan, that's not very nice. go put it back in the water now!" scolded Cathella while scooping Johanna up into her arms.

Brennan nodded his head reluctantly, his lower lip quivering with unshed tears. He threw the frog back in the water and hung his head as his small shoulders shook with silent sobs.

"Don't cry, you two. Let's go home and make some biscuits," answered Cathella, ruffling his hair.

"Can I help?" asked Brennan, wiping his eyes.

"You both can. Grab your shoes and let's get going," said Cathella.

She put Johanna down and took her little hand.

"Race you to the top!" shouted Brennan, running off at lightning speed.

"Oh no you don't! I'm going to win!" shouted Cathella, letting go of Johanna's hand and running after him.

Johanna ran after them giggling and Brennan laughed and ran faster up the hill. Once they got to the top they fell onto the grass, panting for breath.

"I don't know when I last ran like that," smiled Cathella.

Johanna finally made it up the hill and collapsed on top of Cathella.

"Make biscuits," said Johanna, sucking her thumb.

"Yes, we'll make those biscuits," laughed Cathella whilst still trying to catch her breath.

"Cathella, you came!" shouted Patrick, running into the kitchen to give her a hug.

"We made biscuits," smiled Brennan, stuffing one in his mouth as he sat on his knees at the kitchen table with paper and crayons.

Fin walked through the door, wiping his sweaty brow and straddling a chair.

"How's it going?" asked Fin.

"I love them!" exclaimed Cathella, sincerely.

"Sean, see I wasn't lying - Cathella is my friend!" shouted Patrick out of the front door.

A boy not much shorter than Patrick walked through the door. He had red curly hair and freckles on his nose. A grim expression marked his other- wise cute face. Cathella knew he would be the toughest to win over with his immediate reluctance to know her.

"So what, Patrick?" Sean replied with a grumpy tone.

"Hello Sean, I'm Cathella," replied Cathella, handing him a biscuit as an offering of friendship.

He took it and looked away quickly, sitting down with his back to her.

"What do you say?" scolded Fin with a stern glare at his younger brother.

"Thank you," mumbled Sean.

"Sean thought I was lying when I told him you were my friend," taunted Patrick as he stuck his tongue out.

"So what?" shouted Sean.

"Stop it!" barked Fin.

"Where is Jo-Jo?" asked Patrick looking around the room.

"Sleeping," answered Cathella.

"Really? Asleep?" questioned Fin with wide eyes.

Cathella shrugged her shoulders and turned back to her cooking just as the door flew open and Johanna came running out of her room crying.

"What's wrong?" asked Fin holding out his arms for her.

She ran past him and straight to Cathella who picked her up and cradled her close as she sobbed.

"Seems you made another friend," laughed Fin stealing another biscuit.

"Jo-Jo doesn't like strangers," grumbled Sean under his breath.

"Well Johanna likes me, so I must not be a stranger," replied Cathella softly, kissing the girl on the head before handing her a biscuit to eat.

"You can call her Jo-Jo if you want. We all call her that," said Patrick with a wide smile.

"Jo-Jo it is." Cathella felt a warmth stirring in her chest, knowing she was gradually being accepted into this large, loving, but worn-down family.

Susanna came out of her room yawning and rubbing her eyes. She looked much better and well rested - even her colour had returned slightly.

"Look at this place - its so clean!" exclaimed Susanna in shock.

"I hope it's fine?" asked Cathella, nervously.

"Yes, dear lass, it's wonderful. I haven't slept so well in years," said Susanna with tears in her eyes.

"Mamai, she made biscuits," shouted Brennan, waving his in the air.

"Mamai!" yelled Jo-Jo, waving her own biscuit-filled hand at her mother.

"And Cathella has dinner cooking, too," Fin added with a note of pride in his voice.

"I thought I could smell something tasty," smiled Susanna.

Cathella felt herself blushing under all their praise - she hated having too much attention on her.

"It's getting late…I should go. See you tomorrow," said Cathella, gathering up her things.

"Where do you think you're going? You're not leaving without dinner," scolded Susanna.

"Yes Cathella, eat with us!" begged Patrick.

"Why? Let her go," said Sean, moodily.

"Cathella, can we show Sean and Patrick the frogs?" asked Brennan, getting off his chair and taking Cathella's hand.

"There aren't any frogs," answered Sean, turning to face her for the first time.

"Yes, Brennan caught the biggest frog I've ever seen. Would you like to come see?" asked Cathella.

Sean got up from the table and walked out the front door, his shoulders hunched as everyone sat watching him. After a few seconds he popped his head back in.

"Are you coming or were you lying?" questioned Sean.

Brennan let go of Cathella's hand and ran outside to join his brother. Patrick got up and ran after him. Cathella put Johanna down and took her hand before she followed Fin outside. They left Susanna to eat in peace for a few minutes with silence and no kids hanging off of her.

"I think you won him over," whispered Fin, nudging her with his shoulder.

"I like your family, Fin. They're everything I've wished for in a family," admitted Cathella.

"Wait till you meet Dadai!" laughed Fin as he took Johanna from her.

Chapter 5

Ireland 2000

Bella blinked a few times to clear her vision from the blurriness that plagued it. She had read for far too long and her eyes were stinging. She looked up to find Fiona in her bedroom doorway.

"What are you reading all this time?" questioned Fiona walking in and sitting next to Bella on her bed.

"Cathella's journal," said Bella putting it down on the side table next to the bed.

"Are you going to the funeral tomorrow?"

"Yes, I think I will."

"Good. Why don't we go for a walk? You've been lounging around for days," teased Fiona, pulling Bella up from the bed by the arm.

They left the castle and went for a walk around the garden. The gardens were filled with a vast array of different flowers, all beautiful, planted in a pattern that surrounded a cement bench in the middle.

"These are Wylie's babies. He has his own business, you know," said Fiona with pride.

"So he's a plant man?" laughed Bella.

Fiona broke out into giggles, clutching her stomach as she wiped her eyes.

"That's a good one - I can't wait to use it on him," sighed Fiona.

Bella laughed in return and leaned backwards, staring at the stone castle in front of her.

"What makes this place so special?" Bellas asked quietly, closing her eyes and breathing in the aroma of fresh flowers all around her.

"Are you talking about this castle, or Ireland?" Fiona asked, picking up a flower to smell.

"Both…I guess," said Bella.

She was so caught up in her surroundings that she didn't hear anyone else approach.

"What makes your home so special?" Wylie whispered into her ear.

Bella bit her lip to stop from gasping in surprise and glared at Wylie through her sunglasses.

"You have to stop doing that!" exclaimed Bella, pushing him gently in his stomach.

"Don't mind him, Wylie's always been sneaky," giggled Fiona as she twirled the flower between her fingers, watching the two of them.

"Are you going to answer my question?" asked Wylie, ignoring his sister.

He placed his foot onto the bench next to Bella; she turned slightly to face him.

"It's not the home, but the memories that surround the house and the people that live there."

"Exactly. It's the same for us. this castle has plenty of secrets and memories. Some are good, others bad. Lots of people have come and gone and they were all loved by someone in this castle," answered Wylie with surprising heat in his voice.

"But Cathella is gone and she made these memories, so why are you hold- ing on?" asked Bella in confusion.

"Arabella, why don't you tell me why you're holding on to your dadai so much, when he is just as gone as your grandmother," Wylie retorted.

They both stared at the other, neither willing to back down or give an inch. Bella finally exhaled and ran a hand through her straightened hair.

"It's not the same," said Bella sadly.

"Oh, and why isn't it? Just because you never knew Cathella doesn't mean her memories mean nothing," answered Wylie, angrily.

"Stop it! Why do you always have to fight?" cried Fiona, getting up to stand between the two of them.

"He started it," said Bella.

"And I know when to end it!" replied Wylie, walking away without looking back.

"You two are so strange. I've never seen someone work Wylie up as much as you do," said Fiona.

Bella stood and hooked her arm with Fiona's.

"Come on. Let's go eat and forget about him."

She looked back at the bench where Wylie had stood, let out a soft, irritated sigh, and walked away.

⁓⁂⁓

"Catriona, you outdid your self again," smiled Bella, putting her bowl in the sink.

"Thank you, Bella." replied Catriona.

"We love her cooking," Clancy added as he dished up more food for him- self from the large pot in the middle of the table.

"Can you cook, Bella?" asked Fiona, filling the sink with water.

"Yes, I can, and you? Rosie, our cook, used to have me help her when my mother wasn't around," replied Bella.

"Fiona cooking! Maybe if we all want to die," teased Wylie.

Fiona stuck out her tongue and gave his head a light smack. He chuckled and rubbed his head, exaggarating the impact. Clancy looked at Bella with a serious look on his face that looked all too familiar, so she braced herself for some bad news.

"Fiona tells me you are going to the funeral," stated Clancy.

"Are you?" questioned Wylie, a look of confusion on his handsome face.

He was looking at her like she was a puzzle he was trying to solve. Bella stared back at him, her blank expression giving nothing away. She had perfected it over years of confrontations with her mother.

"Yes, I'm going. I'm just not sure what I'll wear."

"I have a few black dresses you can borrow. Come on, lets go try them on. Maybe you will find a handsome man there!" giggled Fiona.

"Fiona, It's a funeral!" scolded Catriona, waving her wooden spoon at her daughter.

"The people are sad, not blind, Mamai. They're allowed to notice us, especially if we look good," answered Fiona, cheekily.

"Aye, where does she come from?" sighed Clancy with a fond grin.

"Maybe you'll find you an Irish man to take home," said Fiona with a sly wink.

Fiona turned to her brother and gave him a knowing look, ignoring the glare he gave her in return, and pulled Bella out the room with her.

After the fun of trying on various dresses came to an end, Bella found herself alone in the library. She curled up in her new favourite comfortable chair and started reading more of the journal. She read late into the afternoon, enjoying finding out new things and getting lost in Cathella's little world. It took her back to a time that was completely foreign to her. She made herself cosy with her shoes off and her feet tucked under her. After some time spent reading, she felt the strange sensation that someone was watching her. Bella peered over the book to find Wylie sitting across from her in the other chair, watching her.

"I don't want to fight," sighed Bella, putting the book down.

"Neither do I. Did you find a dress?" asked Wylie.

"Yes I did, thank you. How do you and your family know Cathella?" questioned Bella, suddenly curious as she tucked the journal down the side of the chair.

"I can't answer that right now," replied Wylie with a grimace.

"And why not? You know, I don't know why I bother being nice to you. I get nothing from you in return. You are so pretentious," spat Bella, her frustration building at his elusiveness.

"Oh! So that's how it is? I don't want to tell you something personal and you get all fancy with your words. I just don't get you, Arabella," said Wylie in a restrained voice as he held back his anger with sheer will.

He stood up, towering over her.

"I just don't get why you won't leave me alone! Stop bothering me!"

"If that's what you want, you got it, lass," said Wylie, caging her in with a hand on either side of the arm rest.

Bella shrunk back into the cushions as his eyes blazed with emotions that scared her with their intensity. He finally turned and stormed out of the room without another word. Bella yelled out in sheer frustration and threw her shoe across the room at the closing door. She heard him chuckle on the other side, getting the last word, it seemed, as usual. Bella sighed and finally picked up her other shoe before walking over to where the other had landed. She picked it up and went to her room.

She sat cross-legged on the bed and dialled her house phone.

"Hello, Mother," Bella said when her mother answered.

"Hello, darling. How are things that side? Have you found yourself a husband yet? And don't even try going to those horrible pubs I've seen in the movies," said her mother in a hurried rush of words.

"Mother, I'm here to sort out Cathella's stuff, not to find a husband or go to pubs."

"You should just come home so we can sort out this whole fashion business. I don't think you can handle running something like that. Your father's lawyers want to have a word with you when you return."

"Mother! I am staying here to sort everything out and then I'll come home and deal with the company myself," seethed Bella.

"Arabella, don't take that tone with me! What would your father think!" scolded Bethany.

"That he's glad I have a mind of my own…" mumbled Bella.

"What did you just say? How many times have I told you that mumbling is a bad habit? You need to go for more lessons with Lady Melody," replied Bethany.

"I have to go, Mother. I love you. I'll see you soon."

"Yes, I have a party to plan tonight. See you soon, dear."

She held the phone to her ear long after the call had ended, tears forming in her eyes. After some time, she put the phone down and curled up in a ball on top of the covers. She fell quickly into sleep, and her dreams spiralled her back into a past she wished she would just forget.

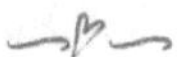

"Daddy why is mommy always angry with me?"

Her father lifted her onto his lap and wrapped his arms around her. Your mother is a vey busy woman, but she loves you so much, Bella."

"Not like you…she says I am loud, and not lady-like. What does lady-like mean?" asked six-year-old Bella, scrunching up her nose.

"It means boring and stiff - you wouldn't want to be that now, would you?" "I want to be like you, Daddy."

"I want you to be you. Never let anyone make you into something you're not."

Bella awoke with a start the next morning, her dream still lingering in the back of her mind. She gently touched the blanket that was now somehow draped over her and snuggled deeper under the covers. Today was Cathella's funeral. At least Cathella wasn't a total stranger to her now - not since she'd been reading the journal. Bella put on the dress Fiona had let her borrow and looked at herself in the mirror.

She turned her straightener on and applied make-up carefully before straightening her hair. She made her way downstairs in search of the rest of the household.

—⚘—

"Bella, you look beautiful. Even if it is for a funeral," Fiona said warmly with that distinctive twinkle in her eyes.

"You two look beautiful," said Clancy standing stiff and uncomfortable in his wool suit.

Wylie sat at the table dressed impeccably in a black suit. Bella sat down next to Fiona, blushing at the intense gaze Wylie was giving her.

"We missed you at dinner last night," said Catriona.

"I wasn't hungry," mumbled Bella.

"We thought something had happened to you. We made Wylie go check on you. He said you were out like a light."

Bella looked down at her bowl of porridge, realising Wylie had put the blanket over her. The increasingly familiar confusion swept over her- why was he nice to her when they hated each other so much?

"We better get going. Girls, you two are going to go with Wylie."

"Can't we come with you, Dadai?" pleaded Fiona.

"Dadai, please take them with you," groaned Wylie as he stood up.

Bella swallowed her last mouthful and tried not to stare at Wylie. She might not like him, but he sure wore that suit well. She looked up at his face and caught the knowing grin on his face. He had known she was staring at him. Bella wanted to slap that smirk off his face.

"I'm the father in this house and I say what goes," said Clancy, firmly.

Everyone looked at Clancy, no one bothering to argue.

He put an arm around Catriona's waist and led her out the kitchen door. Wylie walked towards the door as Fiona followed him. Bella hurried out after them. She stopped outside and looked around. She hadn't seen this part of the castle yet. There was a large swimming pool not far from where she was standing. It was dirty and black, as if it hadn't been cleaned in years.

"You have a swimming pool? A really dirty swimming pool, but still a pool." stated Bella, surprised.

"No one is allowed to use it," declared Wylie, leading them to a large wooden shed where the cars were parked.

They passed a large truck and stopped in front of an expensive-looking, sleek silver Mercedes.

"Why? You don't just have a pool for people to look at," Bella persisted.

Wylie held the door open for her as Fiona was already sitting in the back seat.

"Get in."

Bella glared at him and as she got into the car, she childishly pulled a face at him behind his back. She peered behind her at Fiona who sat still and quiet. Bella rolled her eyes and Fiona just shrugged her shoulders then turned to stare out the window. Bella sighed softly and leaned her head back against the head rest, closing her eyes. She must have dozed off, because when she next opened her eyes the car was stopping. There were already over a dozen cars and families making their way up toward the church. They get out of the car and Fiona grabbed Bella's hand as she pointed towards the church up on the hill.

"It's Riley McPherson's church!" gasped Bella in surprise. Wylie turned to stare at her, his expression puzzled.

"How did you know that?" asked Wylie.

Bella smiled, and the mischievous look in her eyes told him exactly where she got her information from.

"Cathella told me herself," answered Bella, using the same words back on him that he had used to tell her that Cathella would tell her what she needed to know.

She watched his reaction. He still looked slightly confused, but his anger and frustration was evident in his eyes.

"I ask you one question and you can't answer me without some smart remark back," grumbled Wylie, his shoulders looking tense.

"I did, but if you don't believe me then you don't have to."

"Come on Bella, lets go find our seats," interrupted Fiona as she walked toward the church.

Bella followed after her but stopped before the church doors. Bella took a deep breath in and out, her nerves skyrocketing at the thought of entering that church. She felt a warm breath on her neck and peered back over her shoulder to see Wylie standing behind her. Bella pulled herself together and glared at him before walking straight through the doors. He walked in step with her down the long aisle towards the front of the very crowded church. Most conversation ceased as they walked past, audible gasps rendering many speechless. One man stood up and looked directly at her as tears ran down his wrinkled cheeks. He pointed a shaky finger at Bella, his face a ghostly white.

"Cathella, is it you? Are you a ghost?" cried the old gentleman with a slight tremor in his thickly accented voice.

Bella stopped walking, her body bracing and her heart racing. She felt Wylie give her shoulder a slight squeeze.

"Aye, it does look like Cathella, doesn't it? Don't we wish it were true? But no, this is her granddaughter, Arabella McCullen, who has come to say good- bye to her grandmother," Wylie said loudly, addressing the crowd of startled mourners. The old man looked at her with sad eyes and sat back down.

"You can breathe again," whispered Wylie into her ear.

Bella let out the breath she didn't know she had been holding and made her way down the aisle. She sat down next to Fiona with Wylie on her other side and stared straight ahead. She felt ashamed and embarrassed, knowing that these people would rafter have seen the ghost of a dead lady than herself, the actual granddaughter of Cathella.

"They don't know you," whispered Wylie, reading her thoughts.

Bella's eyes flew up to his, her feelings raw and open for everyone to see. "Sometimes I wish it were me in there and her here," mumbled Bella, unshed tears clinging to her eyelashes.

She heard Wylie's sharp intake of breath; her mind racing fast. She hadn't felt like this since her father had died and she'd wanted to bury herself in that hole. All of these people would witness her having a panic attack. She could feel it coming on and was helpless to stop it. She put a hand to her throat, trying to suck in some much-needed air. She sat still, ignoring the waves of nausea assaulting her as her vision started going black. Somebody grabbed her wrist and pulled her up to her unsteady feet. A strong, sturdy arm went around her waist and walked her somewhere. Her mind was spinning and she could barely focus on anything. Someone was talking to her, but she couldn't make out what they were saying.

"Open your eyes!" Wylie said through gritted teeth.

Bella slowly opened her eyes, Wylie's concerned face inches from hers. He had her caged in against the side of the church, away from prying eyes.

"Arabella, I need you to breathe," whispered Wylie, his hand shaking slightly as he moved her sweaty hair from her face.

Bella blinked a few times, her vision blurry.

"Arabella, look at me and breathe!" Wylie said, his whisper rising in volume this time.

Bella swallowed past the bile and watched Wylie taking a deep breath in and out, finally forcing her body to do the same. They kept at it for five min- utes until her breath had steadied and she could see clearly. Wylie ran a hand through his hair, glaring at her. She felt her face heat up with embarrassment.

"What just happened?" asked Wylie, roughly.

"Nothing," muttered Bella.

"That was not nothing."

"Wylie, just leave me alone, please. We're going to miss the service, let's go inside,"cried Bella, filled with shame.

He took a step towards her. Bella stood as close to the wall as she could get.

"I have put up with a lot from you, Arabella. Cathella loved you, so don't you ever wish to change places with her and don't you ever scare me like that again. You nearly passed out," growled Wylie, his body thrumming with tension.

She had never seen him this angry with her before. Bella stared down at her black stilettos.

"Look at me," he spat through clenched teeth.

When she made no move to listen, he took his hand and placed it under her chin, forcing her to look up at him.

"You are so different from Cathella, even if you do look the same," said Wylie honestly, and with a hint of sadness beneath his anger.

"You told me I was just like her," Bella cried, feeling increasingly confused. "So you do listen when I talk."

"All those people were so disappointed when they realised I wasn't her ghost."

"You can either take offence at that or be grateful that you look so much like a woman that was loved by so many that they thought you were her."

"We should go back inside," whispered Bella.

"Fine, but this conversation is not over," stated Wylie, walking away.

Chapter
6

They began calling people close to Cathella up to say a few words. Much to Bella's surprise, Wylie was called last. He stood up there with confidence, gaining everyones' undivided attention.

"As you all know, my family and I live in Scarlett Manor, and we have for many years now. Cathella was the grandmother I never had. She was stub- born and hard-headed, but she had a heart of gold. She made me laugh and told me to dream big, no matter what anyone else said. She loved her gardens and she would have me walk with her through them as she told me stories of her life. Some stories where good, others jut sad. But the one thing that stood out about her was how she loved living and loved people. She suffered a lot of loss and she gained a lot of love from unexpected people. Now...I could stand here all day and tell you about her. That she lost the love of her life, yet still got up every day to raise her family by herself. But we all know how great she was.

We all have our own memories and stories, and most of all, we all miss a woman called Cathella."

As he finished, Bella couldn't help but notice the way Wylie's voice rose and shook with powerful emotion. He wiped his eyes and sat back down next to Bella. She took his hand in hers and gave it a light squeeze. ftings ended off with a couple singing while an old organ was played. Once the service was over, everyone made their way down to the old house that Cathella's aunt and uncle owned for cake and coffee.

"Where is she buried?" asked Bella.

"Come on, I'll show you," replied Wylie as he got up.

He led her towards the other side of the garden where they came across a large graveyard. They ended up at a group of headstones that were set aside from the others, and stopped in front of a specific one. Bella sat down in front of it and gently traced the name, "Cathella McCullen, 1895-2000, Devoted Mother To All."

"Oh, Grandma, I wish I knew you," whispered Bella, laying her hand flat on the stone.

Wylie had left her alone to mourn. She shivered and looked around the graveyard to find the old man from the church standing behind her.

"She talked about you."

"Did you know her well?" Bella questioned, standing up and dusting off her dress.

"Aye, I knew her well. My name is Patrick McCullen."

"Patrick? Is it really you? I've read so much about you and your family. Cathella loved you guys so much. How are Sean and Brennan, and little Jo- Jo?" asked Bella.

"She loved us all. Brennan is at home, he couldn't face today.

Christabelle is in America and Sean passed on a few years ago, as did Jo-Jo", answered Patrick pointing to the tombstones next to Cathella's and Susanna's.

Bella looked down at the tombstones; Sean died four years ago, but the one that stood out was Jo-Jo's dates

"1909-1914... she was only five...'

"Aye , we lost Jo-Jo a very long time ago," answered Patrick.

"No! That can't be! Not little Jo-Jo," Bella sobbed.

Patrick wrapped his arms around her and let her cry in his arms. She cried for the first time since getting here, and not from missing home, but for all the lost people that she never knew.

"Do you think I could come to talk to you tomorrow?" asked Bella, wip- ing her eyes.

"We would love that," said Patrick, staring at her.

Bella turned away from him to look once more at the tombstones. She noticed a smaller stone next to Fin's.

"Who is that?" asked Bella.

"It's little Arabella McCullen. She was just one when she passed away," answered Patrick.

"So much loss in one life. How did she survive it all?"

"Just like we all survive. My house is the same house my parents' owned", replied Patrick.

"Really? That's amazing," answered Bella.

"I'll give you directions. Go down the first alleyway you see..."

"Cut across the meadow, jump over the river and up the hill to the house." Bella finished for him.

"As smart as your grandma was. Come on, let's go get some cake."

"I can see why she loved you so much," replied Bella.

They walked up to the house together.

It looked exactly how Cathella had explained it to be. Fiona ran out the door, grabbing Bella's hand excitedly.

"Hello Patrick, I just need to steal Bella for a bit," said Fiona.

"Why? What for?" asked Bella.

"Trust me," laughed Fiona, pulling her into the house.

She led her over to a group of young people their age.

"Guys, I would like you to meet Bella. Bella this is Brody and Colin, they're identical twins and our age," said Fiona.

Bella smiled and greeted them. So this was why Fiona needed her. They weren't bad looking, with dark brown hair shaved close to their head and hazel brown eyes. Fiona took an instant liking to Colin, which left Bella with Brody.

"So you're Cathella's granddaughter?" asked Brody.

"Yes...I didn't know her well, but I'm trying to find out all I can about her," replied Bella.

"Come by my place and I'll tell you all you need to know," flirted Brody.

Bella laughed at his blatant offer. She hadn't felt this carefree in a while.

—⁊—

But suddenly a strong hand gripped her shoulder. Bella spun around to face a very angry Wylie.

"It's getting late, we need to go."

"I can give you a lift home," offered Brody.

"I promised my Dadai I would bring them home. Fiona, come on we're going," called Wylie.

"Maybe next time," smiled Brody.

"Yes...maybe," replied Bella, coyly.

They reluctantly followed Wylie back to his car. Fiona crossed her arms and refused to acknowledge Wylie. Bella wanted to ignore him, but she was fuming inside from the embarrassment of being treated like a child.

He stared ahead, driving as if nothing was wrong.

"What was that about?" questioned Bella.

"I don't like them." Wylie replied in a clipped voice.

"So let me get this clear - because you don't like them, we can't talk to them?" asked Bella.

"Flirting isn't talking," reprimanded Wylie.

"I am surprised you even know what flirting is!"

"I am telling Mamai that you embarrassed us," shouted Fiona.

"See what she says when I tell her it was the McGuire twins," replied Wylie.

"Ugh, you really are something, Wylie," growled Fiona.

They drove in silence the rest of the way home. Once they got to the castle the girls stormed off inside.

"Girls? Is that you? I made us some tea!" called Catriona to their retreating backs.

They sighed and walked back into the kitchen as Catriona poured them tea.

"Are you alright?" questioned Catriona, looking at Bella.

"I'm just tired. I guess it's been a long day," sighed Bella.

"Funerals do that to you," agreed Catriona.

"Bella met Patrick McCullen today."

"Really? He's a good man," smiled Catriona.

"He said I can visit him and Brennan tomorrow, they live in the same house as they did when they were younger."

"They haven't always lived there, but they can tell you a thing or two about Cathella," replied Catriona.

"Guys, thank you for today, but I'm going to go to bed. See you tomorrow," said Bella, yawning before leaving the room.

Bella woke up earlier than usual as it was still slightly dark outside. She put on a pair of skinny black jeans and a strappy pink top with her black hoodie over it. She quietly made her way to the kitchen in search of food. She switched on the light and let out a startled scream.

"Arabella, it's just me!" shouted Wylie, from his usual spot at the table. "Wylie, what the hell! You gave me a heart attack. Why are you even up?" "I couldn't sleep...and you?" replied Wylie, sipping his coffee.

"I wanted to walk to Patrick's now while it is still early so I'd get there at a suitable time."

"I can drive you?" offered Wylie.

"No, its fine, I like to walk," answered Bella. "It is far."

"I know, I walked here my first day, remember?" stated Bella.

"At least let me walk with you. Mamai will kill me if she finds out you went alone."

"Are you sure? I don't mind walking alone," replied Bella.

"Arabella, I am offering. Now sit down while I get us a proper Irish fry-up."

"You cook?" teased Bella.

"I can cook! Unlike Fiona, I took the time to learn, and Mamai works hard. She needs to sleep in sometimes."

He placed a large plate of food in front of Bella. She looked down at the plate filled with food and her stomach grumbled out loud. There were eggs, bacon, sausages, black pudding, white pudding, sodabread, mushrooms and tomatoes on the plate. Bella picked up her fork and dug in. She didn't look up once, savouring each bite. She felt eyes on her and looked up to find Wylie staring at her. this was by far the best meal she had tasted since getting here.

"this is so good," Bella admitted, her mouth full of food.

"It is?"

Bella smiled and carried on eating. She grabbed Wylie's cup and drank his coffee. He raises his eyebrows in question and she laughed in return. When they were done, they cleaned the kitchen and left the castle.

"Have you had any offers for the castle?" asked Wylie as he casually kicked at a loose stone.

They had been walking in silence for a while now and it had been nice for once.

"No, not yet. But Martin has a good feeling about this couple that put in an offer." said Bella.

She noticed a look of worry on his face before he glanced away from her.

"You'll need to give us some warning…we need to find a new place to stay," replied Wylie.

"I never thought of that."

"Come on this way, it's a shortcut," Wylie said, jumping over a fence.

Bella climbed over the fence and followed him through the field in front of them.

"I used to play here as a little lad…would just run around and pretend to fight the baddies," told Wylie.

"Who won?" teased Bella.

"Hmm that depended on my mood…mostly me," laughed Wylie.

"I grew up in a small house with a little garden but I had a dad who was more than willing to be a king or a knight for me," replied Bella.

"Your Dadai was quite old when he had you?" questioned Wylie.

"They never expected me, I was quite a surprise. My mother had never wanted children but my dad dreamed of having a child.

They did try for years but then gave up, and then one day she found out she was pregnant with me," explained Bella.

"The luck of the Irish, a lucky baby," smiled Wylie.

"No, a blessing. My dad always said it's not luck that made us, but God. So why give luck the thanks for the things that go right and blame God for what goes wrong?"

"He sounds very wise."

"He was."

They arrived at the small river. Bella began looking for a sturdy rock sticking out to jump over when Wylie grabbed her arm.

"It's still early, let's just sit for a bit. Besides there's a bridge over there - your grandfather built it," said Wylie, pointing to a bridge a little further down.

Bella pulled her arm loose from his grip. She looked away and then bent down to feel the water.

"Do you hate me?" asked Bella.

"How can I hate you when you saved my life?"

Bella stood up, confused, and turned to face him. She was just about to ask him what he meant when she heard her name being called.

"Bella! There you are. We heard voices and came to see. And good morning to you, Wylie," greeted Patrick.

"Morning to you, Sir," answered Wylie, politely shaking his hand. They all followed Patrick across the bridge and back to the house.

"Brennan is excited to see you, he got out the old photo albums to show you."

She stopped and took in the sight of the small house before following Patrick inside. An old man walked out of a room already smiling at them.

"Can't be! She looks like Cathella herself," cried Brennan.

"Hello Brennan, I'm Arabella," said Bella, shaking his hand.

"I'll get us coffee," answered Patrick, heading over to the stove.

Bella looked at the black coal stove. She could picture Cathella standing there at one stage. Wylie was sat down next to Bella across from Brennan.

"I saw that little Jo-Jo died when she was five," stated Bella.

"Aye, we were close, me and her, always home together. But that year I had started school and there was no one to protect her. No one blamed Cathella, but she blamed herself."

"But that was many years ago…times best forgotten," added Patrick, placing cups of coffee in front of them before sitting down.

"Patrick says you have a sister in America?" asked Bella.

"Christabelle. Cathella named the lass. Mamai said she had named so many that Cathella could name this one. Chrissie was a real dreamer and wanted more in life," answered Brennan.

"Look – here's a picture of all of us with Cathella." said Patrick handing her a photo.

Bella looked down at the photo.

"You guys were so cute…that must be Sean, and there you two are next to Christabelle and my grandfather…but who's the little girl in Cathella's arms?" questioned Bella.

"That's Arabella. Not you of course, but your aunty. this photo was taken three weeks before the accident," answered Patrick taking the photo back.

Brennan passed her another photo.

"Look how big you all are here! And my dad…he's so young!" cried Bella.

"He was six in that photo - that was the last group photo of us. After that we were all just too busy with our lives, I suppose," replied Patrick.

"Cathella gave us this one - it was her most treasured photo," smiled Brennan passing her another picture.

"That's you," laughed Wylie pointing to eight-year-old Bella sitting on Cathella's lap.

"Oh, I remember this! We were sitting in the library and she was reading me a story. My dad came in and asked me to sit with her for a photo... she was really excited. I saw tears in her eyes and she touched my curls with her soft hands and whispered to me in a loving voice that only angels sit on laps and that I must be one to be sitting on hers," remenisced Bella.

"She was very proud of you, Arabella," said Wylie, placing a hand on her shoulder.

"That she was. The only sad thing is that she never found that scarlett penny." sighed Patrick.

"There it is again."

"You'll find out soon enough, just be patient, lassie."

"Now, is anyone hungry?" questioned Brennan.

"No, we must be going. But thank you for having us," replied Bella, handing the photo back to Patrick.

"You keep it."

Bella nodded her head and tucked it into the small handbag hanging from her shoulder.

"Where to next?" asked Wylie.

Bella's stomach let out a loud growl, and they both stopped and laughed.

"That answers that. I know a great place in town," said Wylie.

Once they reached the fence, Wylie jumped over and waited for Bella. He led her down the alleyway and through the town to a small pub. Bella knew her mother wouldn't be caught dead in a place like this, and if she saw Bella here she would probably faint from sheer embarrassment. It was loud and busy inside, but Wylie led her to a table near the back where it was a little quieter. They could barely talk over the loud music without having to shout. Their waitress was a woman about their age who made her interest in Wylie abundantly clear. Wylie ordered for the both of them, and seemed to barely notice the way the waitress was ogling him.

"You probably get that a lot," yelled Bella.

"Get what?" asked Wylie, leaning toward her to hear.

"Girls staring at you, nearly falling all over you," shouted Bella.

Wylie lifted his eyebrow in confusion. He looked around the room and only seemed to notice now how many of the women were staring at him. He shrugged his shoulders and smiled.

"Guess it comes with the good personality!" teased Wylie.

Bella laughed at his comment and he pretended to be offended in return. The waitress came back with their food. She smiled sweetly at Wylie and leaned in closer than necessary toward him. When she left, they both started to laugh again.

"I can see she loves your personality," shouted Bella over the noise.

"Of course, I didn't have to say a word! It's that good."

They both ate in silence after that, enjoying their food in strangely comfortable companionship. Once they were finished, they left and began the walk back home. They started out silently, but after a while Bella couldn't re- sist the urge to ask him something.

She looked at him and opened her mouth before shaking her head and looking down.

"Just ask."

Bella's head shot up and she stared at Wylie.

"Leprechauns are big here, right? that whole thing about gold and rainbows?" asked Bella.

"Yes it is. People say it's a fairy. A small old man about two foot tall," an- swered Wylie.

"And it's all a myth, right?"

"Well people will always believe what they want. They say he's a shoemak- er, very unfriendly and likes to live alone. He loves gold and if you catch one you can't take your eyes off of them or they disappear. You have to scare them with violence before they'll hand over the gold."

"Sounds a lot like you," teased Bella.

"Me – little!?"

"No, unfriendly and mean," answered Bella.

He looked genuinely offended by her comment, so Bella knocked into his shoulder gently.

"I think I'll call you leprechaun from now on," giggled Bella before running off.

He let out an irritated grunt and ran after her. Bella screamed and ran faster but she was no match for him. He caught her and swung her around in his arms. Bella laughed and Wylie put her down.

"I'm no leprechaun."

"No, just grumpy."

Wylie pulled a face as Bella pulled away and walked off. He stood there for a few seconds before jogging to catch up.

"I hope you can run fast?"

"Why?"

"Because it's about to rain."

Bella looked up just as it started raining.

They both take off in a run until they finally reached the castle entrance. Wylie searched his pockets for his keys while Bella huddled into herself, getting increasingly drenched. He growled and started banging on the door. Bella shivered and Wylie turned to put his jacket around her shoulder which was wet and heavy from the rain but warm inside.

"You're shivering," said Wylie, turning her to face him.

He took his hands and rubbed them up and down her arms in an attempt to warm her up. He stopped rubbing and stared at her with an unreadable expression on his face. Bella realised how close they were standing; their noses almost touching. The rain pouring down around them as their breath came out foggy. Wylie cupped her cheek and leaned down, his lips a breath away from hers. Suddenly the front door swung open and they both jumped apart in fright.

"There you are, we were so worried!" cried Fiona, pulling Bella into the castle.

"We got caught in the rain."

"Come on, let's go run you a bath," replied Fiona.

Bella looked back one last time at Wylie. He was standing in the doorway, his eyes locked on her. She turned to face Fiona and carried on walking.

—⫻—

The bath was perfect; it warmed her right up. Once Bella was dry and warm, she curled under a blanket on the couch in the sitting room in front of the fire with Cathella's journal. What Brennan had said about Johanna's death and Cathella blaming herself bothered her. She needed to know what had hap- pened to Jo-Jo. Something no one dared talk about. Putting aside her con- fusion and mixed emotions about what had just happened in the rain, Bella opened up to the year of Jo-Jo's death, hoping Cathella could tell her what had happened.

Chapter
7

Ireland 1914

Cathella lifted baby Christabelle in the air and twirled her around, relish- ing her innocent laughter. Chrissie was a handful most of the time, but had the look of an angel with her black baby curls and chocolate eyes.

"Ella go to scool?" asked Chrissie, blinking her big brown eyes.

"No Chrissie, only the boys get to go to school. Fin will take Brennan today since it's his first day of school," said Cathella, sitting Chrissie on a chair by the table.

"But why can't I go to school?" moaned Jo-Jo sulkily.

"Oh sweetie, I know it seems horrible now but in two years you'll be in school. And then you'll be wishing you were here with me and Chrissie," answered Cathella as she tugged playfully at Jo-Jo's hair.

Jo-Jo pulled away, her lower lip trembling.

"But Brennan needs me..." Jo-Jo explained with tears running down her cheeks.

"I know he does; but Brennan is a big boy now and he needs to learn to be on his own."

"Jo-Jo don't worry – I'll be home later. Then we can go catch some frogs!" said Brennan as he tied his shoes.

"Frogs, frogs, frogs!" shouted Chrissie, banging her spoon on the tabl

"No! They won't be there then because they'll be sleeping," whined Jo-Jo.

"Brennan come on, we are going to be late," yelled Fin from outside the house.

"Bye, Brennan! Make some friends and work hard."

Brennan nodded his head excitedly and ran after his older brothers. The house was deathly quiet as they all stared at the door. Suddenly, Brennan ran back inside and threw his arms around Cathella. She hugged him back tear- fully. After he left, Cathella sat down and lifted Chrissie onto her lap as she took over the task of feeding her.

"Oh dear...I missed Brennan leaving!" cried Susanna, putting on her jacket in a rush as she left her room.

"Mamai," sobbed Jo-Jo, running towards her.

Susanna stopped and stooped down to hug Jo-Jo. She kissed her on the head and scooped Chrissie up from Cathella's lap into her arms.

"Jo-Jo, don't be sad! Brennan will be home later."

"Mamai go work?" asked Chrissie, giving her a sticky kiss on her cheek.

"Yes, you be good for Cathella," answered Susanna as she put her down.

Jo-Jo followed after her sulkily, so Cathella grabbed her gently by the arm. She glared at Cathella and pulled her arm free.

"Have a good day at work," called Cathella, cleaning Chrissie's dirty face.

Things had changed a lot around here. Since Chrissie had been born, Susanna had found a sewing job in town, which left Cathella alone at home with the children.

"Why does everyone have to leave?" questioned Jo-Jo.

"That's what life is all about. But they always return," smiled Cathella.

Jo-Jo pulled a face and Cathella laughed before beginning to clean the kitchen.

"What are we going to do today?" asked Jo-Jo, standing behind Cathella.

"How about we go for a walk?"

"Frogs, frogs," squealed Chrissie, running around the table with a burst of energy.

Cathella grabbed her and swung her up onto her hip.

"No, actually, let's go into town."

"To town without Mamai!" gasped Jo-Jo.

"Yes, and if you're very good, I'll buy you each a piece of candy."

"I'll go get my shoes," shouted Jo-Jo, running to the room she shared with Chrissie.

Cathella took their hands and walked with them down the hill. Jo-Jo crossed the river alone and Cathella carried Chrissie across. After that, she left them to run their energy off as she kept a close eye on them. Her thoughts were all over the place today. Had it really been two years? She missed her parent's everyday, but being here with these children helped ease the pain. She loved being a surrogate mother to them. She knew that Susanna loved all her children so much, but with a husband like hers it was tough to show much emotion. She worked a lot these days, but they needed the money desperate- ly. Cathella lifted up the end of her dress and ran after the two little giggling girls.

The grass was soft under their feet and the sun was shining down on them. Once they reached the fence, they all stopped.

"Cathella, I can't climb over," said Jo-Jo, clinging to the fence.

Cathella climbed over first and then lifted Jo-Jo over the fence. She picked Chrissie up and kept her in her arms and took hold of Jo-Jo with her free hand.

They walked into town and went straight into the confectionary shop. Chrissie squirmed around until Cathella put her down.

"Candy, candy!" shouted Chrissie, running around the shop excitedly.

Jo-Jo tried to act grown-up and stay still, but after a few minutes she let go of Cathella's hand and joined Chrissie. It took a while, but once they had each decided on their sweet of choice, she took them outside to sit on a bench and eat.

"Where are we going now?" Jo-Jo asked; her mouth was stained a sticky purple.

"How about we go visit my Aunt Attie and Uncle Riley?" replied Cathella, wiping their hands with a handkerchief.

"Yay! Yay!" shouted Jo-Jo jumping up and down.

Cathella lifted Chrissie into her arms and together they walked across the street towards the church.

Once they were safely on the church ground, she put Chrissie down. Both girls ran up the hill and then down the other side towards the little house. They ran straight inside without stopping. Cathella sighed and followed the sound of their voices to the kitchen where her aunt was sitting.

"Hello, deary, you know how much I love seeing them little ones!" cried Attie, lifting Jo-Jo up on her lap.

"Of course Aunty, why do you think I brought them?" smiled Cathella as she took her seat at the table.

"Pour us some tea, lass, I want to give them some sweeties," said Attie. "They just had!"

"Sweets never killed anyone," laughed Attie, handing them a sucking stick and a rag doll each.

The girls went to play with the rag dolls in the next room while Cathella and Attie sat talking.

"What are you going to do with your life, Cathella? I made a promise to your mother. I know you love them, but you can't do this forever."

"I love them, Aunty, and I know it's strange but when I'm not around them I miss them. Sean couldn't stand to be around me, and now he's my biggest helper," said Cathella, honestly.

"I just don't want to see your heart broken, lass…" replied Attie, patting her hand.

Suddenly there was a loud commotion and Riley walked into the kitchen with the girls in his arms.

"Hello my love, I see the McCullen girls are here," said Riley.

"Hello Uncle. We went for a walk," answered Cathella, taking a giggling Chrissie and putting her down.

"They are getting so big!" laughed Riley putting Jo-Jo down.

"They are! I hope you don't mind me bringing them here every few days, just to get out of the house," asked Cathella.

"We love all of you; come anytime," answered Attie, lifting Chrissie onto her lap.

"Where is Brennan?" questioned Riley.

"He's at school," replied Jo-Jo sulkily.

"I see," smiled Riley.

Chrissie let out a yawn and cuddled against Attie, bringing her thumb to her mouth in her characteristic indication of exhaustion.

"We better go before the others get home," said Cathella taking Chrissie from Attie.

"Want botty!" cried Chrissie.

Cathella opened her satchel and took out a glass bottle filled with milk. Chrissie grabbed it happily. laying her head on Cathella's shoulder. They said their goodbyes and then left to go home. Jo-Jo sang and skipped most of the way back while Chrissie slept. Once they crossed the river, she spotted the family car and screamed excitedly.

"Dadai is home!" screamed Jo-Jo, running towards the house.

"Jo-Jo be careful!" yelled Cathella, shifting a sleeping Chrissie to her other arm.

An older version of Fin stepped out of the house. The man had a stern looking face with no softness in it like Fin's had. He always made her feel uncomfortable, but thankfully he was rarely home.

"Hello, Mr McCullen," called Cathella trying not to trip up the hill. The man caught Jo-Jo in his arms and walked inside with her.

"Is Chrissie asleep?" asked Duncan, looking over his shoulder.

"She fell asleep a while ago," stated Cathella, and she left him to put her in bed.

She returned to find Duncan sitting at the table with Jo-Jo in his lap. Cathella heated up the soup she had made earlier that morning for them.

"The boys will be home any minute," said Cathella.

She spoke just at the right time - the door flew open and the boys came running into the house.

Talking and yelling all at once. They stopped talking as they spotted Duncan.

"Dadai!" shrieked Brennan, running to Duncan.

"Hello, lad, how was school?" Duncan said, wrapping an arm around his son's shoulder.

"He got a whipping," Sean replied.

"He didn't know he wasn't supposed to talk," defended Patrick

"What about you, I saw the whipping you got," Sean answered.

"Stop it, Dadai just got home!" ordered Fin as he walked into the house.

Duncan lifted Jo-Jo off his lap and stood up abruptly to face his sons. The boys stopped talking instantly. An ominous atmosphere instantly fell over the usually warm home.

"It seems all three of you need to be taught some manners! No one greeted Jo-Jo and Cathella, and all of you got into trouble at school," shouted Duncan.

"Sorry Dadai, hello Cathella," the boys mumbled in unison

"Go outside and go stand by the tree until I say you can come in," barked Duncan, pointing to the door.

"Dadai not the tree, please...they won't do it again!" pleaded Fin, placing his hands on Brennan's shaking shoulder.

"Finnigan, I am the father in this house and what I say goes," spat Duncan, grabbing Brennan roughly by the arm.

Brennan started crying and Jo-Jo ran over to Cathella and hid behind her. "Stop crying or you'll find you'll be out there all day!" shouted Duncan, shaking Brennan.

"Stop it! All of you just stop it! I made a nice lunch and I want everyone to sit down and eat!" Cathella called out without thinking, shaking with anger and fear.

Duncan turned to look at her as he let go of Brennan, causing the boy to fall to the ground. The father shoved his chair aside and stormed out of the house.Fin stared at her with an unreadable expression on his face. He looked almost angry, but as far as she could tell, she hadn't done anything wrong. Brennan stood up, rubbing his sore arm. The others sat down at the table, all unable to say a word. Cathella placed a bowl of soup in front of each of them and sat Jo-Jo at the table. She hugged Brennan and sat him down.

"On Wednesdays you boys must meet us at the church after school. We'll be spending the day there and don't want to rush home for you. Attie said it's fine and we can call it Picnic Wednesdays," stated Cathella warmly, hoping to lift their spirits.

Fin finished his food without saying anything and walked over to the door. He paused with his hand on the door. His shoulder's tensed as he refused to look Cathella in the eye.

"That was the stupidest thing you could have done. He could have hurt you."

Cathella gasped, putting a hand in front of her mouth. Fin slowly turned to face her, raw emotion shining in his eyes.

"But...thank you," said Fin as he left.

Cathella sat down in the chair he had vacated and let out a sigh she hadn't realised she was holding in; overwhelmed by the hard work of the day and the emotions swirling through her mind.

"We cut up a frog today," said Patrick, breaking the tension.

"Awesome!" shouted Brennan.

"One boy fainted," laughed Patrick.

"So what, some people don't like blood," replied Sean.

"No, you're the only boy I know who doesn't like blood," teased Patrick.

"I do like blood!" cried Sean.

"Fine let me cut myself right now - the blood will pour out all over," said Patrick, picking up a butter knife.

"Stop it!" scolded Cathella. She snatched the knife from Patrick's hand and quickly put it away.

"Ella! Ella!" called Chrissie.

Cathella rubbed at her temples and stood up from the table to look at them sitting around the table. They heard Chrissie calling again and stood up.

"We better go play before Chrissie attacks," giggled Patrick, running out of the house. All their earlier fear seemed to be forgotten, each one following the other.

Chapter

8

Cathella couldn't believe how well her Wednesdays were working out. this was the third Wednesday of her new plan. Something had changed between her and Fin since that day in the house. She would catch him staring at her more and more with an odd expression on his face. When he realised she was staring back he would shut down and look away. Today was like every other Wednesday, but Fin had brought Susanna home for lunch with them. Attie and Riley sat with them under the tree that they had claimed as their own.

"How's work?" asked Riley, looking at Susanna with concern.

"Tiring," Susanna bluntly replied.

Chrissie sat happily on her mother's lap drinking her bottle while the others ran around chasing each other. Cathella and Fin left the others and took a slow stroll around the church. Cathella twirled a flower in her fingers while Fin walked next to her looking tense and nervous.

He suddenly stopped walking, making sure the others were out of sight. Cathella stopped and turned to face him. She smiled and he seemed to relax a bit more.

"Cathella, if I asked you to…go on a date, or something… would you go with me?" asked Fin.

Cathella was 19 to Fin's 21 years of age and this was the first move he had made since the day they had had that picnic two years ago.

"With you?" questioned Cathella teasingly. "Yes." chuckled Fin.

"But why?"

"Well, because you're beautiful outside and inside… I think about you all the time, and I just want to be with you all the time," Fin stumbled through his words, sincerity shining through.

The sky had darkened considerably since they had arrived; all of them had been to busy to have noticed. Before Cathella could answer, it suddenly began raining. Everyone gaftered their things and made their way to the slightly warmer, dry house. After that, it rained all afternoon without stopping. The children played games in the house while the adults sipped coffee. No one was able to go back to work as the possibility of illness hung in the air. In no time, it was dark outside but the rain still hadn't stopped, and it seemed as if it wasn't going to stop anytime soon.Susanna paced around the kitchen, looking wracked with nerves.

"We need to go home!" cried Susanna.

"Not in this weather, we have plenty of room," Attie replied in her sooth- ing voice.

"But Duncan!" shouted Susanna.

"Think about the children," answered Attie, pointing to Chrissie and Jo-Jo asleep on a blanket by the fireplace.

Susanna reluctantly gave in.

The men slept in the sitting room while Susanna slept with Chrissie and Jo-Jo in Cathella's bed. Cathella moved into Attie's room for the night and slept soundly near her aunt's comforting presence. By morning the rain had not let up and it was practically flooding. School had been cancelled, and there was no way of getting to work. They all sat listening to news of the war on the radio, trying to pass time.

"One day I'll go fight," said Fin.

"No son of mine will be fighting," said Susanna with a sharp edge in her voice.

"Mamai, this is our country…and there are people saying the war is headed our way. Many have to go fight." replied Fin.

"You will stay right here." demanded Susanna.

Fin stormed out of the kitchen angrily and Cathella followed him. They stood in the sitting room alone. Fin had his back to Cathella as he stared out the window. She gently touched him on the shoulder and felt him relax slightly.

"She is just worried about you." said Cathella.

"I am a man Cathella, and I have little brothers who need to know that when you are a man you need to fight!" shouted Fin.

"And if you die, what does that prove?" asked Cathella turning her back on him.

Fin sighed and turned to face her. He gently grabbed her shoulders and looked her directly in the eyes.

"I won't die, Cathella."

"I can't lose you," cried Cathella hugging him.

Fin took her arms and pulled her back slightly. He leaned down and kissed her. this was her first kiss and it was nothing like she expected.

"Gross!" yelled Patrick.

They pulled apart to find Sean and Patrick staring at them.

"Go play!" shouted Fin blocking a blushing Cathella from their view.

Cathella felt her face go red with embarrassment; she stepped away from Fin.

"You were kissing," laughed Sean.

Fin ran after them as they screamed and ran off giggling. But then suddenly the front door flew open and Duncan walked in soaking wet.

"Where is Susanna!" demanded Duncan; a thunderous expression on his face.

Everyone heard him and made their way into the room. Susanna, hunched over, came in quietly carrying Chrissie.

"What are you doing here?" asked Duncan.

"It was raining, I don't want them to get sick," Susanna said with fear shaking her voice.

"You are my wife and belong home with me!" screamed Duncan.

"Calm down, brother...it was only one night," said Riley.

"Stay out of this - I am not your brother." spat Duncan, stepping forward with a threatening glower on his face.

Cathella took Chrissie from Susanna and stepped back. He approached Susanna and grabbed her arm, painfully pulling her towards the door.

"We are leaving now." declared Duncan, finality in his voice.

"Leave her alone!" shouted Fin, pulling Susanna away from Duncan.

"Son, step off," growled Duncan.

"No, Dadai."

"Mamai!" sobbed Chrissie.

Duncan stepped forward, raising his fist to hit Fin as he stood firmly in place, his shoulders tense but strong.

"Stop it!' screamed Attie.

"Dadai leave him alone," yelled Brennan pushing Duncan away from Fin. Duncan grabbed Brennan by the shirt lifting him off his feet.

"Lad, you are on dangerous ground," snarled Duncan.

The air became thick with tension as things escalated viciously.

"Leave my brother alone! You are a mean man and I hate you!" screamed Jo-Jo, hitting Duncan over and over with her little fists.

He dropped Brennan and grabbed Jo-Jo's wrist before slapping her through the face. Everyone stood frozen in shock. Jo-Jo touched her cheek and Duncan stepped back in horror. Cathella stepped forward as Jo-Jo stared at Duncan before she ran out of the front door crying.

"Jo-Jo!" screamed Susanna.

Cathella put Chrissie down and ran out in the rain in search of the little girl. She heard her name being called. Cathella screamed out for Jo-Jo, des- peration mounting. A thick mist surrounded them, typical Irish fog, making it harder to see anything. Cathella felt for a moment that she would never find her, her heart dropped at the very idea. It was wet and cold and would be getting dark soon. She heard a loud scream and the sound of a car break- ing the silence that had descended since leavving the house. Cathella lifted up the bottom of her soaked dress and ran through the mist and rain, her heart pounding in her ears and her vision blurring with tears. She found herself in the road, where an older man stood next to his car, panicking and pointing to the ground.

"It wasn't my fault!" cried the man.

Cathella looked down to find, with horror, Jo-Jo lying on the muddy ground, her leg twisted at a horrible angle and blood seeping all around them. She fell to the floor, her hands shaking and lifted Jo-Jo into her arms. There was too much blood to see where it could be coming from and Jo-Jo was letting out soft whimpers.

"Someone help me!" screamed Cathella. She turned to face the man.

"Get help!"

"Jo-Jo," sobbed Cathella ,running a bloody hand through her hair.

"It hurts all over… Cathella. I…I don't hate Dadai, I'm sorry I ran," whis- pered Jo-Jo wheezing for breathe.

"Hush now, don't talk; help is coming."

Cathella rocked back and forth with Jo-Jo in her arms, the girl clutching her hand as blood oozed out of her mouth. this was Johanna and she was only five years old, this was not supposed to happen. Cathella barely felt the cold. She felt like a piece of her was dying inside, along with the little girl in her arms.

Cathella sat in the sitting room; shaking more from shock than from the wet clothes she had on. Sean and Patrick sat with Brennan and Chrissie while Fin stood looking out of the window. The rain had finally stopped and every- one sat silently waiting on news on Jo-Jo. The tension in the air was unbear- able. The doctor had been in and out with bloody material. To much for one little girl. Duncan walked out of the room; his eyes showed nothing but cold emptiness. He looked at every one of them and a single tear ran down his cheek.

"Johanna is dead," Duncan stated with a bluntness that cut through them.

"No!" screamed Cathella.

Jo-Jo's blood was still all over her dress, her last words echoing in her mind. Sean got up and ran to Cathella, sobbing in her arms.

"this is your fault, Dadai!" shouted Patrick.

"Do you think I wanted my little girl to die?" asked Duncan.

"She said she doesn't hate you," mumbled Cathella, rocking back and forth.

Duncan looked at them once more and with sheer horror stormed out of the house, never turning to look back. Susanna stood slowly and moved to leave the room with a slow-motion quality that made her like a ghost. She picked Chrissie up and walked away.

"I never protected her," sobbed Brennan.

"It's not your fault," whispered Cathella.

Riley left the house to get things prepared for the burial. Patrick walked over to Cathella.

"She is dead, she's gone," cried Patrick.

"I know. I should have run faster, I should have..." cried Cathella. Fin faced them for the first time; his eyes red-rimmed, and walked to-

wards Cathella.

"Go to Mamai," he said, ushering them out of the room.

He helped Cathella to her feet, wrapping his arms around her. "Don't ever blame yourself," said Fin with a fierceness that scared her.

"But little Jo-Jo..." sobbed Cathella.

"She loved you," whispered Fin.

"I failed her," mumbled Cathella, looking down at the blood on her dress.

"No! Dadai failed her," cried Fin.

"I held her in my arms and she died, I did nothing to stop it!" shouted Cathella.

"You did everything!" yelled Fin, holding her close.

They stood together, crying for a little girl who hadn't been given much of a chance in life. A little girl whose smile had warmed their hearts.

Cathella squeezed Fin's hand as she looked at the boys huddled together crying. Susanna held Chrissie in her arms while she cried. Duncan hadn't been home seen since the accident and no one expected him to return. It was hot outside but everyone felt cold inside. They watched Jo-Jo's coffin being lowered into the ground. It was a sad day for everyone.

"Do you think she knows how much we loved her?" asked Brennan, tears running down his cheeks.

"Yes, she knew how much you loved her." replied Cathella.

Susanna hadn't said one word since it had happened and held Chrissie like her life depended on it. Chrissie wasn't sure what was going on and no one was sure how to explain it to her. After they each sprinkled dirt on the coffin, they all walked over to the tree and sat down. Patrick looked at Cathella with tears in his eyes.

"Jo-Jo was so little." cried Patrick.

"We need to be strong for Chrissie, she doesn't understand." replied Cathella.

"You won't leave us will you? I don't think Dadai is ever coming back," sobbed Sean.

"I won't ever leave and all you need to know is it is not your fault," answered Cathella.

"Was God mad at us? Was that why He took her?" questioned Brennan.

"God never takes someone unless He needs them for something special."

"But we needed her more…" sobbed Patrick.

"We need to remember all the good times we had with her," whispered Fin.

"Mamai is very sad."

"Mamai needs us to be strong for her, we are all sad. Jo-Jo was our little sister." stated Fin, calmly.

"Do you think she is happy where she is?" asked Brennan.

"She is with all the frogs and candy she can think of," smiled Cathella, wiping her eyes.

9

Ireland 2000

Bella looked up at the tissue being held up to her face. She took it as her face turned red with embarrassment. Bella touched her wet cheeks; had she really been crying?

"What's wrong? Are you alright?" questioned Wylie.

"I'm fine. I just read something really sad," said Bella.

"What was it?"

"Cathella's journal…little Jo-Jo just died," mumbled Bella.

"Her journal! You are reading her journal?" asked Wylie.

"Yes, she was my grandmother," answered Bella, frustrated with him.

"And that's her private property."

"You wouldn't understand," Bella said defensively, getting up.

"That you are reading her personal diary? No, I don't."

"Everything she owns is mine."

"So now you want her things? I really don't want to fight with you, Arabella."

"It's Bella…and neither do I," answered Bella, leaving the room with the journal.

Wylie growled and ran a hand roughly through his hair, frustrated as he watched her go.

Bella put the journal away and found Fiona in the kitchen.

"There you are, I thought you were with Wylie?" questioned Fiona, giving a suggestive look.

"Ugh! No! Why would I be with him?" mumbled Bella sitting down next to Fiona.

"You two looked pretty close in the rain the other day…" winked Fiona with a giggle.

"Don't be silly, you know how we fight all the time."

"Whatever you say. So, since there's nothing between you two, how about a double date with the twins we met at the funeral?"

"I thought your brother said they're bad news or something."

"Oh please; he can't tell me what to do. Wanna come?"

"Sure, why not."

"Good, because I already said yes! And you need to dress smart," Fiona said, trying to make a hasty exit.

"What if I had said no!" Bella shouted to her retreating form.

"I would have convinced you to come," laughed Fiona, disappearing out of the room.

Bella took a deep breath and got up. She decided to go to go up to Cathella's room; the room was a total mess from her last visit.

She sat down on the bed with a better understanding of who her grandmother was. this wasn't just a room but a woman's room, a real woman, someone who had many hardships in her life and still persevered. She picked up a dress lying by her feet and hugged it to her chest. Suddenly Bella heard movement in the doorway and refused to look up, not wanting to accept that she knew who would be standing there. After a few seconds, a gentle hand touched her shoulder softly, and Bella took a deep stuttering breath. She looked up at Wylie, tears running down her cheeks unwillingly. Bella waited for Wylie to tease her but he did something totally unexpected, instead. He sat down and pulled her into his arms. Bella sobbed in his arms. She didn't know why, but she couldn't stop. Wylie rubbed a soothing hand up and down her back. Bella finally opened her eyes and saw that she'd soaked his chequered shirt.

"I'm sorry..."

Wylie tilted her face up and used his sleeve to begin gently wiping away her tears.

"Don't be sorry, Arabella, it's just a shirt," said Wylie.

"It's just that I never knew her...and now I am reading her journal..."

Bella closed her mouth and looked at Wylie, but he had no expression that she could clearly read. She bit her lip and carried on talking.

"It's like, all of a sudden I know her. She's real now - not just someone I met once, years ago..." Bella continued, pulling away to get a better look at his reaction.

"She was real all the time Arabella. I'm just glad that she's real to you now. I'm sorry for shouting earlier on, I was just a bit shocked. Cathella would have wanted you to read her journal," Wylie admitted, a note of defeat in his voice.

Bella smiled and put the dress back down onto the bed gently. She knew Wylie was carefully watching her every move.

"Thank you, Wylie…for letting me cry all over you. I really have to go get ready or I'll be late," said Bella.

"Ready for what?" questioned Wylie.

"A date with Brody.

Bella looked up in time to see the thunderous expression on Wylie's face. She was slightly a taken back by it. In a span of seconds he shut down all of his emotions and left her alone in the room.

Bella returned to her own room and had a nice, long bubble bath. She put on a figure-hugging short red dress with black stilettos. She was just finishing with her make-up when Fiona walked in. Fiona looked stunning in her navy blue strapless dress and black stilettos.

"You look beautiful!" they both exclaimed at the same time. They both laughed and grabbed their handbags.

"Come on, I think I heard a knock. Lets go!" squealed Fiona, pulling Bella down the passage.

Colin and Brody were standing in the foyer while Wylie watched them walk down the hallway. They both let out a wolf whistle at the sight of the boys dressed up in suits. Bella glanced at Wylie who was wearing his usual worn denim jeans and the chequered shirt she had cried on…he still looked better than the other two in their smartest suits. He was staring back at her. Bella felt a blush coming on at being caught staring and tried to shake it off as she walked over to Brody. Fiona took Colin's hand and walked out of the front door with him. Bella took Brody's arm as he raised it to her.

Outside there were two different cars; Bella looked at Fiona nervously.

"I thought we were going together?" questioned Bella.

"A girl needs to feel special, so we agreed to go separately," said Colin, opening his car door for Fiona.

Bella felt uneasy; something wasn't right. She looked at Fiona and saw how excited and happy she was. Bella sighed, trying to put aside her anxiety, and got into the car. Brody got in, gave her a smile, and pulled away towards town.

"Where are we going?" asked Bella.

"It's a surprise..." answered Brody, grinning.

They drove to town and the ride was silent. They end up at the pub that Wylie and her had lunch in just the other day. Bella felt over-dressed for the atmosphere, but Brody blended in with most of the guys who were still in their work suits. The pub felt even louder and more crowded than last time. There was a live band playing on the little stage and a football game on the flat screen.

"this is the best place in town," said Brody, sitting at the same table she had sat at last time.

"I feel over-dressed."

"Nah, you look just fine to me."

They order a whisky each, trying to talk over the music but resorting to shouting.

"So, how do you like it here?" shouted Brody over the music.

"It's beautiful...but I miss home," answered Bella.

"I hope I can make it easier for you."

Bella smiled awkwardly at his flirtatious remark and sipped her Irish whisky. ftroughout the meal, he talked non-stop about working on the boats and topped up their glasses whenever they looked a little low.

By the end of the meal, Bella felt slightly drunk. It was hot and her head was spinning. Brody asked her to dance with him; Bella giggled nervously and accepted. When has she allowed herself to just have fun like this? To let loose and be young again? They gyrated on the dance floor with the masses of other bodies. Bella felt more alive than she had in a long time.

Brody was staring at her with a look of hunger. It gave her the shivers, but she ignored it and carried on dancing. The band finished the song and a man and his guitar stepped up. He started singing a slow song. Brody put his arms around her and pulled her close. His hand kept moving closer to her back- side. Bella grew irritated, and attempted to push him away, but her move- ments felt clumsy. Brody tightened his grip, leaving a sharp pain; she slowly realised that there will be a bruise there tomorrow. Bella pushed his hand away more firmly this time. He had a dangerous look in his eyes and moved in to kiss her; Bella turned her head sideways to avoid his lips.

"Stop!" yelled Bella, pulling away from him finally. "I thought the English liked it easy."

"No! I'm not like that. Just...take me home."

"Stop playing games," growled Brody, grasping her arm tightly.

"No!" screamed Bella, giving him a hard shove before pushing through the sea of bodies.

She made it outside but it was dark and no one seemed to be around. A hand grabbed her from behind and shoved her into the brick wall on the side of the building. Bella let out a cry of pain and pushed Brody away, but he was stronger and forced her around to face him. He held her arms above her head and started kissing her down the neck.

He moved up and kissed her lips. Bella bit his lip and he slapped her in the face.

"Keep still," whispered Brody, ripping the front of her dress.

"Please don't…" sobbed Bella as she tried to break loose.

Another shadow stepped into the alleyway and caught sight of the two of them.

"Hey – what's going on here?" shouted the guy, realising something wasn't right.

Brody got a fright and let go of her for a second. Bella seized her opportunity and kicked him between the legs, then began to run.

She felt sick and dizzy but didn't dare stop running. She wasn't sure where she was going. Bella looked behind her and found she was alone. She had lost her heels along the way and her feet were bleeding. She stopped, finally feeling safe enough to slow her pace, then began to walk until she found the bridge she recognised. She paced across the bridge and pounded on the door till some- one opened up; tears running down her cheeks.

Chapter
10

Wylie slammed the car door so hard that it rattled. He pocketed his keys and walked right into Patrick's house without knocking. Patrick and Brennan were sitting at the table, calmly drinking their coffee.

"Where is she?" asked Wylie, hiding his shaking hands in his pockets.

"On the bridge. She won't come in and she won't talk to us," replied Patrick.

"Wylie, it looks pretty bad. I won't lie. That bastard did a number on her and she needs a friend right now," said Brennan.

Wylie nodded his head. Words had abandoned him. He walked out of the door and looked around. The full moon was high in the sky, making it easy to see despite the darkness. He spotted her sitting on the bridge with her feet in the cold water. Wylie took a deep breath and walked towards her. He made a lot of noise so as to not startle her.

"Arabella…are you alright?" asked Wylie, quietly and slowly sitting down next to her.

She looked up at him and he sucked in a breath. Her cheek was swollen and red and her lip spilt. She has this lost look in her eyes, with dry tears staining her cheeks. Wylie wanted to hold her but knew he couldn't. She was trembling all over. He took off his thick leafter jacket and draped it over her shoulders. It made her look so small and young. Bella snuggled deeper into it. She was staring at the water.

"He said all women are easy," slurred Bella, waving her hands in the air to emphasis her point.

"Come on, lets go inside," croaked Wylie, gently touching her shoulder.

"Don't touch me!" screamed Bella scrambling backwards across the bridge.

"I would never hurt you Arabella; you're just pissed and scared. Let me help you."

"Just because I drank too much doesn't make me easy!" shouted Bella.

"You are not easy, I swear. Now please let me take you home."

Bella eyed him warily and slowly stood up on shaky legs. Wylie saw the torn dress and bruises on her arms and legs; a rage to kill growing within him.

"What happened?" questioned Wylie, standing a few feet away from her.

"Just leave me alone," cried Bella, dropping his jacket onto the bridge as she turned away from him.

"No, I won't leave you, Arabella, tell me what happened?" asked Wylie.

He picked up his jacket and wrapping her in it again. He felt the tension in her rigid shoulders and rubbed soothing circles over her back, not knowing who needed it more.

"He was kissing me. He had me against the wall and wouldn't stop. He tore my dress," whispered Bella, her knees buckling as the tension drained out of her.

Wylie caught her and scooped her up like a bride crossing the threshold. She looked up at him with glassy eyes and burrowed her face into his neck.

"I will kill him…" growled Wylie, walking back towards the car.

"You won't ever hurt me, will you?" mumbled Bella, before falling asleep.

"No, I won't," whispered Wylie. He dropped a quick, light kiss on the top of her head.

He put her in the car and said goodbye to Patrick before going home. Wylie looked at the bruises and cuts on her arms and neck. He clenched his hands on the steering wheel until it hurt. She was fast asleep, dwarfed in his jacket, and he wanted to keep her with him forever.

⸻ ♌ ⸻

Bella woke up with a groan escaping her swollen lip. Her mouth was dry and tasted foul. Her eyes burned as she opened them to the intense light, and her ears were ringing. She sat up slowly and her stomach did a somersault. Bella ran to the bathroom, just making it to the toilet before throwing up. She rinsed her mouth out and looked at her reflection. Her lip was swollen and she had a bruise on her cheek. Her mascara had run when she had cried and her hair was a mess. She knew further down was worse. She didn't want to look at the dress she was still wearing from the night before. She washed her face, noticing for the first time the unfamiliar leafter jacket she was wearing. A blush burned through face as she suddenly remembered what had happened last night with Wylie. Bella threw the jacket onto a chair and crawled back into bed.

After a few minutes, someone knocked softly at the door. Bella grunted in response. The blankets were lifted from her face, and Fiona's worried expression filled her view.

"I am so sorry about Brody. Colin was livid. He almost broke Brody's jaw when he heard," cried Fiona, clutching Bella's hand.

Bella patted her hand soothingly; she could see the displaced guilt wrapped around Fiona like a blanket.

"It's not your fault."

"Yes, it is."

As Bella groaned in pain and Fiona continued to apologise, Catriona walked into the room carrying a tray of food that smelled delicious.

"Wylie told us what happened…are you alright, dear?" asked Catriona, gently touching her bruised cheek.

Yes…I'm more embarrassed than anything else,"

"Don't be. Brody was an ass. Clancy and Wylie went to go and find Brody to have a little talk with him about respecting ladies," said Catriona, patting her leg.

Fiona giggled. Bella smiled weakly in return.

"If you guys don't mind…I want to sleep for a bit more." replied Bella, beginning to lie back down.

"When you feel better, we'll be here."

Bella closed her eyes, trying not to cry. Everything hurt and she just wanted to go home. She slowly fell into a deep sleep, hearing faint voices in the room. When she woke up for the second time her head felt a little better. She licked her dry lips and Wylie handed her a glass of water. Bella thanked him. He was sitting in a chair right next to her bed.

"How are you feeling?" asked Wylie. He stretched out his hand to touch her but then stopped himself at the last moment.

"Much better, thank you," answered Bella.

"Good. Brody's been arrested and charged with assault, so he won't be hurting anyone else anytime soon."

"Why did you come get me?" questioned Bella nervously.

"You are Cathella's granddaughter," answered Wylie, as if that were all the explanation she needed.

"Well, thank you anyway. You were right...no Irish man will like me," replied Bella, biting her sore lip.

"I like you," Wylie said abruptly, staring at her intently.

Bella stared back at him. She couldn't read the emotions in his eyes. Her heart beat faster.

"You're just saying that because I feel so horrible," stated Bella.

"No."

The phone rung suddenly and Wylie passed it to her. She answered to find her mother on the other end.

"Hello, dear! I thought I would find out when you're planning on returning home." said Bethany.

"Hello, Mother. I don't know yet."

Bella looked over at Wylie. He was sitting with his arms crossed, trying not to listen.

"Why do you sound so strange, dear, are you sick?"

"No mother...I was attacked last night."

"By who?!" shouted her mother.

Bella pulled the phone away from her ear; her mother could certainly raise her volume when when she wanted to.

"I went on a date and the guy wouldn't take no for an answer."

"Well what did you do? You must have done something to lead him on."

"You can't seriously think I asked for this!" shouted Bella, refusing to look at Wylie.

"No, dear...it's just the way you dress sends the wrong message at times..."

"I dress fine. It's the men that are the problem."

Bella could barely see through the tears. She clenched the phone tightly. Suddenly the phone was removed from hand without warning. Bella blinked away her tears and looked at Wylie.

"Hello Mrs. McCullen, Bella can't talk right now. When you feel like you can talk to her with respect, you know where to find her," said Wylie calmly before putting the phone down.

Bella heard her mother screaming in the background before the line went dead. She glared at Wylie as he stared back.

"You had no right to speak to my mother like that."

"She had no right to talk to you that way. You deserve better."

They were both glaring at each other when the door flew open and Fiona ran into the room. She sat down on the bed in front of Wylie.

"You look much better," cried Fiona.

"I have to go," mumbled Wylie as he quickly got up and walked away. Fiona looked nervously around the room.

"Would you be mad if I told you I had a good time with Colin?" questioned Fiona.

"No, you have to tell me everything," answered Bella honestly.

"It was magical! We ate by candlelight in this garden...he was here this morning to see how you were," sighed Fiona.

Bella took note of the dreamy look in her eyes and felt a flicker of resentment.

"I'm happy for you," replied Bella.

"Do you want some food?" asked Fiona, pointing towards the tray.

"Let me have a bath first."

Bella had a long soak, trying to loosen her stiff muscles.

She cleaned off all of her bruises and put on a comfortable pair of black sports pants and a blue hoodie.

She made her way slowly to the kitchen, her feet still sore from running. Everyone was already sitting and eating when she arrived. Catriona served her a plate of food.

"You should've seen Brody's face when we arrived! He got such a fright he nearly wet himself," laughed Clancy.

"Thank you," said Bella quietly, blushing again.

"You are one of us, lass, and we keep our own safe. I had to keep Wylie from killing him, mind you. He wouldn't stop and that boy was nearly dead when he was done. He certainly learned a lesson today," answered Clancy.

Bella noticed Wylie's spot was empty and ate her food quickly.

She went to her room and fetched his jacket. Bella knew his room was upstairs, but didn't know where. She made her way up the stairs and walked along the passage. She heard music and followed the sound. She found herself in front of a door that was slightly ajar. Bella knocked and it swung open. The room was as big as hers, but more lived in. Wylie was sitting on the bed with his back against the headboard. He was playing the guitar and softly singing along. Bella stood there, mesmerised. She didn't know how long she was watching until Wylie cleared his throat and she smiled awkwardly.

"Sorry, I didn't mean to pry…I came to give you back your jacket," said Bella, holding it out.

"Thank you."

Bella put it down on the bed. She knew he was waiting for her to leave, but she didn't want to go.

"I didn't know you played and sang." "

It's nothing," sighed Wylie.

"No, it's beautiful, really. Wylie, you could make a career of it," answered Bella earnestly.

"I play because I love it," replied Wylie, looking down at his guitar.

"Would you play for me?" .

He looked up at her as if attempting to see if she was playing some sort of game with him. He saw nothing but sincere interest and sighed.

"Sit down."

Bella smiled and sat down at the bottom of the bed. She crossed her legs and waited. Wylie's fingers moved across the strings with precision. The tune was slow. Wylie opened his mouth and started singing. Bella listened with awe. When he was done, Wylie stopped playing and looked up at Bella to find her gazing at him with an expression he'd never seen before.

"Are you blushing?" teased Bella.

"No, I don't blush," said Wylie, putting down the guitar.

"Please, you can't hide it from me. Don't worry - your secret is safe with me, no one will know you blush," answered Bella.

"And I should trust you?" questioned Wylie playfully.

"Of course you should."

Fiona walked into the room and she gave them a knowing look.

"Bella, you know Martin, the lawyer? He's here," said Fiona. She looked at Wylie once more and left the room.

—♪—

Bella found Martin sitting in the study.

"I didn't expect to see you," said Bella, sitting down across from him.

He looked at her bruises on her face and she noted the look of concern that flashed through his expression.

"It's been taken care of. Don't worry."

"Good...I came to tell you that I found a buyer," answered Martin.

"So soon?" asked Bella.

"Are you having second thoughts?"

Bella thought about last night and shook her head.

"No, I don't belong here. But I do have one request. The new owners are not aloud to kick the McIntosh's out," requested Bella.

"I will discuss it with the buyer," answered Martin.

"Good, so how long will it take?"

"Two months. Then you can go home," smiled Martin.

Bella let Martin out and put her hoodie back on before strolling around the garden.

This was what she had wanted, but why did it feel so wrong For years Bella had never felt like she had belonged anywhere. Her mother was too busy working and her father had tried but it was hard. Now that he was gone, she wasn't sure where she belonged. Bella felt an uncomfortable hint of jealousy toward Fiona and Wylie; they were all so close and they were there for each other. It was nice having someone care for you. It felt strange and unfamiliar, but nice. For once, she didn't have to do this alone. Her dad might not be here to be her king or her knight, but she had Wylie and his family. Two months...that was all she had left here. Bella spotted Fiona sitting on the bench and sat down next to her.

"What're you thinking about?" asked Bella.

"What will happen to us when you leave?" replied Fiona.

"Nothing, this is your home and it will always be your home."

"So why can't you make it your home?" questioned Fiona.

"It's not that easy, Fiona. I don't belong here," replied Bella.

"Cathella didn't either, and she stayed. It's your choice Bella. Irish or not, this is your home just as much as the one back where you came from," Fiona said softly.

"No, this is not home, Fiona. My mother is my home, and one day my husband will be my home," answered Bella.

"But I want this to be your home! I don't have any friends. Only you, and if you go, who will I have?" sobbed Fiona, suddenly overcome by emotion.

"You'll have your family and you have Colin."

"Well then, who do you have?" asked Fiona.

"When I figure it out, I'll tell you," admitted Bella.

They sat in silence for a while just breathing in the fresh air. Eventually, Bella went back inside and sat in her favourite chair with Cathella's journal. ftings were going much better for Cathella since the last time she had read... everyone was still mourning Jo-Jo but they had moved on. She needed to know what would come next.

Chapter 11

Ireland 1916

Cathella felt much older than her 21 years of age. At times, she felt like she had the weight of the world on her shoulders. She was currently sitting at the table helping Brennan with his school work. He was doing well in school for a 9; he was smart and determined. The war was raging on around them, but Fin had said he would stay clear of it. He was the man of the house now, with their father gone and him taking his place as the oldest. Four-year-old Chris- sie was not like her older siblings; she acted like a real little lady, hating any rough play. She sat on the other side of Brennan, brushing her doll's stringy hair. The door opened and Fin walked in smiling - he pulled Cathella into his arms.

"Did I tell you I love you today?" asked Fin.

"I don't think I can remember..." teased Cathella.

"Will this help?" questioned Fin, kissing her on the lips.

Patrick stood in the doorway, his arms crossed and grinning.

"Where is Mamai?" asked Patrick.

"She's sleeping; she wasn't feeling well," sighed Cathella.

"She has been sick a lot lately," said Sean as he came out of his bedroom.

"I know…but all we can do is help her as much as we can and be strong for her," answered Cathella.

"I'm the strongest one here," roared Fin jokingly, lifting Cathella into his arms.

"Fin, put me down!" cried Cathella, hitting him playfully on the shoulder.

They all laughed as Fin put Cathella down but kept his arms around her.

"I have something I need to speak to you all about…" started Fin.

Cathella froze, his arm stll around her, hoping he wasn't about to say what she had been fearing he'd say someday.

"The time has come. this Great War is happening and we can't ignore it anymore. I have to do my part. It's my responsibility as a man, and if the enemy succeeds…well, I don't know how I'd live with myself…" Fin said, his voice quivering with anxiety but with a firmness Cathella recognised as final.

She pulled away from him to sit down so she wouldn't faint; her stomach turning.

"I know it's frightening but we have to be brave. I have to be brave. I hope you'll all understand that."

He looked straight at Cathella as he spoke, but she couldn't find the words to comfort him, or herself.

They all took a seat at the table. No one said a word. Cathella waited for Fin to say more, her hands shaking as she looked up at him.

"How long?" Cathella asked after a long, tense silence.

"Two weeks," mumbled Fin unable to look her in the eye.

Cathella nodded, trying not to cry in front of the children.

"No, Fin! You can't go!" cried Chrissie, running towards him.

Patrick got up and abruptly stormed out of the house without saying anything. Sean got up and followed him out.

"Oh Fin, what are we going to do?" sobbed Cathella.

"Will you die?" questioned Brennan, nervously.

"No I won't, and you have Mamai and Cathella," replied Fin honestly.

"No son of mine is fighting!" yelled Susanna, suddenly walking towards them.

She looked pale and weak, struggling to keep herself upright.

"Mamai I have no choice!" cried Fin.

"I will move in here to help," stated Cathella, attempting to soothe both Fin and Susanna while concealing the panic taking place inside her own heart.

"No child, you've already done far too much for us," said Susanna.

"Please don't argue. You are my family now," stated Cathella calmly as she looked hard at all of them.

"Please live here...you can sleep with me," begged Chrissie, climbing onto Cathella's lap.

"Only if you're sure about this?" questioned Susanna.

"It will be easier, but one of us will still need to work," answered Cathella. "I won't be gone long," replied Fin.

"You be safe - don't be a hero. You have a pretty lady waiting for you when you come home," Susanna said firmly while taking Fin's hand.

"I am going to marry you, Cathella, I promise, and we will live in a castle," said Fin as he turned to fix his eyes on her.

"I know, Fin. you are my Prince Charming," smiled Cathella, tears running down her cheeks.

"I want to go with you," stated Patrick.

"No!" shouted the others in unison.

"You can't stop me!" yelled Patrick. "Not you, too," cried Susanna.

"Patrick, we need you here, while I am gone – you'll have to be the man of the house," said Fin.

"But I want to protect our country, too!" Patrick shouted.

"I need you here to protect your family," replied Fin.

"Mamai is going to need you, and I need you. Brennan will need you to walk him to school," said Sean.

"But I need to be a man and got to war. I should be fighting too"

"You need to be a man and stay here. Don't try to be a hero somewhere else when you can be one right here at home!" said Fin, slamming his fist onto the table.

Chrissie buried her face in Cathella's chest, sobbing softly. Cathella rubbed her back in gentle, soothing circles.

"Fin…please don't die like Jo-Jo," begged Brennan.

"I can't die - Cathella and I are going to get married and make pretty little babies," declared Fin.

"Oh Fin," Cathella cried, trying to be brave.

"I'll write to you everyday and wait for you to come home to me."

"I will read every letter, my love, and answer them when I can." answered Fin.

"I know you will," sobbed Cathella.

"Don't cry, love…I'll be home soon." comforted Fin.

"Why do you have to go?" asked Sean.

"Because they need me, they need men out there," said Fin.

"And what type of man would I be if I didn't go where I'm needed?"

They all stood huddled together on the platform alongside many other families saying their goodbyes. this was harder than anything, seeing Fin in a uniform that meant so much but also meant that he was leaving. Cathella held Chrissie's hand tightly, the little girl sobbing for her brother not to go. Fin hugged everyone goodbye and then pulled Cathella aside and kissed her on the lips gently.

"I love you with all my heart," whispered Fin.

"And I love you Fin. Come home to me," whispered Cathella in his ear before kissing him on the cheek.

"I got you something," said Fin, stepping out of her embrace.

He dug in his uniform pocket and pulled out something small and round, placing it in her hand

"What is it?" asked Cathella opening her hand.

"A Scarlet penny, the rarest thing on earth. I painted it just for you, so that you will know, just like this penny, how rare we are. There is only one of you and me; a love formed by true beauty," said Fin.

"Like a Scarlet penny," smiled Cathella clutching it tightly.

"Now don't you go and lose it. It's worth a fortune in love." Tears ran down Cathella's cheeks.

She would miss him so much.

"Don't cry now, I won't be gone long," replied Fin, wiping away her tears with the sleeve of his handsome uniform.

The train whistle blew and people began to board the train. Fin kissed her once more and turned away.

"Fin!" screamed Cathella.

He stopped and looked back at her as she ran to him. He grabbed her tight, swinging her around before putting her down.

"Sometimes true beauty isn't always what you see, but what you know.

Return to me," whispered Cathella.

She let go of him and watched him get on the train, Chrissie ran towards her and she lifted her in her arms.

"He won't forget us, will he?" asked Chrissie.

"No. Never!" answered Cathella, holding the girl close.

"How do you know?" questioned Chrissie.

"I made sure of it," replied Cathella, watching the train leave.

She made her way back to the others where Susanna sat on a bench crying.

"My son is gone," cried Susanna.

"Mamai, he will be back," said Sean

"I know," replied Susanna, taking a deep breath and accepting Brennan's outreached hand.

She stood up, but stopped when a wracking cough took over as Sean held her up. Cathella looked at her with concern. Nothing would ever be the same again. She couldn't bear to think of Fin not returning or she would have no reason to go on. He was everything to her.

"I will get a job," stated Patrick.

"No," Susanna replied quickly.

"Mamai, stop treating me like a baby! Do you want us to go hungry?" asked fourteen-year-old Patrick.

"Why did your father have to leave?" cried Susanna.

"Why did anything bad have to happen?" questioned Sean.

"Don't be sad, Mamai, I will care for you," said Brennan.

"I know you'll try my darling, but you have school," replied Susanna coughing again.

"Let's go home."

"Don't worry, Fin said he would come back, right Cathella?" Chrissie piped up.

"Right - and Fin has never lied to us," answered Cathella, kissing Chrissie on the cheek.

"Mamai, will you leave us?" questioned Brennan.

"I don't leave the ones I love," said Susanna.

"Good, because you are the best Mamai I know and I love you," said Brennan, hugging her around the waist.

"We all love you," answered Sean.

"Even Cathella loves you!" shouted Patrick, playfully knocking Cathella in the shoulder.

"I know, my angels. We need to stick together to get through this."

"We're a family, even if we are missing a piece of the family. We will be whole again." said Cathella.

"Fin was crying," stated Chrissie, taken aback by her strong brother's sad-ness.

"And you would be too if you had to go to some strange place where you know no one," scolded Patrick.

"What is he going to do?" asked Chrissie.

"Kill people," answered Brennan.

"Brennan!" shouted Susanna.

"But its true!" yelled Brennan.

"Whether it's true or not you, you don't go talking that way around a four- year-old!" cried Susanna.

"Sorry mamai, sorry Chrissie, and I don't think Fin will kill anyone." mumbled Brennan apologetically.

Susanna stopped walking as another cough overtook her fragile body. this time Patrick had to hold her hand so she wouldn't fall over. When she stood up her eyes were watering and her body shook with exhaustion.

'Mamai are you alright?" asked Sean.

"Yes, Son, I'll be just fine," answered Susanna.

Cathella wasn't so sure it was true, but she hoped for the children's sake that she was wrong.

Cathella couldn't believe it had been six months since Fin had walked away to get on that terrible train. She stood on the platform, anxiously waiting for a similar train to arrive.

"Are you sure this is the right one?" asked Chrissie.

"Yes it is…now don't let go of my hand," said Cathella, walking towards the train.

Cathella watched people climb off the train, unable to look away in case she missed him. Their eyes met and he dropped his bag and ran to her.

"Fin!" cried Cathella, holding him tight as he spun her around.

"My love, how I've missed you!" said Fin, kissing her all over the face.

Cathella laughed and hugged him tighter. She stood back and looked into his eyes, they held a lot more sorrow and something else she couldn't quite read clearly.

"Fin, you're home!" yelled Chrissie from next to them.

Chapter
12

Fin stepped back to get a good look at Chrissie. He lifted her up into his arms, giving her a huge hug.

"Have you grown taller?" asked Fin, tickling Chrissie in the tummy.

She squealed in his arms, trying to stop him. Fin bent down, picked up his canvas bag with his free arm and then pulled Cathella close with that same arm.

"How is she?" questioned Fin.

"Not well...the doctor says it could be any day now," whispered Cathella, glancing anxiously at Chrissie in Fin's arms.

They walked home in silence, no words needed between them. Once in a while Chrissie would ask him a question, refusing to be put down. Once they crossed the river, he put Chrissie down and held Cathella's hand tightly. She felt the slight tremors in his hand but said nothing. He had seen a lot over there, but this was their wartime reality, and now it would be Fin's too.

"Fin!" screamed Brennan running towards him.

"Where is Mamai?" asked Fin while he hugged Brennan tight.

"She's in bed…" mumbled Sean from behind Brennan.

Fin pulled his brother into a hug, looking around the room for Patrick.

"Patrick is working, he took up a job," said Cathella, knowing that's who he was looking for.

Fin nodded his head, dropped his bag onto the table, and walked straight pars them to his mother's room. Cathella followed him, knowing he would need her now more than ever. She tried not to cry every time she saw Susanna but it was so hard. Her skin was grey and looked as thin and translucent as paper. Her eyes were sunken and she was unable to speak or move.

"Mamai…it's me. It's Fin," said Fin, taking her bony hand in his large tanned one.

Cathella saw tears in his eyes. If only she could take their pain away. Susanna stayed motionless except for the single tear that ran down her cheek.

"I love you, Mamai," choked Fin, letting go of her hand.

He kissed her on the cheek and walked out of the room angrily with Cathella chasing close behind him.

"Fin!" said Cathella, grabbing onto his arm.

"That is not my Mamai," cried Fin.

"I know, we tried to get to you sooner."

Fin pulled his arm away, walking out of the house.

"Cathella, I'm scared," sobbed Chrissie running to Cathella.

"Let's make biscuits for Fin," Cathella said in a falsely cheerful voice, hoping to distract her.

Patrick walked into the house looking tired and sweaty. He looked around the room at their sad faces.

"Where is Fin?" asked Patrick.

"He went for a walk," answered Cathella.

"And Mamai?" replied Patrick.

"I think she knew it was him," said Cathella, taking out the flour.

A few planes flew low over the house, they were loud and the house vibrated from the pressure. Chrissie hugged Cathella's legs, whimpering and trying to hide behind her. Patrick sighed and ran a hand through his hair as he stared at the closed bedroom door.

"I better get back," stated Patrick leaving the house.

"Come on Chrissie, there's a war going on, don't be scared of some plane!" shouted Brennan angrily.

"Brennan, go play outside," barked Cathella.

"Why? I didn't do anything?" argued Brennan, his hands on his hips as he faced her.

"Listen to Cathella," replied Sean.

"Why? she is not Mamai. I want Mamai!" screamed Brennan.

"Don't talk to her like that," said Fin, standing in the doorway.

He looked exhausted and his eyes were red from crying.

"You are not Dadai," said Brennan, cruelly.

"No I'm not. Dadai left us and Mamai is dying. We are all you've got."

Brennan fell onto his knees crying; Cathella's heart broke for the little boy she thought of as her own.

"Mamai is dying, who will care for us?" sobbed Brennan.

"You know what, I think we need a bridge," stated Fin.

"A bridge?" questioned Sean.

"Across the river. You want to help me?" asked Fin.

"Can I help?" yelled Chrissie, suddenly excited.

"No sweetie, this is a man's job," said Fin.

"I can help." replied Brennan standing up straight.

"Can you now? I don't know…this is a big responsibility," declared Fin, winking at Cathella.

"I'm almost 10, Fin. I can do it!" yelled Brennan, defensively.

"Well show me what you've got," smiled Fin as he headed out the door.

Sean and Brennan ran after him.

"That Fin is something," laughed Cathella.

"Are you going to marry him?" asked Chrissie.

"Chrissie, what a question to ask," giggled Cathella.

"He loves you," said Chrissie.

"And I love him…but right now we're still young," smiled Cathella.

"Love is never young," declared Chrissie, wise beyond her years.

"Oh, Chrissie," laughed Cathella touching her nose with flour.

"Stop it!" giggled Chrissie, wiping her nose.

After everyone had gone to sleep, Cathella went to go sit outside for some fresh air. She sat down and stared up at the stars.

"Trying to count them?" asked Fin, sitting down next to her and taking her hand in his.

They sat in silence for a few minutes; Fin staring at her while she pretended not to notice.

"I almost forgot…" said Fin digging in his pocket.

"What is it?" asked Cathella, accepting the item.

"Love," Fin said as he handed her the Scarlet penny.

"Oh Fin, you kept it!" cried Cathella, holding it tightly.

"Yes, but it was yours to keep," stated Fin.

"I knew you would need it more than me," answered Cathella, kissing him on the cheek.

"You really are something special," stated Fin.

"Were you scared?"

"Yes…but then I would close my eyes and see you standing here waiting for me and I knew why I had to keep fighting," Fin said with a small smile playing at his lips.

"Fin, I worry all the time."

"Don't be scared, my love," replied Fin, putting his arm around her.

⸺⸺

They heard Patrick yelling from inside and got up to go see what was happening.

"Patrick, what is it?" asked Cathella.

"It's Mamai…" sobbed Patrick.

His screaming had woken the whole house. Chrissie stood there crying. Sean lifted her up into his arms as they all made their way to Susanna's room. Susanna lay in the bed gasping for breath, her body shaking all over.

"I'll go get the doctor!" called Patrick, desperation in his voice.

"No, let her go, it's not Mamai anymore," said Fin.

They stared at each other, shocked and overwhelmed, but Patrick finally gave in.

"Does she know how much we love her?" questioned Brennan.

"And need her?" Sean added.

"Why do you think she held on for so long?" asked Fin, looking at Cathella.

"I don't want her to die," cried Chrissie, hugging Sean tighter.

Cathella went closer and took Susanna's hand.

"She is my best friend." whispered Cathella tears running down her cheeks.

Susanna squeezed Cathella's hand lightly. Even though her body had failed her, Susanna was still in there.

"Mamai, please don't die!" shouted Chrissie desperately.

Brennan went to the other side of the bed and took her hand placing it gently on his cheek.

"It's me Brennan…please Mamai," sobbed Brennan.

He let go of her hand and watched it limply fall to the bed.

"Mamai, I love you, please look at me! Just look at me!" screamed Brennan, becoming hysterical with grief.

Patrick placed a calming hand on Brennan's shoulder, but Brennan spun around and shook the hand off.

"We lost them all Patrick, we lost Jo-Jo and Dadai and now Mamai. What did we ever do wrong?" yelled Brennan, tears running down his little face.

"You did nothing wrong," answered Fin. "

We needed them!" Brennan sobbed.

"You won't die, will you Cathella?" asked Chrissie in a shaky voice.

"I hope not," replied Cathella, honestly.

Susanna took a deep, slow, rattling breath. Each breath came slower than the one before. Everyone stood watching her.

"Mamai, you said you loved me, you said someone doesn't leave those they love. Why are you leaving us?" asked Sean angrily.

They saw a single tear run down Susanna's cheek as she took her last breath. The room went quiet except for the heartbreaking sound of crying. Sean put Chrissie down and ran out of the room; they could hear him yelling and throwing things around the room.

They all left the room to go check on him.

"I hate all of you!" screamed Sean, throwing the chair on the ground.

Fin grabbed him from behind and held him until he stopped fighting and gave in to his tears.

"I hate you." mumbled Sean dejectedly.

"Who will care for us?" sobbed Brennan, holding Cathella's hand like a lifeline.

"I will," answered Cathella picking Chrissie up.

"But you aren't Mamai…" replied Chrissie, sobbing into Cathella's top.

"I know I'm not, and I could never be, but I helped raise you and I love all of you," said Cathella, quietly.

"Are you going to sleep in Mamai's bed?" questioned Chrissie.

"No, my darling. Why don't you close your eyes for a bit?" replied

Cathella, rocking her in her arms.

"Patrick, we'd better go get Father Riley," said Fin, heading to the door.

Sean ran out of the house after them, not wanting to be left behind. Cathella sat down with Brennan and Chrissie in the sitting room, the reality of her grief suddenly overcoming her like a tidal wave.

It had been three weeks since Susanna had died. Someone from a chil- dren's home had come to check on them, but Cathella told them she was caring for them. With the Great War still raging and so many homeless, they didn't argue. Fin had a month off before he had to go back. They had settled into a routine, and today was no different to any other. Brennan stopped in the doorway, home from school.

Sean pushed him forward from behind and he hesitantly stumbled into the house.Cathella looked at him and cried out when she saw his purple, swollen eye.

"Brennan!" cried Cathella, gently touching the eye.

Brennan winced and pulled away.

"He was fighting again."

"You have to stop this - it won't bring your mother back," said Cathella as she soaked a cloth for his eye

"I know...just leave me alone." shouted Brennan, running to his room.

Fin walked in the house and came straight to Cathella for a hug.

"Brennan was in a fight again," admitted Chrissie.

"Again!" yelled Fin, headed for his room.

"No, leave him," said Cathella, pulling Fin back.

"What are we going to do? I go back soon...and what about money?" asked Fin.

"We'll all be just fine just as long as we have each other," smiled Cathella, kissing him on the cheek.

She knew she sounded slightly more brave than she truly felt.

"You deserve a castle, my love," cried Fin.

"No...I just need you, and us," said Cathella.

Patrick walked into the house and looked at Fin with a strange expression.

"Fin, are you ready?" asked Patrick.

Fin nodded, and after hugging Cathella, left with Patrick. Cathella felt confused and sat down at the table next to Chrissie and Sean.

"Don't worry." said Sean patting Cathella's hand.

"It's not that easy." answered Cathella laying her head on the table.

Brennan came out of his room and approached Cathella cautiously.

"Cathella, I don't want to hurt anymore," whispered Brennan.

Cathella reached out and put her arms around him.

"None of us want to hurt, Brennan - but fighting won't make it better," replied Cathella.

"I won't fight anymore…I know Mamai isn't coming back," said Brennan.

"No, she isn't, but as long as I am alive, I'll care for you. You can trust me," smiled Cathella.

"Aye, and the English live a long time," teased Patrick, standing in the doorway again.

Fin was nowhere to be seen. Patrick took a seat across from her. Cathella looked up at him and smiled.

"I thought that was the Irish – lucky," laughed Cathella.

"Luckily for you, you are both Irish and English." said Sean.

"Cathella isn't English." cried Chrissie.

"No I'm as Irish as you are," Cathella said, impersonating their accent.

"Stick to your English," teased Patrick.

"Aye, what are you talking about, my Irish is just as good as yours," smiled Cathella.

"No you don't speak well at all," giggled Brennan.

"I thought I heard laughter!" stated Fin walking back into the house.

"Patrick, I need you to watch them tonight so I can show Cathella something," said Fin.

"Aye, I will," answered Patrick before leaving to go back to work.

Cathella got up and went to the stove to start dinner.

She stood with her back to everyone so that they wouldn't see her crying. Fin put his arms around her waist and she leaned back into him trustingly.

"I love how you smell," whispered Fin kissing her neck.

"I am scared," whispered Cathella.

"I know. So am I," answered Fin.

"They are dependent on us," cried Cathella.

"Hush, don't talk, just let us be here together for now," said Fin.

Cathella closed her eyes, taking a deep breath.

"I feel like I can't breathe when you're not here," whispered Cathella.

"When I feel like that, I hold the penny and close my eyes...then I can see you," smiled Fin.

They stood like that for a while, each just absorbing the presence of the other.

⸏

Once it was dark, Fin took out a lantern and lit it before leading Cathella down the hill and out of town. They walked for quite a while before he finally stopped. Fin lifted the lantern up to show her a sign that said, in faded lettering, Scarlet Manor.

"What is this?" asked Cathella, bewildered.

"Your castle," smiled Fin.

"What do you mean?" replied Cathella, thoroughly confused.

"In a year or two we can move in - it'll be ours! But the castle needs work first," Fin said, unable to conceal the excitement in his voice.

"But we can't afford it!" cried Cathella.

"We can! Mamai left me some money, and Patrick and I put more with it We will just pay it off. Once it's done, I will marry you," said Fin.

"Oh, Fin! I love you," sobbed Cathella.

They stood by the sign, holding each other close, neither wanting to break apart and end this wonderful moment of hope.

"Where is the Scarlet penny?" asked Fin, pulling away.

Cathella took it out of her pocket and gave it to him. He got down on his knees and dug a hole by the sign. Fin put the penny in the ground and closed the hole.

"Our love will grow on this land like our love for each other," smiled Fin as he stood up and brushed the dirt from his trousers.

"But you need it for the war," cried Cathella worriedly.

"No, I've got everything I need right here and I'll have to come home for my love," said Fin.

"I don't want you to go..." cried Cathella, trying to be strong.

"Come here when you are sad and then you will know how strong our love is," smiled Fin wiping her eyes.

He took her hand to lead her back home.

"Wait here - I want a last look," said Cathella, running back to the sign with the lantern.

She came running back to Fin, wiping the dirt off of her dress before taking his hand. She stared into his eyes, seeing only love there.

13

Ireland 2000

Bella? Bella, did you hear me?" shouted Fiona, waving a hand in front of Bella's face.

Bella put down the journal and looked at Fiona, not having heard a single word that she had just said.

"Sorry, what did you say?" questioned Bella, yawning.

"Tonight is the Summer Festival in Cork and Colin invited me to go, he said you could come. Please, come with us?" pleaded Fiona with a sad face.

"I'd really rafter not, Fiona. I don't want to be the third wheel," sighed Bella.

"You won't be! Besides, you could invite Wylie and go with him!" giggled Fiona.

"Fiona, you know I don't like him, we fight all the time."

"Exactly, why else would you fight if not that you enjoyed it."

"Fiona, don't be silly," said Bella.

"So are you going to go tonight?" repeated Fiona.

"Going where?" questioned Wylie entering the library.

"Nowhere," Bella answered quickly, glaring at Fiona.

Fiona gave her an evil little grin and turned to face Wylie.

"To the Summer Festival in Cork, I am going with Colin and I want Bella to come with us. She doesn't have anyone to go with - if you took her then our problem would be solved," Fiona said enthusiastically.

"Fiona! I told you I'm not going," scolded Bella, blushing.

"Do you want to go, Arabella? I don't mind taking you."

"I don't want to be an inconvenience to you…you probably have other plans," answered Bella.

"Actually, I don't, and I want to take you. Then you can see how us Irish really dance," smiled Wylie.

"So, it's all settled. We'll be leaving here at six," replied Fiona, skipping out of the room.

—⁊—

Bella looked up at Wylie dressed casually in khaki shorts and a button down black shirt and felt a blush coming on as he gave her a knowing smile in return. Bella stood up awkwardly, feeling slightly disadvantaged with the height difference.

"You really don't have to take me," muttered Bella.

"Arabella, don't start, I said I would take you. Now, let it be."

"Yes, Sir," teased Bella, giving a slight curtsy.

Wylie laughed and bowed in return. They looked closely at each other before Wylie pointed to the journal.

"So, what have you read so far?" asked Wylie.

"Susanna just died and my grandfather built the bridge across the river. He bought this castle for Cathella before returning to the war."

"So you know about the Scarlet penny?" replied Wylie with a raise of a brow.

"Yes, it is so romantic. I wish someone would do that for me." Wylie rolled his eyes and crossed his arms.

"Where is the penny now, anyway?" questioned Bella.

"Gone. Your grandmother wanted to give it to your grandfather before he left for the last time but it was gone. She's been looking for it all these years."

"That's so tragic, that she never found it," Bella sighed.

"I helped her look; you even helped her look when you came to visit with no luck. It was just not meant to be."

"How do you ever get over a love like that?" asked Bella.

"You don't," Whlie responded, bluntly.

Bella looked close at Wylie as he had that odd look in his eyes again. She swallowed nervously and hugged the journal to her chest.

"I'd better go."

Bella left the room and went to her bedroom to sit and think about the coin that was missing. What had happened to it? She would have liked to have kept it. She sighed out loud and collapsed back onto the bed. It had been so long since she had last heard from her mother; not that this was uncommon. Did she even miss home? Or had this become home to her as it had to Cathella? Cathella had stayed because she had family here. But what did Bella have here? She reminder herself that there was no use feeling sorry for herself - that wasn't going to change anything. The door flew open and Fiona walked into the room, collapsing next to Bella on the bed.

"We can't go," mumbled Fiona.

"Why not?" asked Bella, sitting up.

"It's traditional wear only, and I don't have money for a dress," said a dejected Fiona.

"But I do."

"No, I can't take your money!" shouted Fiona, leaping up.

"And why not? We're sisters now, and sisters share. Now lets go shopping!"

"Are you sure?" asked Fiona.

"Come on, we don't have long."

"Thank you so much." replied Fiona, hugging Bella.

Later that afternoon after getting their outfits sorted out, they got ready together. Catriona helped them tie their hair up in the traditional way. She had tears in her eyes as she looked at the two of them.

"You are both so beautiful," exclaimed Catriona, dabbing at her eyes with a tissue.

"Mamai, you're going to make me cry and then I won't look so beautiful," moaned Fiona as she gave her mother a big hug anyway.

"Bella, you look so Irish, all the men will be staring at you!" Catriona smiled and gave her a kiss on the cheek.

"Thank you, Catriona! It's time I looked Irish - I am in Ireland, after all."

"Glad to hear you say that. You look beautiful, Arabella," Wylie announced as he entered the room.

Bella tried not to stare at Wylie or look too flustered. He was wearing tight fitting black trousers and a white shirt that was half-unbuttoned at the front. She blinked and looked around the room to find everyone staring at her.

"It's for one night only!" declared Bella.

"Come on, Colin will be waiting," squealed Fiona, running out her room.

Wylie held out his arm and Bella took it. They walked together to the car.

"Don't talk too much or they'll know you're English…" teased Wylie.

Bella swatted him playfully with her free hand as he ducked out of the way.

"I'll talk as much as I want," laughed Bella.

"Well then be glad that you've got me or you'll be all alone tonight talking to yourself."

"Stop it - men think my accent is intriguing and beautiful," declared Bella, getting into the car.

Wylie laughed and closed the car door for her.

The three of them drove through town and caught the ferry going to Cork.

Just for tonight, the ferry would be open until midnight. The streets were filled with people and performers; the place was crowded. They found park- ing and headed for the evening tent for dancing and food. Bella got out of the car nervously. What if Wylie was right and no one wanted to talk to her? She felt her hands shake slightly and clutched her bag tightly to stop them. Wylie took her hand, prying it from the bag, and kissed her on the palm.

"Don't be afraid…you look beautiful. I was just joking – they'll love you."

Bella nodded her head and Wylie smiled in return before leading her towards the tent. They entered it and Bella stopped to look around in awe. The place was lit with beautifully glowing little lights. On the stage were river dancers and a live band behind them. Bella had never seen anything like this before. Wylie's friends call him over, he looked at them and then at Bella.

"Go," she reassured him,

"I'll wait here."

"Thanks, I'll be right back."

Wylie gave her another smile before heading off to greet his friends. Bella saw Fiona dancing with Colin and smiled. A couple of men approached her and asked her to dance. Bella accepted and found that she was quickly drawn into the dancing. She danced until she was exhausted and sweaty, but surprisingly happy that she came. She couldn't find Wylie anywhere, so she took a seat near the entrance to watch the dancers. Bella suddenly looked sideways and spotted Colin talking to a few friends. Where was Fiona? Bella looked around the tent and saw Fiona dancing with Colin, which meant that it wasn't Colin standing there, but Brody. Bella felt queasy suddenly and uncomfortably hot. She was gripped by the overwhelming sensation that she couldn't breathe. It felt like her lungs were closing up and her head was spinning.

Bella stood up and pushed her way through the crowd out of the tent. What was she supposed to do now? She put her hands down on her knees and dropped her head, trying to take deep breaths, but it didn't feel like the air was filling her lungs properly. Someone touched her shoulder and she let out a shout of fright. Bella turned to face a worried Wylie.

"Are you alright?" asked Wylie, worry written all over his brow.

"I can't breathe! I can't!"

"Okay, just calm down, Arabella. Look at me and follow my breathing."

They stood out there in the dark for some time with the small Christmas fairy lights dangling from trees around them. Music was still playing faintly behind them. Once Bella could breathe properly again, she felt her cheeks heat up with embarrassment and turned away from Wylie.

"Sorry... I saw Brody in there..." cried Bella shakily.

"I know. But he won't hurt you, I promise," replied Wylie.

"It was just...seeing him there, and suddenly I just couldn't breathe. I could feel his hands on my skin and I feel...I feel like I am going crazy," sobbed Bella.

Wylie put his hands on her shoulders, forcing her to turn and face him.

"You are not crazy. this is not your fault, and I won't ever let him hurt you again."

"Colin doesn't scare me even though they look alike. I can let Colin touch me and talk to me."

"They may look alike, but they are nothing alike. And you know that, so don't let him ruin your fun. Please, let's go dance," said Wylie.

"I would rafter not," mumbled Bella.

"Aye I see; for once you're not so brave at all. Well you can stay out here in the dark and I am going to go inside and find me a lady to dance with," replied Wylie, walking away from her and towards the tent.

"Wait!" called Bella.

Wylie turned around, smiling expectantly.

"Make sure she's not some psycho killer that wants to have your babies."

Wylie stared at her for a few seconds before throwing his head back and laughing. He took a step closer to her.

"That may be a bit tricky...maybe you need to help keep an eye on me?" said Wylie, crossing his strong arms.

"No, you're a big boy and you can handle it. I'm fine right here by myself," declared Bella.

"Arabella, don't lie to me. Now come on inside and see what a great dancer I am," pleaded Wylie.

"You won't get me in there no matter what you say," replied Bella, placing her hands on her hips and throwing him a challenging look.

"I don't need to say anything; I just need to do this."

Wylie leaned down and lifted Bella over his shoulder. She hit him on the back repeatedly.

"Wylie, put me down!" screamed Bella, laughing as she kicked her legs.

"Not 'til you say you'll dance with me."

"Never!"

"Fine, let's see what everyone thinks when I come inside carrying you like this!" laughed Wylie, turning to face the tent.

"No! Wylie! You wouldn't dare!"

He slapped her gently on the bum. She stopped with an indignant huff. Wylie chuckled and took two more steps towards the tent.

"Wait! Wait! Fine, you win. I will dance with you!" shouted Bella dejectedly but secretly feeling a warmth burning inside her stomach that she hadn't expected.

He put her down carefully and held out his hand for her to take. "I knew you would come to your senses."

"Yes, but you said a dance - you never said where. We dance out here. Take it or leave it," said Bella, crossing her arms.

Wylie gave her a feral grin and then grabbed her around the waist. He pulled her against him and started slowly moving to the faint music in the background. Wylie twirled her out and pulled her back towards him.

"Wylie!" giggled Bella, breathlessly.

"Hush, you're ruining my dance. When it's your turn, then you can talk," said Wylie playfully.

They danced together until the song inside had ended, stopping with their foreheads gently touching. They were both breathing heavily and staring into each others eyes. Bella took a step back, but Wylie had a firm grip on her. She knew instinctively that Wylie would never hurt her. Bella looked up at him, trying to get a sense of what he might be thinking. He looked down at her then leaned his face down to kiss her. Their lips touched, feaftery soft. Bella sucked in a deep breath. She opened her eyes to see raw emotion in his eyes. He must have seen something reflected back in hers, because he pulled her into a deeper kiss. After a few seconds they come up for air, still staring at each other. Bella knew her cheeks must be blood red.

"That was..." mumbled Bella, but she was cut off by his lips touching hers again.

14

She put her arms around his neck, drawing him closer. He let out a groan and nipped at her lips gently. Who knows how long they would have stood there still kissing, if not for the approaching footsteps that made them jump apart guiltily. They turned to face the intruder, who happened to be Fiona.

"There you guys are! Why do both look like you were caught doing something you weren't supposed to be doing?" asked Fiona, staring at them in confusion

"Fiona, don't be silly. What do you want?" snapped Wylie.

Bella looked at Wylie, his lips still swollen, and touched two fingers to her own. Had Wylie and her just been… kissing?

"Bella, aren't you cold out here? Brody left so I thought you would want to come back in," replied Fiona.

"Thank you, we were just coming inside," answered Bella, stepping forward.

"Arabella, wait! Weren't we talking about something?" asked Wylie, grabbing her arm.

"No, we're finished talking," said Bella, pulling her hand free.

She saw the look of confusion on his face and felt guilty for putting it there. They walked back inside, leaving Wylie alone outside. Once inside the tent, Bella knew Wylie wouldn't be giving up so easily, so she grabbed Fiona's arm.

"Come on, lets dance!" Bella shouted over the music.

She pulled Fiona into the middle of the crowd, trying to ignore Wylie star- ing at her from the entrance of the tent. He has this look on his face, telling her they weren't done yet. The song ended and another started. Bella turned to walk away but was stopped by Wylie. He pulled her into a dance before she could say anything. Bella's hand trembled in his. She knew he felt it, but his jaw was set in stone as they move around the dance floor.

"What happened?" asked Wylie, trying lower his voice so as to not draw attention to themselves.

"Hey, this is my dance and you are ruining it," replied Bella, looking away from his intense stare.

She knew she couldn't keep him quiet forever and the dance would be over soon. The minute it ended, she pulled away and walked straight to Fiona.

"I think we should go home," said Bella, faking a yawn.

"Why, aren't you having fun?" asked Fiona.

"I am, but I'm so tired. I could fall asleep right here," moaned Bella, feeling Wylie's presence at her back.

"Well...okay then," Fiona turned to face Colin and pecked him on the cheek, saying her goodbyes.

Bella sighed in relief and headed to the exit. She felt a warm hand brush along the nape of her neck. Bella shivered and turned to face Wylie.

"You can run, but you can't hide. Sleep well tonight, but tomorrow we talk,"

Bella opened her eyes slowly, looking around her room. She stretched
her muscles as they complained from all the dancing last night. She smiled, remembering her dance with Wylie before her face became hot all over again remembering the rest, and she threw the blanket over her head in an attempt to hide from the memories. Finally up, Bella pulled on her jeans and a cashmere sweater with her black ankle boots. She turned her straightener on and took her time combing and straightening her tangled hair. She wanted to try to avoid leaving her room for a couple hours. Once her hair was straight, she snuck outside to think for a bit, skipping breakfast. Bella sat on the edge of the cliff, her knees drawn up and arms wrapped around them as she considered everything that had happened. She couldn't hide out here forever, which wouldn't be soon enough, anyway. Wylie would find her, and then what? Why had she kissed him? It had felt good…but this couldn't be going anywhere. She would be leaving soon and would never see him again. She suddenly heard footsteps approaching and peered over her shoulder, Bella sucked in a breath. He stood in a pair of dark blue jeans and a navy blue henley. His hands were in his pockets and he looked almost hesitant to approach. He had sunglasses on to hide his eyes, and Bella felt a sudden urge to take them off and see him properly.

"You weren't at breakfast," said Wylie.

"I wasn't hungry," replied Bella.

"I see. So it wasn't to avoid me now, was it?" questioned Wylie.

"Fine, maybe it was," Bella said, burying her face in her knees.

Wylie sighed and sat down next to her. They both took a moment to look out at the view ahead.

"Do you wish it hadn't happened?" asked Wylie, hesitantly.

"Yes and no. I wanted you to kiss me, but it's not right when there can be nothing between us," Bella said quietly, refusing to look at him.

"And why not?"

"We live in different worlds, Wylie. I'm selling this castle and going home. this isn't what I came for," stated Bella.

"What if you are home? No one asks for love, it just happens," replied Wylie.

"I know that, and I know how hard it is to lose that."

"Arabella - I am not going anywhere," said Wylie, pulling her hand free from its tight hold around her knees and giving it a squeeze.

"But I am! this is not my home and…it just won't work," Bella's voice rose now as she pulled her hand free from his grasp.

"And why not? If you love someone, there's always a way!" demanded Wylie, raking a hand through his hair as he became increasingly frustrated with her answers.

"But I don't love you…it was a stupid kiss that meant nothing." She stood up and turned to leave.

"Don't lie to me, I can see it meant something," replied Wylie, with courage in his voice now.

"Well you must be blind, and you said you would leave me alone if you remember clearly," cried Bella.

"I did say that, but that was before, now you don't want me to," replied Wylie, standing up to face her.

"That's not true."

"Oh really?" questioned Wylie, stepping closer to her. He pushed his sunglasses up onto his head.

"Stop coming closer...I'm wrong for you," insisted Bella, stepping back.

Wylie smiled and kept coming towards her; Bella carried on her retreat.

"No you are not. You want me to kiss you," answered Wylie, reaching out and grabbing her before pulling her against his body.

"Please, don't!" whispered Bella, half-heartedly trying to step back.

"Why are you fighting this?" asked Wylie. He gently touched her cheek.

She could feel his hand trembling slightly despite his bravado.

"Why are you pursuing this? You can have any woman you want," replied Bella.

"I want you, Arabella. You're the only woman for me," whispered Wylie, so close to her that the words whispered close against her lips.

"Why do you have to say those things and be so handsome," stuttered Bella, trying to break free.

Wylie suddenly smiled at her with a look of accomplishment, his grin so wide she has the urge to slap it.

"So you think I'm handsome!"

"Wylie!" moaned Bella.

"Can I at least get one last kiss?" questioned Wylie.

"I would rafter have you hating me and us fighting," mumbled Bella.

"What fun would that be?" chuckled Wylie, bending down till his lips touched hers.

Bella sucked in a breath waiting for the kiss to go deeper, but Wylie stepped back.

She looked up at him with confusion.

"Someone is coming," said Wylie ,stepping away from her.

Fiona approached them with a knowing smile; Bella stared at her feet.

"Why do I always find you two together?" giggled Fiona, putting her hands on her hips.

"Fiona, what do you want?" growled Wylie; angry at yet another interruption.

"Why are you so angry all the time? I can see why Bella doesn't like you. Anyway, I came to see if you didn't want to join me, Dadai, and Mamai," Fiona asked.

"Where are you going?" questioned Bella.

"To the Martello towers in Ringaskiddy. We like to go visit there once in a while," answered Fiona.

"I've heard about them...I would love to come. I haven't done anything touristy really yet."

"We're leaving now – and bring a jacket, it gets cold there," replied Fiona, walking away.

Bella looked back at Wylie to find him staring at her with a strange look in his eyes. He stretched out a hand towards her. Bella looked at his hand and walked away. Wylie sighed and walked in step next to her. She could see he wanted to ask her something, but she couldn't take anymore questions. Her head was spinning and she was so confused.

They got into the car and drove in the opposite direction of town. Once there, Bella got out of the car, excited for a distraction from her muddled thoughts. She walked right up to the tower, looking it up and down.

"What is it?" asked Bella.

"A defensive tower," answered Fiona.

"It's twelve-metres high and has two floors.

In the war they would stand up there to see the enemy coming," replied Catriona from behind them.

"It's beautiful. It makes me think…maybe we all have a defensive tower in us to keep us safe." Bella smiled, touching the old stone.

Fiona had followed her parents further down the path. Bella loved the feel of the stone under her hand as she looked up at the tower.

"Yours is particularly high. When will you stop seeing me as the enemy and let me in?" whispered Wylie from beside her.

Bella shivered slightly as he was right by her ear, his breath breathing over her like a ghost.

"Yeah, well, maybe you need one too, or you could end up feeling broken inside."

"Will you ever let me in yours?" asked Wylie, walking next to her.

"Do you even want me to answer that?" questioned Bella, looking up at the tower once again.

"Arabella, the world is a beautiful place and all you see is the ugly in it… why is that?" persevered Wylie.

"That is so not true Wylie; I can't believe you would say something like that!" Bella hissed, now walking away at a faster pace.

"Name one thing that's beautiful," demanded Wylie staring her down.

"The castle is beautiful, Ireland is beautiful."

"So you do think Ireland is beautiful - then why can't you stay?" asked Wylie.

"Because I don't want to," insisted Bella.

She looked up at his crestfallen face and walked away, surprised at how guilty she felt.

She looked up at his crestfallen face and walked away, surprised at how guilty she felt.

She wasn't being totally honest, but she needed him to think that she was. Bella found Fiona sitting on the grass setting out their food for a picnic.

"He really likes you, you know," said Fiona.

"I know Fiona…but I am leaving when the castle is sold," replied Bella.

"Please don't hurt him. I love you both, and I know he can be a pain in the butt…But he is still my brother and I don't want him hurt…" Fiona's voice cracked as she hugged Bella tightly.

"He won't be the only one getting hurt," whispered Bella under her breath.

The others joined them and they sat to eat lunch under the tree.

As they were driving away, Bella looked out of the back window at the tower once more. Did she really have a defence tower up, and if so, would she let anyone in? These were the thoughts that were confusing her. She needed to stop thinking like this and enjoy every moment…

Once they got back, Bella went straight to her favourite spot and picked up the journal. Everyone else was busy with their own business and no one would bother her for a while. She opened the journal to the last page she had read, preparing herself to be absorbed back into the past.

Chapter
15

Ireland 1917

"Wifey where are you?" called Fin, entering their bedroom.

"In here!" laughed Cathella, rubbing her swollen belly.

They had been living in Scarlet Manor for over a year now. Fin had kept his promise and married Cathella soon after. Now they were expecting their first child and Fin was home from his last tour for the birth of their child before going back. Fin had been notified that his father was deceased and had left them some money; enough to finish the castle off. He had made sure that they built a bathing pool especially for Cathella. She had cried when she saw it for the first time while Fin smiled on with an immense feeling of accomplishment. Over the last year, they had kept up their charade of passing the penny between the two of them. It had become a game of sorts. Fin dropped his satchel in the room and walked over to where Cathella was sitting on their bed.

"I think this is yours," said Fin, holding the Scarlet penny between his fingers.

"Why, yes it is," giggled Cathella.

"And…how do you suppose it got inside my bag?" questioned Fin teasingly.

"Oh, it must have fallen in!" laughed Cathella, trying to snatch it away from him.

"I think you're lying, missus!" said Fin, leaning down and caging her in with an arm on each side.

He started placing kisses on her neck and all over her face, missing her lips on purpose. Cathella grabbed his cheeks and kissed him. He let out a loud laugh and stood up straight.

"Okay, fine, I put it there," admitted Cathella, sitting up.

"thought so. Now come on, let's go swim. It's a hot day and Chrissie is waiting," replied Fin.

"She can wait, I've missed my husband," answered Cathella, putting her arms around his neck.

"You know I want to, but no seven-year-old is going to wait. We'll have plenty of time later," smiled Fin, kissing her on the lips.

"Alright…but it's your loss if I'm too tired later. Don't blame me," teased Cathella.

She was eight months pregnant and felt very round; but with the help of the older children she managed to get around. Fin held out a hand and pulled Cathella to her feet. Chrissie came running into the room wearing her swimming costume.

"Let's go!" cried Chrissie, eagerly pulling Fin by the hand.

"You get going and I'll get my swimming costume," said Fin, prying his hand free from her grip.

Chrissie ran out of the room, calling for the others. Cathella walked towards the door and stopped to look at Fin.

"You better hope this is a boy or you're going to have two little girls telling you what to do."

"I don't care what it is, as long as you're their mother," answered Fin.

"You say that now," laughed Cathella.

"I'll say that everyday," replied Fin, going into the bathroom.

Cathella went downstairs to the kitchen, where 10-year-old Brennan sat in his swimming costume with a now 13-year-old Sean. Patrick was seventeen now and worked full time - he worked late most nights.

"You look like a whale!" laughed Brennan affectionately.

"No she doesn't! She's beautiful!" cried Chrissie, sticking out her tongue towards her brother.

"No fighting; it's hot and I'm tired," ordered Cathella while she slowly made her way toward the back door.

She went over to the bathing pool and slowly climbed in; the cold a welcome sensation on her overheated, stretched skin. Chrissie ran past her and jumped in, followed by her brothers. Cathella laughed and swam over to them. Chrissie wrapped herself around her like an octopus. Fin appeared and dove into the water, popping up next to Cathella. He took Chrissie from Cathella and threw her into the water playfully. At that moment, Patrick walked out of the house, still in his work clothes. He looked at all of them splashing around and then dived in, clothes and all.

"Patrick! your clothes!" cried Chrissie.

"I forgot all about my clothes! It just looked too wonderful not to join in!"

"You are silly," laughed Chrissie, splashing him in the face.

"I guess I am…maybe I should go put on my swim suit?" asked Patrick, swimming toward the steps.

"No - it's too late now!" shouted Chrissie, swimming over to him.

Cathella suddenly let out a painful moan. Fin swam over to her quickly and put his arm around her.

"Are you alright?" asked Fin.

"I think the baby is coming…" cried Cathella, clutching her stomach.

Fin helped her out of the pool and dried her off.

"Patrick, go get the doctor!" yelled Fin, delicately leading Cathella inside.

"Sean, you keep Brennan and Chrissie busy," gasped Cathella, clutching her stomach as another contraction hit.

"Are you feeling alright? It's a month early…" replied Fin, beginning to panic despite his best intentions.

"I'm fine…" answered Cathella, patting his hand reassuringly before taking another deep gulp of air.

—ℓ—

"She is beautiful," said Chrissie, touching the little hand as it flaired around.

"She looks so fat and red," stated Brennan scrunching up is nose.

"She is Arabella McCullen, your niece," answered Cathella, kissing her daughter's newborn head.

The baby had thick auburn hair like Cathella and the clear blue eyes of a newborn. Fin took her from Cathella with pride shining all over his face.

"She looks like her Mamai," Fin declared, grinning.

"Fin, we have a daughter," cried Cathella, touching the end of the pink blanket hanging down from his arms.

"I am going to be the best uncle ever!" declared Brennan.

"No, I am," argued Sean, giving Brennan a push.

"I get to be the only aunt," smiled Chrissie with pride.

"As the only aunt, would you like to hold her?" asked Fin.

Chrissie's face lit up and she opened her arms welcomingly.

"We are a family…all of us." said Cathella, yawning with intense exhaustion.

"We are. And she is just the first of our next generation," answered Patrick, taking her from Chrissie who now sat sulking.

"You'll all get a turn. Arabella will be the most loved little girl!" replied Fin.

"I just realised you have to go back so soon…" sobbed Cathella; her emotions fluctuating wildly.

"Not for a month, remember…." said Fin, lovingly. He leaned down and kissed Cathella on the head.

"You did great. You were fantastic," whispered Fin.

"I love you."

They stared at each other lovingly, forgetting about everyone else in the room.

"Do you think she'll like the cot I made her? I'll carve her name onto it," asked Sean, nervously.

"I think she will love it because you made it just for her," answered Cathella as she scooped Arabella back into her arms.

"You will still love us the same, won't you?" questioned Brennan, his fear of abandonment rearing up.

"Of course; and Arabella will love you just as much," declared Cathella, taking his hand and stroking the skin reassuringly.

"Don't worry, when Fin is gone, we'll all be here for the both of you," stated Patrick.

—✒—

Cathella kissed Fin goodbye once more.

He had one-month-old Arabella in his arms while they waited for the train. The others had stayed home to give them time alone. Patrick served as driver, but he sat in the car waiting for them from a polite distance. Cathella had the Scarlet penny in her hand, tears running down her cheeks.

"I love you, both of you," said Fin, kissing Arabella on the cheek.

"We will miss you so much…" sobbed Cathella, taking the baby from him reluctantly.

She gave Fin one last hug, dropping the coin in his pocket. this was harder than the other goodbyes because they had a daughter now, and they both knew that he would miss out on so much.

"I love you, Fin," said Cathella.

"I'll be home soon," answered Fin, wiping her cheeks with his uniform sleeve.

"She won't know you…"

"With a Mamai like you, I doubt that," smiled Fin, taking Arabella's little hand in his.

"I will make sure she knows you love her," stated Cathella with determina- tion in her voice.

"That's my girl…now go, before I start to cry," scolded Fin, softly.

Cathella held back her tears and watched him board the train, steeling herself against the waves of grief and longing. Once he was out of sight, she went back to the car.

"Is he gone?" asked Patrick, tapping the steering wheel nervously.

"Yes…" sobbed Cathella, hugging Arabella to her chest.

She was silent all the way home. Once they got home, she placed Arabella in her cot and collapsed onto her bed, allowing herself to cry freely at last.

Eventually she awoke to Arabella's newborn whimpers and pulled herself up to go see to her. When she arrived in the nursery, Patrick was already there with the baby in his arms.

"I'll tell her all about her Dadai," said Patrick.

"Thank you, Patrick," replied Cathella.

"Jo-Jo looked like her at this age," stated Patrick.

"I still miss her," answered Cathella.

"We all do…and this is a new beginning for all of us. this little girl is going to be great," smiled Patrick, kissing her on the head.

"You're truly the brother I never had Patrick…I hope you know how much I appreciate you," said Cathella.

"I know!" Patrick grinned cheekily and threw her an affectionate wink.

Chapter
16

Another month had passed, and Arabella was steadily growing. She was held constantly by everyone. Cathella sat in bed watching her sleep on the bed next to her, comforted by the warmth of her body. Patrick walked in and sat silently next to her on the bed with the baby between them. Sean walked into the room.

"What are you all doing here without me?" questioned Sean, jumping on Cathella's bed.

"Quiet! You'll wake her, you brute," scolded Patrick, shoving his brother away.

"Oh Patrick, she's just a bairn - she won't break! Calm down; there's nothing Uncle Sean can't do," laughed Sean.

Arabella opened her eyes and let out a cry. Patrick picked her up.

"How about a smelly bum?" asked Patrick, passing Arabella to Sean.

"Now that there is a Mamai's job."

"I thought there was nothing you couldn't do?" teased Patrick, getting up with Arabella still in his arms.

"Oh, shush you boys, give her to me. I'll go change her," smiled Cathella, holding out her arms.

"No, Uncle Patrick isn't a fraidy-cat like Sean. He can do it himself," said Patrick, softly placing the baby down on the bed.

Patrick bent over to the task of changing her while Sean pulled funny faces to try to tempt a gummy smile out of Arabella. They heard footsteps and looked up; Chrissie came running into the room.

"Cathella, Brennan is being rude!" shouted Chrissie.

Cathella opened her arms, welcomed the small girl onto her lap and wrapped her arms around her. Soon she would be doing this with her little one. She felt overwhelmed with indescribable love.

"Ignore him. You just sit here with us."

"Cathella I don't have to call you mamai, do I?" asked Chrissie.

"No, of course you don't! You had a mother who loved you so very much.

But no matter what, I will always love you as much as I love Arabella," answered Cathella honestly, kissing Chrissie on the head.

Brennan walked into the room with a beautiful teenage girl following behind him. She had long, thick blonde hair and blue eyes, taking them all by surprise. Patrick stood up as she entered, suddenly appearing more nervous than his usual self.

"Cathella, she was at the door," said Brennan.

"Hello my name is Macy…I've just come to bring Patrick his wages…" the girl said, timidly.

Patrick lifted Arabella into his arms and went over to her, taking the envelope. They all noticed her odd accent. It sounded American.

"Hello, Macy, I'm Cathella and this is Christabelle, Patrick's sister." answered Cathella, trying to compensate for the room's awkward silence.

"Sorry for not introducing everyone...my brother Brennan opened the door for you, that's Sean and this little baby is my niece, Arabella..." mumbled Patrick, noticeably uncomfortable.

"She is so beautiful! Do you mind if I hold her?" Macy asked.

"Sure," said Patrick, gently handing her over.

"But you better not drop her," scolded Brennan, ever the protective uncle.

Patrick glared at him and whacked him on the side of the head. Macy giggled at the two of them.

"Macy, would you like to stay for supper?" questioned Cathella.

"I don't want to impose!" said Macy, smiling at Arabella gratefully.

"Not at all; we would love you to stay," replied Cathella.

"Okay...I just have to go tell my papa. He's in the car waiting. He wanted to make sure Patrick got his wages after missing work yesterday," answered Macy, handing Arabella back to Patrick.

"I'll go with you!" shouted Patrick abruptly, passing Arabella to Brennan who stood the closest to him.

Cathella made her way downstairs and placed plates of corned beef and cabbage on the table in front of each chair. Macy sat next to Patrick at the table. They couldn't take their eyes off each other; sneaking side glances the whole time.

"Patrick, do you want to kiss Macy?" asked Brennan, bluntly breaking the tension.

"Brennan! Stop it!" yelled Patrick, turning a deep shade of red and kicking his brother under the table.

"Brennan, leave your brother alone or Macy will never come back," scolded Cathella.

"I like your family," smiled Macy sweetly.

"I think you're pretty," said Chrissie, shifting her chair closer to Macy.

Sean stared at Patrick angrily and Cathella carefully watched him. He barely ate his food and didn't say a word throughout the meal despite the chatter around him. Suddenly, Sean got up and left the room.

Cathella excused herself and followed him, already suspecting what might be bothering him. She found him sitting against the wall in Arabella's room, staring at the sleeping baby. Cathella sat down next to him, quietly waiting for him to say something.

"He is going to leave us," declared Sean after a long silence

"What do you mean, Sean? Patrick loves us." Cathella said, reassuringly.

"Don't you see it? They're in love, and in a year they'll be old enough to marry..." cried Sean.

"I think that's a bit hasty!" replied Cathella.

"He has a way out, Cathella. He'll care for her alone, and I am going to have to be the man in this house," Sean blurted out, angrily.

"Patrick doesn't want out, surely?" cried Cathella, stung by his words.

"We all do! Fin got lucky because he's away all the time anyway," declared Sean.

"How dare you? Fin loves me, and all of you. He never would have gone if he didn't feel he had to," said Cathella.

"I wake up everyday and know that Mamai and Dadai aren't coming back," confessed Sean, tears running down his cheeks against his will.

"You can have any future you want! Some of us never had a choice...and if I did, I would do all of this again, despite everything that's happened, because I wake up each morning grateful that I am not alone and that I have a family."

"But all everyone does is leave or die."

"I know, I do understand...I pray everyday that I don't have to leave, that nothing bad will happen to us again. Sometimes memories are all we've got left," Cathella replied, putting her arm around Sean in an attempt to comfort his shaking body.

"But what if most of them are bad?" asked Sean.

"Then they aren't worth remembering. Your brothers have done a lot for this family...they deserve happiness," stated Cathella.

"I know, and I want him to be happy, I just don't want him to leave me," answered Sean.

"No matter what happens, he will always be your brother. Come on, lets go back before they come looking for us," Cathella said with finality, standing up and reaching out a hand for him.

Sean stared at the crib for a few seconds before looking at Cathella.

"Cathella, how do you go on living?" asked Sean.

"That is how I go on. You, the other children, all of you are how I go on," answered Cathella, pointing to Arabella in the cot.

Cathella went back to the kitchen to find Macy and Chrissie washing the bowls while Patrick and Brennan were preparing tea and biscuits.

"Is Sean okay?" asked Patrick, concerned.

"Yes he is…but I think he might need his brother for a few minutes." replied Cathella, taking the pot of water from him.

Patrick nodded and left the room. They stood in silence, working together.

"Macy, do you like Patrick?" inquired Cathella, understandably curious.

"Yes…but please don't tell him, not yet, anyway! Do you think he likes me?" replied Macy, nervously.

"I think he likes you a lot! You're welcome here anytime. Did you know that this castle is a lucky castle? It was bought with pure love," Cathella said, smiling at the younger woman.

"Really? How do you know that?" asked Macy.

"Fin, my brother, he bought this castle for her. He loves Cathella and they have a Scarlet penny together. It's like magic." said Chrissie.

Cathella supressed a smile at the simple, magical way that children express profound truths.

"That is so special…I hope I find love like that one day," sighed Macy with a dreamy look in her eyes.

"It might be sooner than you think," whispered Cathella, watching the two boys reappear.

They all sat back down to enjoy the tea and biscuits.

"Macy, how long have you lived here?" asked Sean.

"We moved here two years ago. My dad had a great job opportunity here." said Macy.

"Where do you come from?" questioned Chrissie, her face full of crumbs.

"America," answered Macy.

"What is America like?" asked Brennan.

"Like home…it's big and has lots of buildings. It's not green like here in Ireland," stated Macy.

"I want to go to America one day!" declared Chrissie.

"Not until you're older," warmed Cathella.

"Are you going to go back?" asked Patrick, hesitantly.

"No, this is home now and I like it. It's so quiet and beautiful here," answered Macy.

"Not quite so quiet here!" laughed Cathella.

"Yes; Arabella cries all night," complained Brennan.

"Or because you kids are so chatty all the time," teased Cathella.

"My family can be a bit much at times…" admitted Patrick.

"I like that; my parents are quiet and don't do much," replied Macy.

"I can be your little sister if you want?" offered Chrissie.

"Who would want you as a sister?" sneered Brennan.

"Everyone loves me, just not you!" shouted Chrissie.

"Stop it, don't make Macy regret visiting," scolded Cathella.

"He started!" cried Chrissie.

"You are such a baby…" shouted Brennan.

"I would love to have you as a little sister," said Macy, trying to break the tension.

"I better go take Macy home; it's getting late," replied Patrick, getting up.

Arabella started to cry, so Sean got up to go see to her. Chrissie asked to be excused with Patrick, leaving Cathella and Brennan alone at the table.

"I don't really hate Chrissie…" stated Brennan.

"I know," answered Cathella.

"It's just fun to see her get cross," laughed Brennan.

"Come help me clean up, you silly boy," smiled Cathella.

"I think they like each other a lot," stated Brennan.

"I think so, too!" said Cathella, genuinely happy for Patrick.

They all had it so rough, and they all deserved to be happy.

Chapter 17

Ireland 2000

Bella let out a loud yawn and put the journal down. It was nearly lunch time and she was feeling overwhelmed by everything that was going on. She now knew why her grandmother loved this castle so much. this castle was bought with love; it was Scarlet Manor after all. It's very structure and name symbolised love. She thought of Colin and Fiona…were they in love? She then pictured Wylie and shook her head as if to clear the image of his face from her mind; they were barely speaking at the moment, let alone in love. Bella needed to get out for a bit, to breathe in the fresh air with no one bothering her. She put on her shoes and grabbed her purse. Pulling on her coat, she walked out of the front door and down the path leading to the main road. She stopped walking when she heard her a voice persistently calling her name. Bella turned to face Wylie - he was walking from his truck that was parked a few feet away. The back was filled with plants and compost. Bella licked her lips without meaning to.

Wylie had removed his shirt and his muscles were gleaming in the sun. He stopped in front of her and crossed his arms.

"Arabella, where are you going?" Wylie questioned

"Town."

"Alone?" replied Wylie, raising an eyebrow.

"Yes, alone. I am not a child and I can care for myself. Now, if you will excuse me..." answered Bella, angrily turning to leave.

"I didn't mean it like that!" shouted Wylie, but Bella was already walking away.

She walked down the road, taking the the shortcut that Wylie had showed her last time, trying not to think of how much fun they had had that day. She arrived in town just after midday, her stomach growling in protest at the late hour. Bella got herself a pastry and sat on a bench to eat. She finished her meal and then took a slow walk around the town. She saw that the church gate was open and walked through. Wylie had told her that it wasn't used anymore – it only opened for special occasions. She found the old tree that was mentioned in the journal and placed a hand on the bark. Not a leaf in site; the tree was bare and unloved. She slowly walked around the tree, sliding her hand along the bark. Her fingers grazed over something carved in the tree. She took her hand away to have a look. The tree had seven names carved in it: Fin, Cathella, Patrick, Sean, Brennan, Jo-Jo and Christabelle. It looked like they had been carved into the bark with a knife. It was untidy and old but still clear enough to be read. Bella could not believe it - after all these years there were those precious names, carved by her own grandmother or grandfather. She touched it once more and then walked towards the old house.

It wasn't locked and seemed to be empty, so Bella walked inside. It smelled musty and damp. She hadn't had a good look the last time she was here. this was the place where Cathella had spent those first few years in Ireland; the house that Jo-Jo had died in. So many memories…so many stories! She walked down the passage and turned into the first bedroom she found. It had a small metal bed in it and a wooden dresser. The room was bare besides a chest of drawers and a large mirror on one wall. Bella sat down on the bed looking for anything her grandmother might have left behind. She noticed one of the drawers looked slightly open and pulled it out to see what was inside. The drawer was empty except for a musty old dress. Bella picked it up and nearly dropped it in fright. The front of the dress has a large dark red stain on it that could only have been blood from many years ago. Shock set in as Bella realised that this must be the dress Cathella had worn the day Jo- Jo had died. Bella put the dress back and ran out of the room. Why had her grandmother kept that? Was it true? Did she really blame herself for the death of the little girl? Was that a reminder of what had happened that day? All of these unanswered questions with no way of getting answers…Bella was fed up and frustrated; she just wanted to know why everything had happened the way it had.

Bella walked along the road back towards the castle. It was getting chilly outside; the weather changing drastically. She rubbed her hands up and down her arms in a mostly ineffective attempt to generate some heat. The road was abandoned and silent. Bella looked around nervously. A car hooted from behind her, causing her to jump in fright. She turned around to see Wylie in his truck, laughing. He slowed down to crawl his truck along next to her but Bella ignored him and carried on walking.

"It is going to rain soon!" Wylie shouted, peering up at the sky.

Bella looked up at the grey clouds looming above and then at the warm car with Wylie in it. She carried on walking faster; there was no way she could allow herself to be so close to him.

"Arabella, don't be silly. You could get sick," said Wylie, driving slowly next to her.

"That's a chance I am willing to take. Go home Wylie. I don't need you," spat Bella, stubbornly.

"That may be so, but who do you need, Arabella? No one wants to be alone," Wylie responded, sounding aggravated.

"Maybe I do want to be alone," answered Bella, climbing over the fence to get away from Wylie.

She was being childish and she knew it, but she didn't want to be alone in a small space with Wylie. She watched the truck drive off and stopped running; now out of breath and slightly warmer than before. He must think she was totally insane.

—⁊—

Bella laughed at herself. She stopped by the river to take a break. Had she really run this far? Suddenly angry, she picked up a few pebbles and threw them into the river, watching them sink.

"I like to come here and think myself, you know," said a kind voice from behind, startling Bella.

She turned around to face Patrick and sighed in relief, her heart still beating fast.

"It is a beautiful river, isn't it?" answered Bella.

"Aye it is. Dadai bought us this house because of it. He barely took note of the house, just saw this river and said, 'I found us a home.'" answered Patrick, smiling at the distant memory.

"Did you ever miss him after he left?" asked Bella.

"He wasn't a good man, Bella...but he was my Dadai. He did love all of us and he did love Jo-Jo, she was his first little girl and it broke him when she died."

"I think the guilt drove him away," said Bella, watching the water.

"Aye, it would have driven many a man away. Mamai tried her best for all of us after that. Life was hard for us, but we never doubted that we were loved," answered Patrick.

"I found your names carved in the old tree by the church." smiled Bella.

"We did that the day before Jo-Jo had died."

"I wish I had a family like you did...maybe things would be different now," sighed Bella longingly.

"But you do! The McIntosh's love you. You have Brennan and I. Open your eyes and look around, child."

"The more you love, the more you have to lose."

"Aye, but if you don't love at all, you never grow."

"Thank you for talking to me. I always seem to feel better afterwards. I can see why Cathella loved you so much," said Bella hugging Patrick.

"You make my heart flutter, child, come visit anytime. I see the rain is coming and my old bones don't like the cold. D'you want to come in from the cold?" replied Patrick, turning to leave.

"No...thank you, though."

Bella watched him walk away and sat down for a few minutes to think. After what felt like barely a moment, a single raindrop landed on her nose and dropped onto the ground. Bella looked up as another landed in her eye. She blinked it away as more appeared. She groaned out loud and stood up quickly, looking for shelter. There was nothing around but Patrick's house and she didn't want to intrude.

She started running across the field; rain soaking through her clothes and shoes. She should be used to this by now, she thought to herself. Why was she always caught in the rain? Bella climbed the fence and power-walked down the road; her exhalations appearing like smoke in front of her as she puffed heavily and her skin covered in goosebumps. The truck sounded nice by now. She should have swallowed her pride and taken the ride. A small whimper snatched her attention away from her thoughts. Bella looked around. There was nothing there. She shrugged her shoulders and carried on walking. The whimper was louder this time, followed by a small whine. Bella saw a large rock by the side of the road and walked over to it; the sound seemed to be coming from that spot. She cautiously peered around it and found a small black ball of fur shivering. She bent down and touched it. Two big round eyes stared back at her. Bella smiled and picked up the puppy.

She wrapped his shivering body in her arms and hurried the rest of the way back home. She knocked on the door, shivering and praying someone would open up soon. Fiona opened the door with a shocked cry and pulled her inside.

"Look at you!" cried Fiona shutting the door.

Bella ignored her and opened her arms to reveal the puppy. "Look what I found."

"A dog?" questioned Wylie.

Bella looked up at him standing in the passage, leaning against the wall with his arms crossed and a thunderous expression on his face.

"I need to get him dry and fed," declared Bella, walking towards the linen cupboard and pulling out a dry towel.

"But what about you? You'll get sick!" shouted Fiona, wrapping another towel around Bella.

"He'll die if I don't warm him up!" yelled Bella, wrapping him tightly in the soft towel.

She walked into the kitchen and poured him some milk in a bowl, then placed the dog down to drink it. When he was done she picked him up and left the kitchen. Bella walked into sitting room. A fire was blazing in the room. She stood as close as possible with the puppy in her arms.

"You need to change," stated Wylie as he stepped into the room.

"The puppy needs me," cried Bella protectively.

Wylie took the dog from her and placed it securely on the armchair. Bella protested, but Wylie grabbed her up into his arms and carried her to her bedroom.

"Wylie, let go!"

"Go change," demanded Wylie, blocking her exit.

"And if I don't?" questioned Bella.

"Then I'll do it for you."

Bella stared at him to see if he was joking. He had that stern look in his eyes again; one she was coming to recognise as concern concealed by anger. With a loud huff, Bella threw her hands in the air and stormed into her bathroom.

She put on dry clothing, finally feeling more human again, but in her hurry to get to the dog she forgot her socks. She ran back to the sitting rom, but found it empty. Bella sighed and made her way to the kitchen where she discovered Wylie drying the puppy.

"I see you found a dog!" said Catriona.

"Yes, isn't he cute?" smiled Bella, taking him from Wylie.

Catriona laughed and turned back to her cooking. Bella took the puppy and walked back to the sitting room. She curled up in the chair with the puppy in her arms and let out a yawn.

The puppy was curled against her, fast asleep and exhausted from the newfound comfort. Bella was drifting asleep when she felt someone touching her feet. She opened her eyes sleepily to see Wylie holding her feet.

"What are you doing?"

"You don't have socks on."

Bella watched him put a pair of socks on her feet. She smiled sleepily and mumbled a thank you before drifting back off to sleep. Wylie sat back with her feet across his lap, gently massaging them. How had he fallen in love so quickly with the one woman who hated everything about the one place he loved? She would go home, and what would he be left with? He opened his eyes and gazed down at her sleeping face. Could she ever love someone like him? She let out a small whimper before trying to curl in a ball. Wylie sighed before getting up. He lifted her and the puppy into his arms and took her to her bed. He tucked her in and gently kissed her on the head. Wylie gently put a hand on her cheek and took a deep breath.

Chapter
18

Bella awoke to someone licking her face. She sat up suddenly, causing the puppy to go tumbling down her body. Bella giggled at the sight of the puppy struggling to stand up again. He let out a yelp and climbed back up to lick her on the face again. She gentle pushed him away before there was a knock on her door and Wylie walked in, already dressed as usual for the new day. Bella yelped and pulled the covers up as she glared at him.

"What are you doing here?" asked Bella.

"I came to see if you slept alright."

"And that's all?" questioned Bella, suspicious.

"Do I need any other reason?" replied Wylie leaning down across the bed and caging her in.

Bella swallowed and leaned back while Wylie smiled and moved in closer. She steadied her breath, trying to think of something to say, but she was speechless. He was staring at her so intensely with that smouldering gaze.

Bella put her hands on his chest to push him away, feeling hard muscle against her hands.

"Could you give me room to breathe?" squeaked Bella.

Wylie gave her a wild smile before moving forward. She knew she was in trouble now. The puppy jumped up and licked Wylie in the face, stopping him. Bella threw her head back and laughed. Wylie straightened up and picked the puppy up.

"Have you got a name for him?"

"Not yet."

"It better be Irish - he is an Irish dog, you know," stated Wylie predictably, placing him in her arms and leaving the room.

Bella slowly made her way to the kitchen. She was feeling sluggish and her head was sore. Everyone was seated around the table and they all took turns holding the puppy.

"Are you keeping him?" questioned Fiona, tickling his tummy.

"Yes, I think I am going to…but he needs a name." said Bella.

"What about Shamrock?" replied Clancy.

"Or Leprechaun."

Bella looked at Wylie to see his wide grin. She blushed slightly and carried on eating.

"He'd end up being called Leper for short, that wouldn't be nice," answered Bella.

"Oh right, that isn't very cool." "Lassie?" added Catriona.

"I like that but it doesn't suit him…maybe I should call him Ireland," smiled Bella.

"No that is unacceptable," chuckled Wylie.

"Oh, and do you have a better name?" questioned Bella.

"Yes I do. He can be called Corkun," declared Wylie.

"Corkun! I think it suits him," smiled Bella, kissing the dog on the nose.

Bella ate quietly, listening to the conversations going on around her. She was in no mood to talk; her head getting worse.

"Mamai, I am going to Colin today. He wants me to meet his parents," said Fiona, the excitement obvious in her voice.

"Yes, love, but behave…and do make plans for us to meet them, too," answered Catriona.

Bella put her bowl away and left the kitchen.

Her headache had intensified and her eyes were burning slightly. Maybe she needed some fresh air. Bella walked outside and sat on the bench while Corkun chased butterflies. She closed her eyes, trying to stop her head from spinning. When she opened them, Wylie was walking towards her.

"You again," said Bella, exhausted.

"I just want to check on you and ask you…if we could be friends," replied Wylie, sitting down next to her.

"Just my friend?" questioned Bella.

"Yes," answered Wylie sincerely.

"And if I happened to go on a date - you would be fine with that?"

She saw the murderous expression cross his face before he quickly hid it and gave her a fake smile.

"I am a grown man! I can handle it."

"Alright, we can try the whole friend thing," smiled Bella holding out her hand for him to shake.

He took it and gave it a slight shake but didn't let go afterwards. Bella looked down at their intertwined hands. Wylie was rubbing her wrist soothingly. She looked up and saw the raw desire in his eyes.

A slight panic over- took her. He gently put his free hand on her cheek, drawing her closer.

"Say I must stop and I will…" whispered Wylie into her lips.

Bella knew she should say no, but his lips looked so inviting. She could still remember their last kiss. She leaned forwards, touching her lips with his. He let out the breath he had been holding in and closed the distance between them. Bella let out a moan and wrapped her arms around his neck while his arms made their way around her waist. She felt safe and cared for in his arms. Corkun let out a loud cheery bark and Bella opened her eyes, jolted back into reality. She quickly pulled away and jumped up to put as much distance between them as she could. Wylie was staring at her with a combination of want and need; his eyes glazed over and his lips swollen.

"We can't do this!" cried Bella, quickly stepping back.

"Arabella, just let this happen between us!" pleaded Wylie.

"No!" shouted Bella, swaying on her feet as her head spun.

"We can take it slow."

"No, I can't do this."

"I won't force you Arabella; but you need to decide what you want," answered Wylie, sadly.

"Let's just be friends."

"Fine, but no shaking hands this time." teased Wylie.

Bella tried to smile, but all she could see were black spots dancing in front of her eyes. She felt arms around her. Her stomach was rolling strangely and her ears were ringing.

"Arabella? Arabella, are you alright?" asked Wylie, holding her up.

"I think I am going to be sick…" mumbled Bella before she passed out.

Bella woke up and groaned in pain at the brightness in the room that seemed to be burning her eyes. Catriona was sitting on the bed holding a cold wet cloth over her forehead. Her throat was dry and sore. She stared at Catriona in confusion.

"You have a high fever," stated Catriona in her soothing, gentle lilt.

"I feel horrible…" stuttered Bella, trying to hold the tears back.

"I know, child, it was the rain I suppose. Try to sleep as much as you can…you gave us quite the scare," answered Catriona, holding a straw to her lips.

Bella sipped the water and looked around the room.

"Where is Corkun?"

"Wylie took him for a walk. Now you rest, child, and try not to worry," Catriona reassured her, getting up.

Bella closed her eyes. her head hurt far too much to get any more sleep. Her stomach rolled again and she got up, just making it to the toilet in time. Bella lay down on the cold tiles in the bathroom; tears running down her cheeks. The cold tiles felt good on her hot skin. She closed her eyes in an attempt to calm her stomach. She suddenly felt large hands lifting her up and cried out, craving the comfort of the cool tiles.

"Arabella, the floor is to cold." whispered Wylie carrying her back to bed.

"Mmm, feels nice," mumbled Bella.

"I know, darlin', but it will make you worse."

Wylie gently placed her back in the bed and dipped the cloth in water again. He gently rubbed it on her face.

She smiled weakly up at him before falling asleep. He carried on for a while, simply because he didn't want to leave her. When she had collapsed outside, he had nearly had a heart attack. He had run inside with her, screaming for his mother. She had calmed him down and made him take the dog for a walk. He came back to check on her and when he saw the bed empty, his heart had skipped a beat. The small groan from the bathroom had signalled her whereabouts and he had instantly calmed down. He felt at peace sitting here with her, listening to the steady beat of her heart.

He must've dozed off watching her because he awoke to his head hurting from the awkward angle he had fallen asleep in. Another whimper from the bed grabbed his attention - that was the sound that had pulled him from sleep. He touched Arabella and pulled his hand away from the sheer heat coming off her body. Wylie knew he needed to cool her down fast. He walked into the bathroom and ran a shallow cold bath. She would hate him for this, but it needed to be done.

—⟨⟩—

Bella felt like she was drowning, everything was dark around her and the water was filling her lungs. She opened her mouth to scream, but nothing came out.

"Arabella, shh! Open your eyes, love," said Wylie, pouring water gently down her neck.

Bella opened her eyes, panicking, to find herself lying in the bathtub in her clothing with the water freezing.

"Cold…" moaned Bella.

"Just a little longer, I promise. You were over-heating and I needed to cool you down," whispered Wylie, rubbing a hand through her hair soothingly.

After a few more minutes, he stood up.

"Can you get out yourself? Should I call Fiona to help you?" asked Wylie.

"No I can do it, thank you."

Wylie nodded and left the bathroom. Bella groaned and stood up. Her muscles were aching terribly, but her head felt clearer and her stomach more settled. She pulled off the wet clothing and dropped them to the floor. She put on a pair of her pyjamas that she found neatly folded on the countertop. Bella shuffled out of the bathroom to find Wylie pacing the room anxiously. He started walking towards her, but Bella held up a hand to stop him. She made her way to the bed and slowly climbed in. Wylie handed her a glass of water and she sipped at it slowly. Her stomach didn't flip over, so she carried on drinking. Wylie walked into the bathroom and came back with her wet clothes, heading for the door.

"Wylie, don't leave me," pleaded Bella, embarrassed by her outburst.

Wylie turned around and gave her a huge, warm smile.

"Never, Arabella. I just want to go put theses in the washing machine, then I'll be right back."

Bella nodded her head and watched him walk away. She picked up the piece of toast on a plate next to her and slowly nibbled on it.

By the time Wylie returned she was exhausted again. The pain medication seemed to be taking a toll. Bella watched Wylie sit awkwardly in the small chair trying to get comfortable and patted her bed gently. He looked at her with confusion, Bella just shrugged.

"I'm cold and that chair looks uncomfortable. Friends cuddle when they need it."

Wylie laughed before kicking off his shoes and crawling into the bed next to her.

Bella rolled over to face him and placed her head on his chest. He wrapped his arms around her and she fell asleep feeling truly safe for the first time in years.

By morning her fever was gone and she felt much better. Bella ate some breakfast and Fiona sat with her while Wylie went to do a job in town. He came back later that day and sat in the chair reading Cathella's journal to Arabella. She listened to him quietly as the sound of his smooth voice and soft accent lulled her to sleep. Corkun was brought in once in a while, and everyone came in regularly to keep her company. She watched movies with Fiona until bedtime, then Fiona left and Wylie entered the room to check on her.

"Thank you for last night," whispered Bella, blushing.

"Anytime, Arabella," smiled Wylie.

"Don't look at me like that!" cried Bella, hiding her face.

"Like what?" asked Wylie, genuinely confused.

"Like that! I'm sick and look a mess but you look at me like...well, like I'm beautiful!"

"You are beautiful, even when you're sick," Wylie said calmly, as if it were obvious.

"Don't lie to me."

"I told you, I won't lie to you. I would kiss you but I don't want to get sick myself," replied Wylie.

"Then I am glad I am sick...friends don't kiss."

He stared at her and she smiled.

"The type of friends we are don't kiss," laughed Bella.

"I could risk it," teased Wylie.

"Don't you dare!" shouted Bella, throwing her pillow at him.

He caught it and threw it back at her. Bella quickly hid it under her body. Wylie jumped onto the bed and tickled her until she finally surrendered and gave him the pillow.

He settled back in his chair with it behind his head.

"Finders keepers."

"You are such a kid at times," giggled Bella.

Wylie pouted and Bella sighed before settling into the bed. She looked at Wylie watching the television and bit her lip.

"Ask me."

Bella jumped slightly, alarmed by his uncanny ability to read her mind. She blushed and stared at the television.

"What was your life like, you know, growing up here in Ireland?" asked Bella, nervously refusing to look at him.

"Normal, I guess," answered Wylie, honestly.

"A little more information would be nice."

"Only if you answer my question first. What's the worst thing that has ever happened to you, besides your father dying?" questioned Wylie.

"Seeing the look in my mother's eyes the first time I failed at something. She wanted me to be perfect, and the more I tried, the more I failed."

"That's horrible; a parent should love their child no matter what."

"Tell that to my mom! By not marrying a lawyer or a doctor I'm trashing the family name."

"She must want you to be happy, though?"

"Enough about me. You haven't answered my question."

"It was like a fairy tale. Growing up in the castle was awesome. My friends loved to come visit, and Cathella never minded. She loved the noise that they brought with them, but I know she missed her home, even though she never spoke of it. What do you miss about your home?" asked Wylie.

"Hamburgers and chips - I miss that," yawned Bella.

Wylie laughed and looked at his watch.

"You better go sleep - it's late."

Bella yawned again, struggling to keep her eyes open.

"You never told me what your worst day was…" replied Bella, falling asleep.

"The day you left…" whispered Wylie as he walked out of the room.

Bella awoke the next morning feeling much better. She picked up the jour- nal and opened it to the last page Wylie had read from. Before she could start, Corkun ran into the room. Bella bent down and lifted him onto the bed with her. He barked and licked her face. Corkun curled into her lap and fell asleep right away. Bella rubbed a hand through his hair as she read the journal.

19

Ireland 1918

Fin walked into their bedroom and caught the little body that threw her- self at him. He chuckled and peppered her face with kisses.

"Look at you, Arabella - my little princess!" Fin said, throwing her in the air and as she laughed out loud.

She had just turned one and was a real handful at times. Well, most of the time.

"She always tries to act innocent around you," replied Cathella, kissing Fin on the cheek.

"Never, not this little girl, she's as sweet as pie," laughed Fin, tickling her tummy.

"Dadai! Dadai!" squealed Arabella as she gave him a wet kiss on the cheek.

"Come on - it's time for her bath," stated Cathella, holding out her arms.

Fin had been home for three months now and they planned on having family photographs taken.

"Let me do it - you go get ready for the family portrait," said Fin, walking to the bathroom with Arabella.

Cathella took the penny out her pocket and kissed it. She placed it on her side table. Moving to the wardrobe, she took out her Sunday best dress and put it on while Fin bathed their little girl. Fin had to leave once more; just one more tour and then he would be home for good. Cathella was beyond excited to finally have her husband home forever. Chrissie knocked on the door and Cathella opened it to find the little girl in her favourite pink dress.

"They're here!" exclaimed Chrissie, dancing around in glee.

"Go make sure your brothers are ready and let Patrick know he can go see Macy after the pictures are taken," replied Cathella, quickly neatening Chrissie's hair.

"He loves her," smiled Chrissie, running off to go taunt her brothers.

Cathella laughed and headed for the bathroom.

"Fin - hurry up!" called Cathella, fluffing her curls once more in front of the mirror, just in case.

Fin walked out of the bathroom holding Arabella, who looked pristine in a white dress with her hair tied up in pigtails. Cathella took her from Fin so that he could get ready and kissed her baby girl on the cheek. Once Fin was done, they walked downstairs together.

—🖋—

A photographer stood in the entrance with his camera on a tripod while Sean and Brennan stood asking him questions, all of which he answered patiently. Chrissie danced into the room dragging Patrick along. He looked at them with a grumpy expression. Fin laughed and hooked an arm around Patrick's neck, pulling him towards the wall. Everyone stood against the wall as close together as possible.

Cathella stood on one side holding Arabella, while Fin stood next to her with one arm around her and the other around Patrick's neck. Chrissie stood in front of Cathella and Sean next to Patrick with Brennan in front of them. The man took several different photographs as they stood in different positions. Fin took one alone with his daughter, and one with all his siblings.

When they were done, Patrick kissed Cathella on the cheek and left to see his fiancé. Once everyone had left to get on with their day, Fin stood in the entryway with his arms around Cathella, holding Arabella close between them.

"I love you two with all my heart and nothing will change that," declared Fin, kissing Cathella on the nose.

"Ow!" cried Arabella pushing Fin away as the hug became too tight for comfort.

Fin laughed and took her from Cathella. She laid her head on his shoulder with her thumb in her mouth. Sean walked into the room and handed Cathella the Scarlet penny.

"I found this with Chrissie; you'd better keep it safe," said Sean while making his way toward the kitchen.

Cathella put it in her pocket before Arabella could see it and potentially shove it in her mouth.

"Let's go for a walk," said Fin, looking relaxed and content.

He took Cathella's hand and led her to the garden by the side of their home. They stopped by the cement bench. Fin put Arabella down and sat down next to Cathella. He put his arm around her, holding her close as they watched Arabella wobble around, ocassionally tumbling over before clambering back onto her little feet. Cathella took the penny out of her pocket to look at.

"It's love," answered Cathella with affection.

He took it from her and kissed it before slipping it into his pocket.

"Don't you forget…I nearly lost it a few times, so I think it's safer here with you," warned Fin.

"Mamai, swim?" asked Arabella, her white dress now covered in grass stains.

"Not today," replied Cathella.

"Want!" shouted Arabella; a tantrum rapidly brewing.

"Mamai said no, Arabella, come sit by Dadai…" said Fin, holding out his hands.

"No!" yelled Arabella, clumsily running off.

Fin watched her run away. He winked at Cathella and ran after Arabella. She looked back at him chasing her and let out a scream before running as fast as her little legs would take her. Fin caught her and rolled with her on the grass so that she landed on top of him. Cathella watched them play and gently put a hand to her stomach. She still had to tell Fin he would be a father again…well, at least she thought so. All the signs were there that she was pregnant again. She watched them roll around, considering how difficult it would be to get those grass stains out of the pretty dress. Fin stopped playing and picked her up. He placed her over his shoulder and made his way back to Cathella.

"Down! Down!" cried Arabella kicking her little legs.

Fin placed her on Cathella's lap grinning.

"Dadai naughty," scolded Arabella, pointing a chubby baby finger at him.

"No, Mamai is silly," teased Fin.

"No!" shouted Arabella wrapping her arms around Cathella's neck.

"I love you, Arabella," said Fin holding out his arms for her.

She eyed him warily, one of hair ties had fallen out and her curls were full of grass. Fin pretended to sulk and Arabella stood up before jumping up into the air. Cathella gasped but Fin caught her and spun her around. Arabella giggled and kissed him sloppily on the cheek.

"It's nearly dinnertime," stated Cathella with a sigh, standing up.

"No, play Dadai." pleaded Arabella.

"Mamai, we are playing." added Fin pouting.

"Mamai also wants to play, but without Arabella…" smiled Cathella taking Fin's hand.

He laughed and bent forward to kiss her on the cheek.

"Kiss me!" shouted Arabella, grabbing onto Fin's cheeks.

Fin smothered her with kisses all over her face as she giggled and fought him off playfully.

—⁊—

It was still dark as they both woke up to Arabella calling them. "Mamai, Mamai." sobbed Arabella from her room next door. Cathella sat up but Fin gently pushed her back down.

"I'll go," said Fin, pulling himself out of the warm bed.

He came back with Arabella in his arms. He put her in the middle of the bed and got back in. Cathella turned to face them. She smiled as Arabella cuddled against Fin, both of them falling back asleep.

There weren't many mornings like this left with him having to go back in a week. Cathella touched one of Arabella's red curls and wondered if any of her children would have Fin's black hair. It seemed like they had just closed their eyes before Arabella was wide awake again and ready to play. She jumped up and down on Fin until he sat up.

"Chrissie, are you awake?" called Fin.

Chrissie came running into the room, still in her nightgown.

"Please take Arabella?" begged Fin, passing her over to Chrissie.

"Come Arabella, let's go play," replied Chrissie, carrying Arabella out of the room.

"Why did you do that?" questioned Cathella.

"I think my wife needs some quality time, too..." smiled Fin, grabbing Cathella and pulling her closer to his body.

"I think so, too..." giggled Cathella.

They stayed in bed for a while before heading down for breakfast. Patrick stood by the stove making them breakfast while Sean kept Arabella busy with blocks.

"We made breakfast," said Sean setting the table.

"I see - thank you!" answered Cathella, sitting down.

"Where is Chrissie?" asked Fin as he carefully lifted Arabella up from the floor.

"Her and Brennan are busy playing a game, she said Arabella wasn't playing nicely," laughed Sean.

"Swim!" cried Arabella, pointing to the door.

"The next child will not be born in the swimming pool," scolded Fin, playfully.

"She wasn't born in it!" protested Cathella.

"Might as well have been," sighed Fin as he placed her down on the floor.

Cathella ate her food, her stomach slightly queasy. She needed to tell Fin her secret without any interruptions.

"Can you watch her for a bit, Sean? I want to talk to Fin alone," said Cathella, taking Fin's hand.

Fin looked at her with worry but she shook her head. He followed her up to their room, closing the door. Fin sat on the bed and while Cathella paced nervously.

"What is it?" asked Fin.

"I...well, I'm fairly sure I'm pregnant..." said Cathella, turning her back to him.

"You are?"

Cathella heard the excitement in his voice. She turned to face him and saw pure joy on his face.

"You aren't angry? I know money is tight...and you're leaving for another couple of months," cried Cathella nervously.

Fin grabbed her by the arm and pulled her onto his lap. He wrapped his arms around her.

"I love you Cathella, and I want as many children as you do. Arabella is too spoiled being an only child; a little bairn will do her good," whispered Fin, kissing her neck near her ear.

Cathella shivered pleasantly and he smiled into her neck.

"Fin, I'm so happy! I was scared you wouldn't be pleased," admitted Cathella.

"Nothing you do could ever make me unhappy," smiled Fin.

"I love you so much Fin, please don't leave next week," murmured Cathella into his chest.

"It's the last time and then you'll be stuck with me forever," said Fin, kissing her tenderly on the cheek.

They sat together for a few wonderful moments just holding each other close. Suddenly, the bedroom door flew open. Sean ran in, red in the face and out of breath.

"We can't find Arabella...everyone is looking!" shouted Sean, wheezing for air.

"What happened?" asked Fin helping Cathella off his lap.

"I put her down for a second and then she was gone...I swear it was a second," cried Sean.

They all ran out of the room and spread out to search each room for her. Cathella went outside, suddenly filled with a sense of terrible foreboding, to look at the bathing pool. She peered all around and noticed something float- ing in the pool. Cathella screamed and immediately jumped in, swimming over to Arabella. Everyone came running outside. Fin took Arabella from Cathella, lying her down on the soft grass. Patrick lifted Cathella, shocked and shaking, out of the pool, and Sean ran without saying a word to call for the doctor. No one knew how long she had been under the water for, but her lips were blue and she wasn't moving.

"Is she breathing?" cried Cathella, grabbing Fin's arm as her chest seized up in terror.

Fin put his ear to her small chest. Hearing nothing, he started to push on her chest and breathe into her mouth.

"Arabella, please don't die...no...don't die..." murmured Cathella, rocking back and forth.

"I can't get her to breathe!" shouted Fin, refusing to stop.

Brennan and Chrissie held one another, sobbing for the little girl, but Arabella hadn't taken a single breath. Cathella took her little hand, giving it a squeeze.

"Please, someone please help her..." sobbed Cathella.

20

Sean led the local doctor towards them. Had they really been doing this for that long? Cathella had no sense of how much time had passed. The doc- tor pushed Fin aside and bent down to examine Arabella. He looked at them and stood up. Fin wrapped his arms around Cathella. She was trembling more from fear than coldness.

"I'm so sorry, she is gone. There was far too much water in her lungs," said the doctor, signalling for another member of his team to approach.

"No! That's my baby! Keep trying!" yelled Cathella, trying to get closer to Arabella.

Fin held her back, knowing in his heart that it was too late for their little girl.

"I'm sorry. You tried, you did your best, but she's gone, God bless her," the doctor said somberly.

"No! Don't take her!" screamed Cathella, become hysterical and fighting Fin to push past him.

She is gone," sobbed Fin, holding tighter onto Cathella.

"Leave me alone, my baby needs me! She needs her mother!" "Cathella, stop it, please..." said Fin.

Cathella fought him, but he held on tight. He forced her to look him in the eyes.

"She is gone," whispered Fin, tears running down his cheeks.

Cathella fell against him, weeping for her little baby. Shock and confusion came over her in terrible waves. She desperately wanted her baby girl back. Arabella would never sit on her lap again, never call her Mamai or give her little kisses. She would never feel those small arms wrap around her neck and be woken in the night by her baby girl....it couldn't be real. Fin lifted her into his arms and carried her to their room. He helped her out of her wet clothes and into something dry then put her in their bed. The doctor gave her a mild sedative, mindful of her new pregnancy. She felt nothing but numb- ness. All she wanted was to die with her little girl. Cathella cried and cried, her heart completely broken.

The door opened and Sean stood in the doorway, his face also streaked with tears. She looked at the eighteen-year-old boy standing there, broken and guilty, and did the one thing that she could. She lifted her blankets up and waited for him to get in the bed with her. They lay together in the bed weeping until they finally fell asleep wrapped in each other's arms. It was comfort and reassurance they needed. When Cathella awoke, it was dark outside and for a momen she thought it had been a horrific nightmare. But Sean was still asleep in her bed and she knew in her heart it was real. She tried to take a deep breath but couldn't. Everything was closing in on her and she couldn't breathe.

Cathella got out of bed and pulled her boots on in a hurry. She went downstairs and then outside the back door. She stood in silence and sitllness, simply staring at the stars and moon. It looked the same as it did last night. Why did these things still look the same when everything was so horribly, irreversibly different? She buried her face in her hands and stood alone, weep- ing. A noise not far off startled her. Cathella followed the sound towards the pool. Fin stood by the pool throwing his mug into it. He threw a metal chair and seemed to be searching for something else to throw.

"Fin..." whispered Cathella walking towards him.

He turned around and saw her standing in the moonlight. Fin let out a whimper and fell to his knees. He let out a heart wrenching sob; one after the other. She could barely see him in the darkness, but saw his large frame shak- ing. Cathella knew they needed each other to get through this. She walked over to him and stood quietly looking down at him. His face was covered in tears. Fin looked up at her with the most broken expression she had ever seen on her husband's face. Cathella stepped forward and Fin wrapped his arms around her. She ran a hand soothingly through his shorn hair. She stood mur- muring over and over that they would be alright, attempting to comfort him somehow. this was worse than when Jo-Jo had died; this was how Susanna must have felt. Nothing they have ever felt before could ever have prepared them for this intensity of despair. Today they had lost a child while another was growing inside of her; how was that even possible. What if this child died, too? She couldn't bear to lose anyone else she loved. She looked over at the bathing pool and shuddered in despair. They would never use it again. Patrick approached them, looking younger than his twenty years of age.

"What are we going to do?" asked Patrick, his voice cracked and hoarse.

"The only thing we can do," answered Cathella, closing her eyes.

"She won't ever grow up…" cried Patrick.

"She was loved, that's all that really matters," replied Fin through hiccups. Cathella suddenly looked at Fin and hugged him to her chest.

"I just remembered…you're also leaving," sobbed Cathella.

"No, I won't go. Not yet," said Fin, kissing her wet cheeks.

"Please, don't ever leave me," whispered Cathella, shivering all over.

Fin stood up and wrapped his arms around her.

"Hush my darling, lets not think about it now. Lets go to bed."

"Sean is in our bed," said Cathella.

"I'll go wake him," said Patrick, leaving them outside.

Cathella looked at the bathing pool and, in an uninvited flash of memory, saw her baby floating again. She closed her eyes. Fin took her hand and led her away from the bathing pool and the bad memories it now held.

Cathella went to check on the others before going to bed. She found Brennan and Chrissie sleeping in one bed and left them there to grieve. They had each other and that was all that truly counted. Today was a tragedy, but they were alive. Tomorrow would be hard; so would many more days to come. But growing in her stomach was their second chance, and she would make sure nothing happened to her new baby. She had failed Arabella, but she would not fail this baby.

It was exactly five months from the day that Arabella had died. Sometimes, it felt like it had happened only yesterday. Fin hadn't gone back straight away, but now he had to. The war was almost at an end, and he was needed. Cathella only prayed that he would be able to come home in time to see their next child born. Everyday, getting up was harder, but with Fin it was possible. She missed Arabella with all her heart and prayed that this was a boy, simply because she couldn't bare another girl who would remind her of the loss.

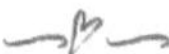

She sat eating her breakfast at the table in the kitchen, watching Chrissie get ready for school. Chrissie walked over to her and gave her a quick hug and kiss before leaving for school with Brennan. After that, Fin walked into the kitchen and sat down next to her. He placed his hand on her swollen stomach, feeling for kicks.

"Are you alright?" asked Fin, rubbing her stomach.

"I miss her so much…" admitted Cathella, placing her hand over his.

"So do I, Tomorrow, I leave. Will you be alright?" asked Fin with his arm wrapped around her shoulders.

"No, I won't be. I need you, Fin," sobbed Cathella, unable to conceal her pain.

Would this torturous grief ever go away, or would it hurt every time she thought of her little girl?

"Want to go for a walk?" asked Fin, strategically changing the subject.

She nodded and let him help her to her feet.

They walked over to their favourite bench and sat down.

"Do you have to go?" asked Cathella, clutching his hands in hers.

"It's the last time, I promise," answered Fin.

"I know, but I'm scared Fin...I don't want to be alone. And what if, well, what if something happens out there..." cried Cathella.

"You're not alone - you will have the Scarlet penny and all of the others," said Fin.

"No, you need it!"

"Lets not talk about it now," stated Fin, kissing her on the cheek.

Cathella nodded and sat with him outside. She could see them doing this one day when they were old – the thought gave her a small glimpse of happi- ness after months of misery.

After a while, they got up and Cathella went up to her room to go lie down. She thought about the penny and felt compelled to feel it in her hand. Cathella got up and searched the last place she had placed it, but it was gone. She began to panic, throwing everything out of the cupboards in search of it. Fin walked into the room a and found her frantic.

"What's wrong, angel?" asked Fin, pulling her into his arms in a warm embrace.

"I can't find the penny."

"It's alright."

"No, it's not. It's gone, Fin. Everything I love is gone," sobbed Cathella into his strong chest.

She could hear the steady beat of his heart, the rhythm like a drum. She tried not to think of war, of battle.

"Hush, my love, we will find it," whispered Fin soothingly.

"No, we won't. I lost it and now there's nothing to keep you safe..." cried Cathella.

"I will be safe, no matter what."

"No, no you won't. We need the penny."

Fin gently held her in place and searched her eyes intently.

"Is that all our love is?" questioned Fin.

"No, it isn't. The penny has always brought you back to me and it keeps you safe!" yelled Cathella, trying to breath through her panic.

"No, you brought me back."

"But where is our love now?" asked Cathella.

"Right here! We don't need a penny," answered Fin, touching his chest where his heart was.

Cathella deflated a little at that while Fin held her tight.

"Oh Fin, we lost our little girl," sobbed Cathella, broken.

"I know we lost her," sighed Fin leaning his head against hers.

"Please don't you die too, I need you - and so does our baby," cried Cathella.

"I have to come back; now that there's no penny, I need to prove it to you." answered Fin, reassuring as ever, kissing her on her tear-stained cheeks.

"You have to come back."

"No matter what, our love is stronger than anything or any distance. It's definitely stronger than a penny."

"Our baby needs his Dadai. Don't be a hero over there, Fin…be my hero here," answered Cathella.

"Don't think about me being gone - think about me returning," smiled Fin.

—⟨ρ⟩—

Cathella held newborn Scott McCullen in her arms, unable to watch the coffin being lowered in the ground. Fin was gone and she was alone without her love. Her son would never get to see his father or know how deeply he was loved. Patrick put his arm around Cathella but she barely felt it. She gave him the baby to hold and got down on her knees. Cathella threw a handful of dirt onto the coffin.

"Fin, why didn't you come home to me?" asked Cathella, quiet as a whisper, still sure he could hear her.

"He tried to…" answered Sean.

"Not hard enough, or he would be here. The penny is gone and it wasn't there to protect him!" yelled Cathella, getting up, anger filling her aching body.

"I'm sorry…" said Macy.

"I don't want your sorry! I want my husband. I want our love! Who is going to love me?" sobbed Cathella.

She knew people were staring but she couldn't stop. She had believed him when he said he would return.

"We love you! Scott does, too," answered Brennan.

"It's not the same. We were meant to grow old together. He was only 28!" cried Cathella.

"Let's go home," said Chrissie in a soft voice.

"Where is home? The castle was bought with love and now that love is gone."

"No it isn't gone. Scott is proof enough of that," replied Patrick.

"Until he dies!" spat Cathella, furious.

"Don't talk like that, Cathella!" yelled Sean.

"I am sick of everyone dying around me," yelled Cathella.

Patrick handed Scott over to Macy and took Cathella's hand. He led her to the old tree where they had once had their picnics. Cathella touched the tree and all the anger suddenly left her. She felt the tears running down her cheeks; rage replaced by raw grief.

"I feel like I can't breathe without him," sobbed Cathella.

"I know…" replied Patrick, quietly pulling her into a hug.

"He said he would come back."

"I know he did and I'm certainly sure he tried, but many men didn't come back. Too many to count. It's awful, I know, but it's true.

But Cathella, you are still here, and you are still alive.”

Cathella felt hot and dizzy all of a sudden. Was this how an attack of hys- teria felt? She fell to the floor, attempting to take deep gulping breaths with no success.

“Help me to live...” sobbed Cathella, scratching at her neck.

Patrick placed a soothing hand on her neck.

“Just one breath at a time,” whispered Patrick.

“We will all help you,” said Sean.

Chrissie and Brennan stood next to him.

“Help me to breathe when I feel like there’s just no point,” cried Cathella.

“Just take another deep breath,” said Patrick in a soothing tone.

“This was not meant to be my life. I was not meant to be a widow!” yelled Cathella, feeling the air filling her lungs again with a fresh burst of anger.

“We weren’t meant to have lost our parents, but we did. Life is hard and just like you told me once, we just need to go on, remember?” answered Brennan, stepping forward.

“Why so much pain? The Scarlet penny would have kept him safe, it was love...” whimpered Cathella.

“No, Cathella, no. You are love, not a stupid wee penny,” scolded Sean angrily.

Macy bent down and placed the tiny Scott in her arms. He had his daddy’s black hair and nose.

“This is love,” said Macy, quiet but certain.

Cathella looked down at her son. Macy was right. this was the product of their love. She felt a small spark of hope as her son stared back up at her, those same curious eyes as his father...

“Scott, your dadai loved you so much,” said Cathella.

"Now Scott, your mamai loved your father even more," stated Brennan, placing a hand on her shoulder.

The others formed a half circle around her and Scott, like a wall defending her from the pain that surrounded them.

Chapter
21

Ireland 2000

Bella dropped the journal onto her lap as tears streamed down her cheeks. So much loss in one year, how could a person survive that? How would you get over losing your husband and child? Bella picked up a tissue and wiped her eyes, but the tears wouldn't stop coming. Was she crying for Cathella's loss or her own? Her father had died last year just like Cathella had lost her child and husband. Bella stood up, leaving the journal on the chair and made her way to Cathella's room. She opened the chest of drawers, pulling everything out. The penny had to be here somewhere. It was last seen in this room. She pulled out another drawer and threw it across the room in anger and frustration. Bella fell to the floor crying. She wished she had never read that journal. The door opened and without looking up, she sensed that it was Wylie standing there. He must really think she was a nutcase. She looked up at him through her tears and saw concern reflected back at her.

"They died…Arabella and Fin, they died," sobbed Bella, hugging one of Cathella's dresses to her chest.

"That was a long time ago, Arabella," answered Wylie, crouching down in front of her.

"Don't call me that - I am not Arabella! I am Bella and I don't know why I was ever given that name!"

"You'll find out soon enough. Your grandmother always called you Arabella," answered Wylie, twirling a lock of hair around his finger.

"I don't want to go on anymore, the pain is too much, Wylie. People die all the time and leave us behind."

"I know, and life isn't fair, but you've been given a chance to live and love, Arabella, and the ones who died gave you that chance," replied Wylie.

"What if I don't want to live?" asked Bella.

"Then you wouldn't be here," stated Wylie, cupping her cheek.

Bella took a deep shuddering breath and leapt forward into Wyle's arms. He caught himself before he fell back and wrapped his arms around her. Bella slowly calmed down, embarrassed by the outburst, and mumbled an apology before pulling back.

"Will you help me pack her things back up?"

"Yes I will; but I want to show you something first."

Bella took his hand and let him pull her to her feet.

He walked them to the next room - the door to this room had been closed since she arrived. Wylie turned the handle and the door creaked open. Wylie switched on the light and stepped back. Bella took a step forward; unable to do anything but stare.

"Don't hold on forever," said Wylie.

Bella looked at the wooden cot with an old dusty pink blanket still lying in it, and took in the rag dolls and blocks scattered across the floor. Towelling nappies and a little dress lay on a changing table in the corner.

"Arabella's room," whispered Bella.

"Your grandmother could never let go. She loved your dadai but he had to live in the shadow of a ghost."

"I didn't know," Bella murmured as she ventured futher into the room.

"I know. It's time to let go, Arabella. Don't hold on to an empty room," said Wylie, leaving her alone in the sad space.

Bella walked over to the cot that Sean had beautifull hand-craThed and rubbed her fingers across the name Arabella engraved on the side. Bella took a deep breath and looked up at the ceiling, hoping her voice would reach past the ceiling to somewhere far higher.

"Dad, I will always love you."

She looked around the room once more and switched the light off.

—♫—

Back in Cathella's room, Wylie had empty boxes lying all over and was sitting in the middle of room, packing clothes into one. Bella sat down across from him and started packing another one. She remembered her mother doing this to her father's things and how angry she had been, how she'd said that her mother hadn't loved her father. But her mother had refused to stay imprisoned in her pain. It was time for Bella to let go, too. Some time later, Fiona walked into the room and sat down to help them pack. They sat in comfortable silence together, gently folding the precious, antique objects and clothes and carefully packing them away. Bella realised that her father had grown up fatherless and he had survived, so why was she finding it so hard?

Unlike him, she had at least had the chance to get to know her father. Bella shook those thoughts away, overwhelmed, and helped Wylie carry the boxes down to his truck. Bella stopped walking mid-step and looked at the murky pool.

"You said it's time to let go. Cathella never let go, and I think this pool needs to be used again. It shouldn't be a tragic memorial left to decay. It was built with love," said Bella.

"But Arabella…" started Fiona.

"It was an accident, Fiona. It's a pool, not a coffin. We could use it and remember how good things can still come from even the most terrible tragedies," argued Bella.

"I agree. I'll go find someone to clean it," answered Wylie, taking the box from Bella.

"No, I want to do it. But I will need your help. We need to get a pump to suck out the water first."

"I'll go get one now while I go drop this off," answered Wylie as he climbed into the truck.

Fiona and Bella went back to Cathella's room to finish up the packing. Bella stooped down to look under the bed and noticed a piece of folded paper in the corner. She squeezed under the bed and pulled it out. It was actually an envelope that had become yellow and curled over the years. It looked un-opened, with Cathella's name written on the front.

"Open it - I don't think Cathella knew it was there. It must have fallen down the back of the bed!"

Bella sat down on the floor with her back against the bed and read the letter out loud to Fiona.

"My Dearest Cathella,   *14 July 1918*

I know you are sad right now, and so am I. But this baby is our new beginning. our second chance, and together we will raise him or her. I leave tomorrow and I know you're scared. So am I. I want to come home to you and our baby, but if I don't, it will be alright, because this castle was bought with love, filled with love, and that love will never die. I know you are worried about the penny but it is in a safe place where our love is planted. I was too scared to take it with me this time. I love you, Cathella, and our wee Arabella will always be our little girl, but she is gone and we aren't. We have to move on, Cathella. If I could write how much I love you, I would. You saved me when I thought my life was over. You showed me what life could be and a happiness I will never forget. Each day with you was like a day in Heaven. If I don't come back, I will be in Heaven with our little girl, making sure she knows how much she was loved. That day I saw you alone on the road when you were 16, I knew I was going to marry you, and I'm so glad I did. I don't regret one day of our life together. When Mamai died, you were the one that stepped in - I couldn't have done that alone. You are the one that showed me the world through your eyes, and I will forever be grateful. Don't hold on to the past and don't worry about me - us Irish live a long time.

Love, Finnigan McCullen, your husband and true love"

Bella put the letter down and looked at Fiona.

"That is so terrible…she never got to read it!" cried Fiona, tears welling up in her eyes.

"He hid it," replied Bella.

"Hid what?" asked Wylie, walking into the bedroom.

"The Scarlet penny. I found a letter he wrote Cathella before he left and I don't think she read it."

"Strange, why would he hide it?" questioned Wylie.

"He said it's in a safe place," added Fiona.

"But Cathella looked all over for it," replied Wylie.

"It is a mystery. Come on, let's go sort out the swimming pool."

She placed the letter on the bed and walked out of the room.

They helped Wylie set it up so that the pump sucked out the water. Once that was sort- ed, they went inside for lunch, suddenly ravenous. To Bella's surprise, it was homemade hamburgers and chips. She looked over at Wylie and smiled.

"You said you missed it - we hope it tastes like home," replied Wylie, smiling shyly as he sat down.

Bella was speechless. These people were so nice to her; what was she giving them in return? She swallowed past the lump in her throat and sat down. They were all looking at her, waiting for her reaction. Bella took a bite. It tasted nothing like back home, but she couldn't decide if it was better or not.

"It tastes really good," answered Bella, eating another chip.

"I'm going to town after lunch," announced Clancy.

"Can I go with you, Dadai?" asked Fiona.

"Yes, but you need to hurry up," replied Clancy as he finished off his lunch.

They all ate their lunch in silence after that. Bella put her empty plate away and went outside to check on the progress of the pool. It was about halfway, and would take another couple of hours. She went back inside and read more of the journal.

It was mostly about her father growing up, but with less of the excitemend and happiness that had marked Cathella's earlier writing. She found herself pulled back into the old Manor world again and lost track of time.

Chapter
22

Several hours later, Wylie walked into the room, casually whistling. He stopped in front of Bella.

"Its empty."

She left the journal there and followed Wylie outside. The bottom of the pool was covered in thick dark green sludge and grime. Corkun was bark- ing and pouncing on flowers a few feet away. Bella kept an eye on him and slipped on long, thick gloves. Wylie helped her put on a set of large yellow gumboots and did the same for himself. She slowly walked down the slimy steps and headed over to the largest object she could lift by herself. Wylie lifted the metal chair out of the pool and let out a hiss of pain. Bella dropped the object and rushed over to Wylie.

"Are you alright?!" asked Bella.

"I'm fine..." lied Wylie.

The blood was pooling under the glove. Bella pulled a face and grabbed his hand.

"I am alright, please, it's fine."

"No, you are not, you're bleeding!"

Bella pulled Wylie behind her and up the stairs. She took off her gloves and then his. He let out another agonised hiss. He had a semi-deep cut from the metal chair on one finger.

"Come on, lets go clean it," replied Bella.

"No, it's fine. It will heal itself."

"Don't act all brave! Now, move your butt before I make you."

Wylie arched a brow and Bella gave him a hard shove.

"You are so bossy."

She made him sit by the table and tracked down the disinfectant and plas- ters. She sat down, dipped the cotton wool into the disinfectant, and took his large hand in hers.

"this is going to sting…"

"Doesn't it always," mumbled Wylie.

"You're a bad patient," teased Bella.

"If I'm good, do I get a lollipop?" pouted Wylie.

"Don't push it," laughed Bella, gently sticking the teddy bear plaster on his finger.

He looked down at it and scowled. Bella giggled and kissed the spot over the plaster.

"We'd better go clean up now."

"If there was water in that pool I would throw you in," joked Wylie, following her outside.

"Oh, please, you would never do that," said Bella, pushing him forward.

"You're asking for it!" smiled Wylie, trying not to stumble.

Bella gave him another push and then ran past him before he could grab her. She heard him behind her. She let out a loud shriek just before he wrapped his arms around her from behind and they both fell forward. Wylie rolled at the last second, causing her to land on top of him.

Bella laughed and looked down at him. She tried to get up but Wylie grabbed her wrists and rolled her over so that he was now on top.

"Wylie, stop!" pleaded Bella playfully.

He moved his hands to her ribs and tickled her until she cried for mercy before rolling away. They both lay on the ground for a few moments, panting for breath. After a few seconds, Wylie stood up and held his hand out for her. Instead of taking it, Bella grinned mischievously and swung her leg up, knocking him off his feet. She laughed and stood up. Wylie stared up at her as if he had something he wanted to say but wasn't sure how to word. Bella left him lying there and put her gloves back on. She heard Corkun barking and just knew he was following Catriona around as usual.

"Corkun!" called Bella, but the puppy took no notice of her.

It took them all afternoon to clean all of the junk out of the pool, and tomorrow morning they would scrub it with disinfectant before they refilled it.

After supper, Bella sat down to watch a movie with the family. Halfway through, the phone rang, interrupting the relaxed scene. She ran to pick up the phone. It was Martin, the lawyer. He told her that someone had bought the castle and would move be ready to move in in two weeks. She put the phone down and looked around at everyone. Wylie was staring at her, disappointment written all over his face. This was what she had wanted wasn't it? If that was the case, why did she feel so horrible about it? Bella sighed, said goodnight to the family she had unexpectedly come to love, and excused herself to go to bed.

—♪—

Bella got up early to finish cleaning the pool.

Corkun happily ran around the garden while Bella got ready with her safety gear. Wylie appeared beside her soon after wearing an old button-down black shirt and shorts, with sunglasses covering his eyes. She hated when he wore them; she knew by now that he did it to hide his emotions from her. She took a deep breath, and together they started on the pool in silence. By lunch time the pool was clean. Wylie set everything up so that the pool would be filled up with clean water.

Bella decided to go for a walk to think things over while she waited. She had learned so much about her grandmother from the journal; like how she got her name. Her father had promised his mother that he would name his daughter Arabella and his son Finnigan; it was a promise he had kept. So many things made sense to her now. She stopped by the old entry sign by the road and thought about the new people moving in. They needed to know what this place was, and she would have to make that happen.

She jogged back to the castle and found Wylie in the kitchen drinking coffee. Bella asked him for some black paint, and he carried it back to the old sign with her. She handed him a paint brush and together they repainted the letters 'Scarlet Manor'. Bella looked over the finished product with pride with Wylie standing next to her. She smiled mischievously before picking up her paintbrush and smearing it along his cheek. He grabbed her wrist, tak- ing the paintbrush and turning it back on her. They fought with the paint; getting splashes of black all over themselves and their clothing. Bella grabbed the bucket of paint; ready to pour it on him. Wylie held her arms to stop her, paint spilling all over them and the ground.

Bella stumbled back towards the sign and tripped over a large rock in front of it. Wylie dropped the bucket and tried to grab her. She fell onto her bum, laughing. Wylie pulled her up with concern written all over his face.

"Are you alright?" asked Wylie checking her for any signs that she might be injured but finding nothing.

"I tripped over this stupid rock…" giggled Bella, throwing the rock across the road.

She suddenly noticed a piece of cloth in the ditch and picked it up. Bella opened the cloth up and stared down at the unmistakable item.

"The penny!" cried Bella.

"Arabella, you found it!" shouted Wylie, pulling her into a huge bear hug.

"He said he put it where their love was planted, and he bought this land with love!" squealed Bella, quickly trying to clean it up as much as she could.

"We need to go tell the others!" said Wylie, grabbing her hand.

Together they ran back to the castle and straight into the kitchen where everyone was busy sorting out dinner.

"Arabella found the coin!" yelled Wylie lifting her hand in the air.

"It was buried under a rock by the sign," replied Bella, showing them the coin.

Fiona jumped up, running to Bella. She took the coin and walked over to her father.

"Look, Dadai, it is real," smiled Fiona.

"That's all well and good, but you two are dripping paint in my house. Go hose off out back," scolded Catriona, pointing to the back door.

They looked down and walked out of the back door. Bella walked over to the pool to check its progress.

Wylie came up from behind her and grabbed her, jumping into the pool with her. She came up for air and turned to face him, splashing water in his face.

"I said I would throw you in!" laughed Wylie, splashing her back.

Bella tried to jump onto his back and push him under the water, but he was too strong and turned to catch her. Bella laughed and swam towards the steps. She got out of the pool, the cold air hitting her immediately, and she started shivering. Wylie got out and stood next to her, his satisfaction obvi- ous. Bella glared at him.

"There's no towel, smarty-pants," cried Bella, shivering.

"I'll be your towel," declared Wylie, grabbing her and wrapping his arms around her.

"You're just as wet as me!" shouted Bella, pushing him away.

"At least you won't get wetter," smiled Wylie teasingly.

"Stop it," giggled Bella pushing him back.

"Fiona, please get us towels!" shouted Wylie through the open door.

"Wylie, don't yell," laughed Bella.

Fiona walked out with two towels, and she handed Bella the coin. "

this belongs to you," said Fiona.

"It's not Scarlet anymore," replied Bella.

"Do you need paint?" asked Wylie with a devilish grin.

Bella clutched it tight in her hand and wrapped the towel around her body. She went inside and changed into dry clothes before heading to the armchair to read what was left of the journal alone. She wanted to get to the end of the story before time ran out and she had to leave.

Chapter
23

Ireland 1981

Cathella felt overwhelmed and nervous. Today was the day she would meet her granddaughter for the first time. Her son's family had flown to Ireland just so that she could meet her. The girl was eight-years-old already and feisty, from what she heard. Her son told her that she had red curls just like her and the same eye colour. Her only grandchild would be here today in this very castle. Had time really flown that much? It was lonely being in this place by herself all the time; she missed the con- stant sounds of laughter and chatter. Scott had kept his promise and named his daughter Arabella, but she was called Bella for short. Cathella didn't worry about the details, all she wanted was to see the little girl that would remind her of another little girl she used to know. She hardly saw the others now that they had all grown up. They all had children of their own and grandchildren to care for. Patrick had lost his wife recently; left with only his two daughters and three grandchildren.

Sean spent most of his time visiting his three children and seven grandchildren in all different parts of the country, and Brennan lived with Patrick as his son had moved to America with his three children. Chrissie had moved to America as soon as she could after hearing about it form Macy. Last she heard, the girl was expecting her first grandchild from her only daughter. All in all; it was a lonely life here for Cathella. Patrick tried to visit as much as he could, even though his schedule was so busy. Cathella wished she still had the Scarlet penny to show her granddaughter, but it was still gone after all these years. It was still a mystery as to how it had disappeared. Days like these, she longed for Fin the most, mostly because he had missed out on so much. When she felt extremely alone, she would walk around Arabella's room hoping to feel something, or to catch a glimpse of a shadow on the wall.

The sound of knocking at the door brought Cathella out of her thoughts and down the stairs to open it. Tears blurred her eyes as she took in the sight of her only son and his family. Her little Scotty was a grown man now; almost too old to be called little anymore in her mind.

"Mom!" said Scott, hugging his mother close.

He was almost 50 now, where had all the years gone for them?

"Scott, you are home!" cried Cathella, refusing to let him go, just in case it was all a dream.

"Hello, Cathella," replied Bethany, stepping forward to greet her mother- in-law.

"Bethany, it is so good to see you again. Please, call me mom. No matter our age, we will always be mothers," smiled Cathella as she embraced Betha- ny.

Scott stepped aside and put his arm around a young girl.

"We would like you to meet our daughter, Arabella."

Cathella was suddenly at a total loss for words. The little girl was beautiful.

"You must be Arabella..." said Cathella in a shaky voice.

"People call me Bella, but you can call me Arabella if you want," replied Bella, shy and quiet.

The little girl stepped forward and hesitantly wrapped her arms around Cathella's waist. Cathella had missed the sensation of a small body against hers. this was something she would remember forever.

She led them inside and showed them to their room. Bethany was already on the phone to someone back home while Scott apologised and started unpacking. Bella followed after Cathella, wanting a tour of the place. She had a long list of questions about the castle and Ireland. Cathella soaked in every minute of it; she felt more alive than she had in years. They ended the tour in the library, with Cathella a bit winded from walking. She sat down in her favourite chair to take a breath. Bella strolled slowly around the room, gazing at the large collection of books in awe.

"Have you read all these books?" asked Bella.

"Yes my dear. Would you like to read one?" replied Cathella.

"I can't read very well yet, could you read me a story?" questioned Bella, finding a children's book that she didn't recognise.

"Yes I can," Cathella smiled as she took the book from her.

Bella took a cushion off the other chair and sat down in front of her grandmother. She loved the soothing sound of her Irish accent as she read to her. Scott walked into the room and took a photo of them.

"Bella, I want to get a photo of you with your grandmother - go sit on her lap!" said Scott excitedly.

Bella got up and carefully climbed onto Cathella's lap. Her grandmother had such soft hands that made her feel safe. They wrapped around her nicely, not like her mother's cold hands. Her mother walked into the room, disap- proving of Bella on her grandmother's lap.

"Bella, your grandmother is an old woman and I told you that young la- dies don't sit on laps. Now, go take a bath and get ready for bed," said Bethany, tapping her foot impatiently.

"I told her to sit there for a photo," replied Scott.

"Don't encourage her, it is so hard to re-teach her all this nonsense she's learned from you."

"Do they always fight?" whispered Cathella.

"Only when I don't listen," answered Bella.

She kissed her grandmother on the cheek and went to her room to bathe.

She had to do it herself. After her bath, her father tucked her in and said goodnight.

Bella lay in the large bed by herself, the shadows on the wall giving her the shivers. She hated sleeping by herself; usually she slept by their cook Rosalie when she got scared.

The wind howled and rattled the windows. Bella bit her lip, trying to keep the scream in.

—⚘—

She got out of bed and ran for the door. The passage was still lit up. Bella sighed in relief and followed the lights. She found her grandmother still in the library, bent over a book, writing something. Her grandmother put down her book and looked at Bella with concern.

"Grandma, I got scared..." sobbed Bella

"There is nothing to be scared of," answered Cathella, opening her arms for the little girl.

Bella ran into her grandmother's open arms.

"Please can I sleep by you? Mama doesn't like it when I wake her," pleaded Bella, teary-eyed.

"Yes you may. Come on - lets go up to my room, then," replied Cathella, getting up with a little difficulty.

They walked up the stairs together to Cathella's bedroom. She lifted Bella up into the bed and then got in herself. Bella quickly snuggled against her, scared that Cathella would changer her mind.

"Your accent sounds strange," whispered Bella sleepily.

"That's because I wasn't born here...I came here alone, when I was just a teenager," replied Cathella.

"Without your parents?" gasped Bella.

"Yes, without them," smiled Cathella, her hand running through Bella's curls.

"Weren't you scared? I would never come here without my daddy," stated Bella.

"Sometimes you have to do things you don't want to do."

They laid there in silence for a few minutes before Bella spoke again.

"Grandma, I like this castle. One day I want a castle just like this one."

"Maybe one day you can have this one," replied Cathella, kissing her on the head.

"I would like that a lot...and I would care for it and love it..." answered Bella, drifting asleep.

Cathella lay in the bed unable to sleep as she held this little girl. She had missed out on so much with her own daughter when she had lost her. Scott knocked on the slightly open door and she gestured for him to enter.

"There she is. She has a mind of her own, that one," said Scott, sitting on the bed and gently touching Bella's cheek.

"Reminds me of you," answered Cathella.

"Mom, I am so sorry it took me so long to come home. I really wanted to, but the ghosts around here, well, they can be too much. It's just that…you live in the past, while the present is passing you by," admitted Scott sadly.

'I never knew you felt that way, son. I love you, and I only want what's best for you."

"I know that now, Mom. having a child of my own taught me that," smiled Scott, taking his mothers hand.

They sat in the room together, watching Bella sleep.

"Do you still miss her?" questioned Scott.

"Yes, but I know she's gone and never coming back, and neither is your father. You look just like him…it makes me miss him even more…" Cathella confessed with tears running down her cheeks.

"I get so scared sometimes that I'd have to leave her and that she would have to grow up without me. She's my whole world, and I'm not so young anymore."

"No matter what happens; she'll always have the memories of how much you love her," smiled Cathella patting his hand.

"But will that be enough? Anyway…enough depressing talk - get some sleep, Mom. And I love you, I know you did the best that you could," answered Scott, getting up.

Cathella nodded her head and watched him walk away. She thought about what he had said. Was she the reason he had left?

24

The next morning they took a slow stroll towards town. Cathella held Bella's hand with Bella skipping and singing along side her. In town, Scott lifted Bella onto his shoulders and showed her all his favourite shops he had missed since leaving. Bella asked a million questions and wanted to take something home for everyone. Scott led them down the old alleyway and helped the ladies over the fence.

"Still today, no one uses the real entrance," said Cathella, breathless.

"This way is more fun, and the other is all the way at the other end of town!" laughed Scott.

"Where are we going, Dad?" asked Bella, tapping him on the head.

"To visit family," said Scott.

"Do we really have to walk through all this thick grass? It's ruining my skirt..." moaned Bethany.

"Enjoy the fresh air!"

"Who are we visiting?" asked Bella.

"Your father's uncle," replied Cathella.

They all walked across the bridge, Cathella stopping on it. Bella turned her head and saw her grandmother standing there. She made her father put her down and ran over.

"What's wrong, Grandmother?" asked Bella.

"Your grandfather built this bridge," stated Cathella, running her hand across the wood.

"It's beautiful," replied Bella taking her grandmother's hand in hers.

"Yes it is, and the man we are going to visit helped to build it," answered Cathella, leading them off the bridge.

They walked the rest of the way up the hill together until they reached the front door.

It opened to the sight of an old man with red hair and faint freckles across his nose.

"Scott, is that you?" asked the man, smiling.

"Sean, you're an old man now!" laughed Scott, hugging him.

Cathella stepped forward and received a warm hug. She introduced him to Bella.

"This is my granddaughter, Arabella," said Cathella with pride in her voice.

"Hello, dear, I am Sean, your uncle," Sean said amiably, shaking her hand.

"Hello, I'm Bella. Aren't you my daddy's uncle?" replied Bella.

"A smart lassie, like her father. Come inside and I can tell you all about how naughty your father was," answered Sean, leading them inside.

"Did you really build that bridge?" asked Bella.

"Aye I did, and your grandfather helped me," replied Sean.

"More like you helped him," teased Cathella.

Sean laughed and made them some tea.

"Where are the kids?" questioned Scott, looking around the empty room.

"Here and there. I'm on a break for a bit."

Cathella grew tired easily, so they started the walk back home to the castle after a chat with Patrick and Sean. On the way home, Bella saw a boy and girl playing in the field and ran over to them. She climbed up onto the fence as they cautiously approached.

"Hello, my name is Bella McCullen." called Bella. The little boy climbed up and sat next to her.

"Hi! I am…"

—◈—

2000

Bella was so busy reading that she hadn't noticed the dark clouds looming above. Rain suddenly came down in torrents, soaking her and the journal before she could read another word. Bella jumped up from the bench and ran back towards the castle. She was hugging the journal to her chest to protect it from any further damage.

She stopped inside and made her way to the sitting room to assess the extent of the damage down to the journal. Wylie heard a loud commotion and followed the sound towards the sitting room where he finds Bella soaking wet on the floor and crying. Wylie ran towards her, worried that she had been hurt. He lifted her chin and looked into her eyes.

"What's wrong? Did something happen?" asked Wylie, searching her for anything out of place.

Bella lifted up the soggy journal and showed it to him.

"The journal is soaked…and now I'll never know how it ends," sobbed Bella, fresh tears running down her cheeks mingling with the water already there.

"Arabella, it's alright," answered Wylie, grabbing a blanket off the chair and wrapping it around her.

"No it's not - it's wet and ruined and I need to know what happens next."

"No, it isn't ruined; I'll make a fire while you change and leave it to dry there. Then when you're done changing, I'll tell you what happens next in the story," Wylie said, taking the journal from her.

"How would you know what happened next? The children were going to tell me who they were!" shouted Bella, standing up and throwing the blanket aside angrily.

"Because I am that boy and Fiona is that girl," replied Wylie, standing in front of her.

"How did you know I was reading that?"

"I check your progress when you put it down."

"Why would you do that? Tell me now, please? Tell me everything!" demanded Bella.

"Not 'til you're properly dry, you don't want to be sick again," argued Wylie, staring her down.

Bella groaned and threw the blanket off of her, leaving the room in a hurry.

When she returned, there was a fire blazing and Wylie was settled comfortable in the one chair. Bella looked around the room. Wylie patted the spot between his legs. Bella glared at him. He laughed and pulled her down. She fell half on top of him.

"Wylie, stop it."

"My story - my rules. Now settle down nicely and I'll tell it to you."

Bella climbed over him and settled between his legs. It felt surprisingly comfortable. He pulled her back against his chest and wrapped an arm around her waist.

"this is the story of how you saved my life," smiled Wylie, massaging her scalp.

Bella looked up at him, confused, waiting for him to go on and tell her what had happened.

1981

They were both straddling the fence facing each other.

"Hi, I'm Wylie McIntosh and this is my little sister, Fiona," said the boy cheerfully, pointing to his sister standing near him.

"Why are you playing here alone?" asked Bella.

"Come on Bella, we need to go," called Bethany impatiently as she approached them.

"But Mom - I want to play with my new friends," whined Bella, crossing her arms.

"Maybe you should listen."

"Nah, they don't mind. How old are you?"

"I'm ten-years-old and my sister is eight," answered Wylie.

"I'm also eight," beamed Bella proudly.

Cathella approached the fence, placing an arm around Bella.

"Wylie, who is your father?" questioned Cathella, growing curious.

"Clancy ma'am," replied Wylie nervously.

"And where is he now?" asked Cathella.

"Dadai is looking for work...we've got no money and Mamai is looking for food," mumbled Fiona honestly.

"You don't have food?!" cried Bella, her mouth hanging open.

"And no house…" added Fiona.

"Mom, they have no house or food! Grandmother, please can they live by you in that big castle? You said you're all alone," begged Bella.

"Bella, don't be silly," snapped Bethany in a stern voice.

"But, Mom, we're supposed to love our neighbour, right? And Grandmother said the castle was bought with love. Please, they could probably help you and work for you," pleaded Bella.

The children stared at Bella in shock while Cathella watched the children's reactions.

"Bella, say goodbye now…" Scott said, beginning to feel awkward at the tense scene.

"No, I won't leave 'til you say yes!" screamed Bella.

Scott walked up to her and lifted her off the fence. She put up a fight but he was stronger.

"No! Let me go!" yelled Bella kicking him in the leg.

"That's enough young lady!" shouted Scott.

He hardly ever shouted at her. Bella's lower lip trembled.

"Bella, it's alright, we will be fine. Dadai said Uncle will care for us 'til they get money," replied Wylie sincerely.

"Are you really going to break up a family?" questioned Bella defiantly.

Cathella walked up to the boy and looked him up and down.

"Wylie, would you like to live in my castle?" asked Cathella.

"Yes, ma'am…" answered Wylie, confused.

"Go get your mother and father and come to Scarlet Manor - it's just up the road from here. I'll speak with them there about an arragement we can make," said Cathella.

"Scarlet Manor! we know where that is," said Wylie, jumping off the fence.

"My grandfather bought it," added Bella.

"Can I come with you now?" asked Fiona shyly.

"Please, can she?" begged Bella, looking up at her grandmother with a forlorn expression.

"Yes she may, if it is alright with her brother," replied Cathella.

"Mother, you can't do this…" warned Scott.

"I am living in the present - just like you told me to, Scott," answered Cathella sharply as she began to walk away.

Wylie looked at Bella and smiled.

"Bella you are special, d'you know that. Mamai said you will know a jewel when you see it; and you are a jewel," said Wylie.

"I like you…even if you are Irish," stated Bella.

Fiona took Bella's hand and together they walked back towards the castle. Wylie ran off to go get his parents; their life changed from that moment, all thanks to a little girl called Arabella McCullen.

25

Ireland 2000

Bella snuggled deeper into Wylie's warm body and peered up at him. Corkun had joined them a while ago and was now asleep in her lap.

"You thought I was a jewel?" asked Bella, shyly.

"I still do," answered Wylie, softly resting his hand on her cheek.

"Don't be silly."

"Arabella, I'm not," Wylie replied, leaning down and kissing her upside down on her lips.

Bella didn't realise until that moment how much she had missed his touch. She wrapped her arms around his neck and pulled him closer, deepening the kiss. After a few seconds, reality hit and Bella pushed him away.

"Wylie, stop!" cried Bella, pulling away from him.

She got up and stood as far away from him as possible without leaving the room, crossing her arms as if to defend herself from his affection.

"Stop what? You want me, Arabella, so why are you fighting this?" questioned Wylie mirroring her pose.

"I am not a jewel, I am wrong for you," squeaked Bella, holding the tears back.

"Why do you think that?"

"I am a bad person and I don't deserve you," cried Bella, hugging herself.

"Stop saying that! You saved my life again when you came back. I was all alone, mourning Cathella, and then you showed up and I fell for you and came back to life."

"No, I destroyed it - the castle is sold, Wylie, and I'm leaving in a week."

"What do you mean, a week?"

"Exactly as I just said. It's to late for us – I'm leaving," stated Bella.

"No! I love you, Arabella." Wylie said, approaching her like a predator would it's prey.

Bella stepped back nervously. "I don't want you," lied Bella.

"Don't do this to us," begged Wylie, giving her the space she wanted.

"I already have," replied Bella running out of the room.

She fell onto her bed crying. She did love Wylie. But she had sold the castle and now it was too late for them. He would hate her even if he didn't mean to.

—⋅ℐ⋅—

She picked up the phone and dialled home, needing to hear a familiar voice. Her mother answered with the same tone she always used when she was annoyed.

"Mom..." sobbed Bella.

"What is it, darling?" asked Bethany, sounding sincerely worrried for the first time.

"I need you," cried Bella.

Her mother talked to her for a while until she had calmed down and the plans had been made to come get her. She lay with her face buried in the pillows and ignored the persistent knocking on her door.

"It's me, Fiona," pleaded the voice.

The door opened and Fiona sat down next to Bella rubbing soothing circles over her back. Tears ran down her cheeks; she did nothing to stop them.

"Do you love him?" asked Fiona.

"Yes," answered Bella truthfully.

"Then why are you leaving?"

"Because I sold the castle, Fiona, I did the one thing he didn't want me to do and he'll just hate me forever."

"He loves you," replied Fiona, as if that solved everything.

Bella wiped her eyes and sat up. She looked blankly at Fiona until she dropped the subject.

"Tell me about you and Colin."

"I think he's the one for me. He's smart and funny and looks at me like he really loves me," answered Fiona blushing.

"Sounds like you love him," smiled Bella.

"Yes, I do, but I think it's too soon to tell him."

"It's been three months, and if it's real love I doubt it will fade; nothing can keep that apart. If I learned anything from my grandmother, it's that you should love fully and not conditionally," answered Bella.

"But isn't that what you're doing to Wylie? You're saying his love is conditional, and I know my brother - he has changed since you got here. He isn't so grumpy anymore. Your grandmother was his best friend and when she died I thought he would, too, but now I see life in him again."

"I didn't know that."

"He doesn't talk much, but with you it's different. Cathella was the same, she only spoke to Wylie."

"I'm glad that she had someone…even if it wasn't me."

"But who will he have when you leave?" questioned Fiona.

"He has his family… he has you."

"Do you think he would talk to me the way he talks to you? You probably know more about him than I do. I've never heard him sing properly or seen him so playful all the time. He had to be so grown up and serious when we were children and you showed him a different kind of life."

"At least I gave him that and I'll never forget him. He showed me love when I thought I would never love again," admitted Bella.

"Think about what you are doing, because I don't want to lose my sister for good," replied Fiona leaving the room to give Bella space to think.

—❧—

"I'm going to Cork to pick up my mother today." Bella announced as she entered the kitchen with Corkun following close behind her.

"You can't go alone - take Fiona with you."

"Sorry, I can't. I have plans with Colin," apologised Fiona.

"I'll be alright on my own."

"That won't do; what will your mother think of us? Take Wylie with you," answered Catriona.

"No, he has plans."

"No I don't, and I actually want to take you somewhere in Cork before we fetch your mother."

Everyone stared at her, waiting for her to answer him. Bella sighed and he gave her a triumphant smile.

They left right after breakfast and caught the first ferry out. They sat quietly in Wylie's car, both lost in their own thoughts. Once they reached the other side, Wylie drove in the opposite direction of town.

"Where are we going?" asked Bella, peering at him through her sunglasses.

"Have you ever heard the Irish use the word Blarney?" questioned Wylie.

"Yes."

"Well, it's not just a word but an actual place called the Blarney Stone - and we're going there," replied Wylie.

"What do you do there?" questioned Bella, sceptical.

"Kiss a stone."

Bella peered over her glasses to see if Wylie was teasing her. He was staring ahead with a straight face.

"You what? Why?" laughed Bella.

"The Blarney Stone is a block of blue stone that's built into the battle- ments of Blarney castle. They say Blarney means flattery or coaxing talk." said Wylie.

"So why do you kiss it?"

"Legend says that the builder of Blarney Castle was involved in a lawsuit, and he asked the goddess Cliodhna for assistance. She told him to kiss the first stone he found. So on the way to court he did just that. He pleaded his case and won; the stone is said to import the ability to deceive without offending."

"So now people kiss it!?"

"Exactly. It is dirty and old ,but it's just something that is done. It's tradition. You can't go home without having done it. The tricky part is that to kiss it you have to hang upside down..." replied Wylie, taking a quick glance at her to see her reaction.

"Sounds dangerous."

"No, there'a always someone there helping you, and I'll be there to keep you safe."

They drove in silence the rest of the way. Once they got there, Wylie took Bella's hand. He led her to an instructor and asked him to help them.

"So – who's first?" asked the man.

"You go first," said Bella.

Wylie handed her his sunglasses and put on the protective gear. He followed the instructions and kissed the stone quickly. Nothing magic seemed to happen. Bella stared down at the stone and shivered. It still looked dangerous.

"I don't think I can do this!" cried Bella, stepping back.

"I've got you."

She gave the stone a quick kiss and sat up just as quickly. Wylie laughed and helped her out of the gear.

"That wasn't too bad now, was it?" asked Wylie, leading her to a bench.

"Let's just say I won't do that again anytime soon."

Wylie pecked her on the lips and stepped back before she could even register that he was kissing her. She touched her lips and looked at him.

"Just in case kissing the stone wasn't enough luck," he explained.

"Very funny. My mom will be here soon. Let's go to the airport."

26

At the airport, she spotted her mother right away and ran towards her. Her mother doesn't look that pleased to be here.

"Mother, I am so glad you came!" cried Bella, leading her to Wylie.

"I had to! You sounded like you would end up in the hospital if I didn't come," answered Bethany.

Bella rolled her eyes and introduced her mother to Wylie. They got back in the car and drove back to the harbour. Once they got to the castle, Bella led her mother to her room and left her to freshen up. She waited outside the door and, when her mother appeared, took her to the kitchen.

"Hello Catriona, it has been a long time," said Bethany in an awkward, polite tone.

"Yes, it has been! How was your trip?" asked Catriona while she served everyone beef stew for lunch.

Her mother pulled a face at the food but took a seat anyway, ever mindful of her etiquette.

"Hello Clancy, you look the same as ever."

"Aye, it has been a blessing having your daughter here with us," he replied warmly.

Lunch was dominated by an awkward silence..

After lunch, Bella took her mother to the sitting room for a chat. Corkun tried to jump onto her lap. She laughed and picked him up. Her mother looked at the dog like he was a disease.

"This is my Irish dog, Corkun." said Bella.

"I can see that."

"I'm so grateful that you came."

"I am your mother after all. Is that man the reason you're so upset?" asked Bethany.

"Yes, Mom. I love him but...we won't work."

"And why not? If you love him then what's the problem. He is quite handsome, he probably isn't a lawyer, but he'll do."

"I sold the castle that Cathella left me."

"Well that's alright, you wouldn't want to stay here forever, would you?"

"No, I want to go home."

"I will tell you one thing - you know what's right in your heart. I see how he looks at you, and to find a man that loves you like that isn't easy," replied Bethany sincerely.

"Maybe he isn't the right one for me."

"If he's all you think about and you miss him when he isn't around, then he just might be the right one."

"Can we just go home? this was all a mistake."

"Alright...but you can't bring the dog."

"He is my puppy, Mom."

"And it's my house and I don't want a dog. Now, if we're done talking I would like a little nap. Tomorrow will be a long day for the both of us."

"Have a nice nap, Mother."

Bella took a walk around outside, possibly for the last time ever. She spot- ted Wylie standing near the cliff and turned away, but he has already signalled her over.

"So that's it? You leave and I get no say?" asked Wylie.

"Yes that is it. It's my life and my choice."

"Arabella, don't do this to us."

"Just stop it! You don't want me to stay. It's just the fear of not having me here that's upsetting you," replied Bella.

"Stop fooling yourself – you're just as in love with me as I am with you."

"So what if I am? I'm still leaving, and new people will be living here by next week," answered Bella with a coldness she instantly regretted.

"So you made a mistake by selling this place, so what?"

"And it can't be undone. Please can Corkun stay here with you? My mom won't let him come back with us and I don't want him to starve,"

"Do I have a choice?" questioned Wylie resentfully. Bella stared at him.

She was trying to absorb as much as possible to remember later when his face would be thousands of miles away. She gave him a sad smile and walked away.

Bella was standing outside the airport with Corkun in her arms. Her mother had already checked in. Fiona stepped forward and wraps her arms around Bella.

"I am going to miss you so much," cried Fiona.

She stepped back and took Corkun from Bella.

"Fiona, you will always be my sister, no matter where we are in the world," replied Bella before wrapping Fiona in a huge hug.

Clancy and Catriona gave her a hug and kiss, then left with Fiona to sit in the car. Wylie took a hesitant step closer towards her.

"Please don't go."

"Don't make this harder than it already is."

Bella wrapped her arms around his waist, wanting to burrow into him.

"I love you." murmured Wylie in a husky voice.

"Sometimes love means letting go," whispered Bella.

She kissed him on the cheek and stepped back. He grabbed her arm gently pulling her back.

"Or holding on."

"No it doesn't."

"Arabella, you're scared - so am I. But love can keep us together through all our doubts and fears."

"Not this time."

"Can I have one last kiss?"

Bella stared at his lips. She really wanted to kiss them. But if she did, she wouldn't get on the plane. Bella shook her head and ran inside the airport. She had done the hardest thing in her life by leaving. She had lost the love of her life because she was so scared of loss. None of it made any sense.

Chapter 27

South Africa 2001
Four months later...

Bella stood in her new office overlooking the city. Since being home, she had thrown herself into the clothing company, Pennies. She had been told that her grandmother had started it after Scott was born to bring money in, and it just grew from there. It had grown to the point that Cathella didn't have to work herself; just keep an eye on things and ensure that everything was runnning smoothly. Bella had started her own journal, writing about her trip to Ireland. Not a day went by that she didn't think of Wylie and his family. She missed him as much as she missed her father. Sometimes it felt like she was being consumed by her guilt and yearning for him. It was true when Cathella had said that it was hard to breathe when her loved ones were no longer around. Most days she wanted to stay in bed and reminisce about all of those moments with him, but instead she worked herself until exhaustion hit each night. Her phone suddenly rang, shaking her out of her depressing, faraway thoughts.

The sound of the familiar voice on the other end nearly made her weep.

"Bella, it's Fiona! How are you? I can't believe it's been so long," Fiona said in her usual fast-paced, Irish lilt.

"Fiona, I thought I'd never hear your voice again!"

"I miss you so much, please come back," begged Fiona.

"I can't Fiona, I'm sorry. I have a company to run."

"Not even for my wedding?"

"Wedding? You're getting married? It is to Colin, right?"

"Of course it is! And I need my maid of honour to be at the wedding," begged Fiona.

"When is this wedding? I wouldn't miss it for the world," asked Bella.

"In a month - we wanted it as soon as possible. When can I expect you to come? Oh, and please tell your mother to come along, too!"

"I will tell her! We'll come in a few days to help and I'll make a plan for us to stay in a hotel in town."

"Don't you dare, Mamai would never hear of it," argued Fiona. "It's not debateable - do you want me there or not?" asked Bella.

"Fine, but I want you smiling in all the photos," teased Fiona.

"Of course I'll be smiling. Fiona, how is Wylie doing?"

"The same as you, I suppose. If we even get a 'hello' out of him, it's a miracle." Bella winced, feeling guiltier than ever.

"Sorry, I didn't say that to make you feel bad. Just think about your happiness first. I have to go but I can't wait to see you!"

⁓ℬ⁓

Bella left work early for the first time and went straight to her mother's house. She found her mother on the phone shouting at some poor caterer.

"Mother, we've been invited to Fiona's wedding in Ireland."

Her mother puts down the phone and turned to her with a smile.

"A wedding in Ireland? Tell them we're coming! When is it?"

"A month away, but Fiona asked for our help."

"I'll pack right away."

Filled with excitement, adrenaline, and nerves, Bella quickly tracked down a travel agency and organised two tickets for their flights, as well as bookings for a small hotel in town. She went upstairs to find her mother. Her mother stood in front of her wardrobe directing the cleaning lady on what to pack. Bella rolled her eyes and sat on her mother's bed. She saw the family portrait of them from two years ago and swallowed back the tears.

"Do you miss him?" asked Bella. Her mother turned around, shocked.

"What a question to ask! I loved your father; it was devastating to lose him."

"But I never saw you cry."

"I cried all the time…just not in front of you. I needed to be strong for you. We couldn't both be blubbering all over, could we?" answered Bethany.

"I didn't want you to be strong…I wanted us to cry together," explained Bella.

"I am sorry if you thought I didn't miss him. You two had a special bond that, to be honest, made me a little jealous. He loved you in the way I couldn't," answered Bethany.

"Mom, I know you love me. You came to Ireland because I needed you and look at you now – packing to leave again to be by my side."

"I am so sorry for not loving you like you needed. I just want what was best for you."

"I missed you growing up. You were there but I was too scared to approach you. So I went to Dad, and when he died I just had no idea what I would do."

"You have me now and forever. I love you Bella. I know that your father was proud of you. I'm proud of you, too - for going there alone and doing what you thought was best at that time. There's no use dwelling over what could have been; just keep moving forward," answered Bethany, hugging her daughter for the first time in a while.

"I am scared to see Wylie," mumbled Bella.

"Do you still love him?"

"Yes I do...but I love him enough to give him up."

"You are so special Bella, don't forget that, and maybe you should start thinking that you just may be exacly what's good for him. Besides, you're getting too close to 30 now and I want some grandbabies!"

"I forget how smart you are, Mom. But I made my decision and I need to stick to it."

"I was married in Ireland...it was so beautiful." smiled Bethany.

"You, in Ireland? I never knew that. How did you and Dad meet anyway?" questioned Bella.

"I was 21 and still living at home, normal for girls like me with a strict father back then. My father came into a lot of money suddenly and decided to take us on vacation to Ireland since he had always wanted to go there for some reason. My brother Jackson was only 14 at the time and we were pretty close. We were so excited to be leaving the country and finally be going overseas."

"So you went there and met Dad?" asked Bella.

"Not exactly…so we were staying in a hotel, actually the very hotel we're going to be staying in this time. One day, Jackson and I snuck out for a walk because we were bored in the hotel. We followed the road leading out of town, wondering where it would lead us. Then it started to rain - something we weren't used to happening so suddenly. We took off running but somehow got separated. I stopped to look for my brother everywhere but he was gone, and I knew my father would be furious with me for losing him. I sat down on a rock by the side of the road and started to cry. It was still raining but I didn't care; I would rafter die than face my father."

"He sounds mean."

"He was, but only because he loved us. Maybe that's why I'm so hard on you…"

"So what happened next? You were in the rain…" questioned Bella.

"Right, I was sitting there and I heard a car stop a few feet away. I could just picture my father's angry face in my mind yelling at me, so I refused to look up. But to my surprise, it was a young man, the most handsome man I had even seen. He had black hair and blue eyes with a kind smile. He told me his name and asked me if I had lost something. I told him I had lost my brother and he told me that I was in luck, because he had found a boy who had lost his sister. I got up and followed him to his car and got in to find my brother soaking wet," replied Bethany.

"So you got married after that?" questioned Bella.

"No, no, my father wouldn't hear of his English daughter marrying a poor Irish man, no matter what sort of house he came from. We fell instantly in love and I snuck out every chance I could to see him. Cathella was sweet about the whole thing but she hated that I was deceiving my father.

So, one day she phoned him and told him everything. My father gave me the biggest whipping of my life and locked me in the room. My mother was a small, soft person but she didn't agree. She let me out, saying true love was never to be locked up. She helped me arrange everything with Cathella behind my father's back. We got married in the McPherson's church. My father found out and was livid but there was nothing he could do. So he decided, if this marriage was going to work, Scott would have to come back here with us and work for my father. Scott loved me so much that he said goodbye to his family and mother and came here with me."

"Love was so tough in those days!" declared Bella.

"Love is pretty hard today, too, wouldn't you say?"

"Mom, if Wylie loved me, wouldn't he find a way that we could be together like Dad did for you?"

"Would you really want him to leave his family for you?" questioned Bethany.

—❧—

Ireland
A month later...

Bella stared down at her figure-hugging champagne-coloured strapless dress. It was a stunning dress made by her own company. Fiona was wearing one of their wedding dress designs. She watched as Catriona helped the bride button up the back of the dress. Fiona looked stunning and everyone agreed that Colin was a very lucky man. They had found a priest willing to hold the wedding at the McPhersons church. Bella had managed to avoid seeing Wylie the whole time she had been here, but today it was inevitable.

"You look beautiful! Colin is so lucky," said Bella hugging Fiona.

"I couldn't have done it without you…and that dress is so you!" smiled Fiona, nervous and trying not to cry.

"We'd better leave for the church now!" announced Catriona.

She stopped and looked at Fiona, tears running down her cheeks.

"Look at you…my little girl getting married."

"Mamai, you'll make me cry and my makeup will run," warned Fiona anxiously.

"Sorry, child, I shall try my best to control myself."

They all laughed and piled into the car that would be taking them to the church. Bella hadn't seen the castle since returning and she wouldn't let any- one bring it up. She knew she was avoiding everything. But by tomorrow, she would be leaving for good this time, so what use would it be to get tangled up in memories and emotional turmoil? Clancy was standing outside the church when they arrived with the rest of the bridesmaids. All of the groomsmen were standing on the opposite side. Bella's eyes tracked them until she finally laid eyes on Wylie. Unsurprisingly, he stood out from the rest. She looked up at him to see him staring back. Bella blushed and turned her back on him, suddenly overwhelmed. Why did he have to look so hand- some in that tuxedo? The music started and each girl paired up with one of the men to begin the bridal procession. Bella wanted anyone but Wylie, but that old Irish luck wasn't on her side this time. She felt him touch her arm and inhaled a deep, shaky breath. Bella looked up into his crystal blue eyes and was unable to say anything. They walked down the aisle together. She could feel the warmth coming off of his body. Bella wanted to grab him and hold him forever; thankfully their arrival at the front of the church cleared aside her thoughts.Colin looked at Fiona with tears in his eyes.

The service was beautiful; many people left crying.

Afterwards, they headed towards the large tent that they had rented for the reception. Bella was seated at the family table with her mother and Wylie; this was the closest they had been since their walk down the aisle. She knew he was staring at her but Bella was unable to do anything about it without causing a scene. Fiona and Colin had their first dance together and to a raucous round of applause, after which everyone else rose up to join in. Bella found her mother dancing with some old man and smiled. At least she was having fun. Fiona grabbed Bella's hand and dragged her onto the dance floor.

"You did great!" shouted Bella.

"I am married!" squealed Fiona, hugging Bella tight.

They laughed and danced with the rest of the bridesmaids around them. Bella turned to go back to her seat but walked straight into something hard. She looked up to find Wylie's eyes gazing down at her and stepped back abruptly, shocked. He caught her before she could stumble and pulled her against his body. Bella stood there, tense in his arms, his breath fanning over her neck.

"Just let me have this dance?" whispered Wylie; a hint of uncertainty and desperation in his voice.

Bella nodded her head and felt his body instantly relax against hers. They moved slowly across the dance floor without an inch of space between them. Bella had her arms around his neck. She noticed that he had bags under his eyes and felt thinner than he had the last time she had seen him. His hand was shaking slightly where it was on her back; she wasn't the only nervous one. She took a deep breath, taking in his natural scent that always reminded her of a forest, and sighed.

"You look beautiful."

"Thank you…you don't look too bad yourself," replied Bella breathlessly.

"Corkun is really big now," smiled Wylie.

"I've missed him."

"And me?" questioned Wylie.

The silence between them was awkward and stilted, Bella pulled away a bit.

"Wylie, lets just enjoy this dance, please…" begged Bella.

She saw the raw intensity in his eyes dimmer at her reply. It felt like the song went on forever after that. The minute it ended, Bella walked away from Wylie.

She found her way outside and stood in the cool breeze trying to clear her head. Bella walked up to the tree in the front and she saw one leaf slowly growing on the dead tree. She remembered all the things her father told her about new leaves and felt tears prick her eyes. She heard footsteps approach and, as always, knew he was behind her, but she can't look at him just yet.

"Are you thinking about the last time we were outside with music?" asked Wylie from right behind her.

If she took one step back, she would be close against his chest.

"There are some beautiful women in there - go dance with them," stated Bella.

"I don't want them," whispered Wylie, placing his hands on her shoulders.

"I… I… uhm, have to go inside now," babbled Bella, nervously.

"No, first you need to tell me why you gave me the Scarlet penny."

Bella swallowed and looked down at the penny in his hand.

"I thought you should keep it," lied Bella. "What if I don't want it?"

"Then I'll take it back," said Bella, turning around to take it.

Wylie lifted his hand higher in the air, causing her to stumble. He wrapped his arm around her to hold her up. Bella had her hands on his chest. She looked up at him.

"I never said I didn't want it," Wylie whispered in her ear.

Bella felt a shiver go through her entire body. She knew he was going to kiss her. She wanted this just as much as him. She wanted one more memory to take home and play on repeat in her head at night. His lips were warm and soft against hers. Bella grabbed the front of his jacket. She was scared he would leave her wanting. He let out a laugh and kissed her again. Deeper and longer, like this was the last time he would ever get to taste her. They pulled apart and looked into each other's eyes. Bella started to panic.

"I..I.." she mumbled, looking for words.

She touched his cheek. He leaned into it. Bella pulled her hand away and ran back inside. Bella searched the crowds of people until she finally found her her moth- er and begged her to leave. She found Fiona and Colin and promised to see them at lunch tomorrow before she left. Bella walked back to the table to collect her handbag. Wylie was standing near the table staring intently at her. She grabbed her purse and left. Back at the hotel, her mother, sensing her pain, let her sleep in the bed next to her her for the first time in her life.

Chapter
28

The next morning, Bella found herself all alone in the hotel room. Her mother had left her a note that promised to meet her for lunch with the oth- ers. Bella turned to find the phone and accidently knocked her hand bag off the table, spilling all its contents all over the floor. She sighed and got out of bed to pick everything up. Bella noticed something odd and picked it up. It was the Scarlet penny. How did that get there? Her heart beat faster and her palms started to sweat. What did this mean? Why did Wylie put it in her bag? She threw everything back into the bag and quickly dressed before leaving the hotel.

Bella went for a walk to Patrick and Brennan's house. She wasn't sure if they knew that the penny had been found. Bella knocked on their door and waited for them to answer. She suddenly felt nervous. Brennan answered the door with a smile and led her to the kitchen table. Patrick was already seated at the table with a cup of tea.

"Hello, dear child. We thought you went home?" asked Patrick.

"I did, but I came back for Fiona's wedding. I'll be leaving later this evening," replied Bella, sitting down.

"So what brings you to us old folk?" asked Brennan, handing her a cup of tea.

"I wanted to show you this," answered Bella, taking the penny out of her pocket.

Patrick stared at it for a long time, tears falling freely down his cheeks.

"It cannot be...after all these years," cried Patrick, taking it from her.

"I found it before I left the last time I was here, it was by the sign for the castle," Bella told them as she sipped her hot tea.

"So that's where he put it," smiled Brennan.

"You knew he had hid it?" asked Bella.

"Of course - it couldn't have just disappeared. I saw Fin holding it once and looking out of the window with a sad expression on his face. I knew he must have hidden it to keep it safe."

"I wish Cathella had found it."

"Without Fin it was just a penny. It was their love that made this so spe- cial. this penny stays with the one you love when they go away and then it brings them back to you. That's what they believed." answered Patrick.

"I left it with Wylie when I went home."

"Why? Did you want him to atking it to you?" questioned Brennan.

"No, I just wanted him to keep it!" cried Bella.

"And now you have it again...what will you do with it?" asked Patrick.

"I suppose I'll do what I'm meant to do - give it to the one I love. But not so that he will come back to me; I just don't want it," replied Bella.

"I see, you know what's right then. I know Cathella would have wanted you to keep it or use it like she did."

"Thank you for loving my grandmother."

"She's the one who loved us so well. We will always be grateful," Brennan answered.

"I would love to stay, but I really need to go. It was so nice seeing you again, and thank you for the wisdom."

She headed straight to the pub for lunch. Everyone was already there. The only open seat was across from Wylie. Bella shook her head, shocked by her bad luck, and took a seat. Her mother was deep in a conversation with Clancy and Catriona barely noticing her arrival. Fiona turned to face Bella and grabbed her hand.

"I'm going to Hawaii for my honeymoon!" squealed Fiona.

"Ah that's lovely, I hope you enjoy it."

"Oh, I will, my husband and I are to have a craic." smiled Fiona.

Bella sputtered out her drink and gulped in clean air.

"A what?" asked Bella, red in the face.

"It means fun!" laughed Colin, an arm wrapped around his wife.

"Right, I don't think I should use that one back home," laughed Bella.

Bella looked up at Wylie who was staring out of the window looking distant and lost. She wanted to take his hand and tell him it was alright. But that would cause more confusion.

"So, what are we eating?" questioned Bella, facing the others.

"We're having the Dublin Lawyer," replied Fiona.

"Seriously guys, you're losing me."

"It's lobster cooked in butter, cream and whiskey," explained Wylie, opening his mouth for the first time since she has arrived.

It seems like everyone had noticed and was now looking carefully at the two of them. Wylie stood up, pushing past the others.

"I can't do this."

Bella was torn between staying and chasing after him.

She remembered the penny in her pocket. Suddenly decisive, she got up and ran after him. He looked over at her with such sad eyes that she nearly cried.

"Wait…can I get a hug goodbye?"

"Bella, stop! Can't you see what this is doing to me?" shouted Wylie.

"Just one hug," pleaded Bella.

He stepped forward, his arms hanging by his side. Bella wrapped her arms around him, trying to savour the moment. She dropped the coin into his jacket pocket and stepped back. Wylie looked at her for another moment and then walked away.

Bella stared out of the airplane window at the green fields and valleys below, her heart breaking with each second as they grew smaller. Her mother took her hand and gave it a squeeze.

"He still loves you," said Bethany.

"I know he does, Mom, but.."

"But what? You're scared? Don't you think I wasn't scared the day I married your father; because I was," replied Bethany.

"Mom, I really don't need a lecture right now. I'm hurting enough already."

"I am sorry, dear," answered Bethany.

"So am I," sobbed Bella.

It was a week later and Bella felt no better. She could still smell him and feel his touch all over. She couldn't shake the feeling that she had made a terrible mistake that she had no idea how to fix. Someone suddenly rang the door bell, so she waited for one of the staff to answer. The bell carried on ringing persistently, so Bella sighed and got up to answer. It was probably a salesperson making a cold call. She walked downstairs ot find the house completely empty. Where was everyone? She pulled open the door, intent on chasing the irritating person away. Bella stopped and just stared at Wylie standing before her; unable to do anything but drink him in. She couldn't comprehend the fact that he was standing right there, right outside her house. He smiled sheepishly.

"Can I come in? It was a long flight."

Bella stepped aside and closed the door behind him. The minute the door was closed Wylie pulled her into his arms. Bella stood there like a statue, trying to remember how to speak.

"Just let me hold you..." trembled Wylie.

Bella snapped back into reality and wrapped her arms around him. They stood together in the semi-darkened entryway simply holding onto each other. Wylie finally let her go and stepped back. He seemed reluctant to lose contact with her completely; keeping a hand on her arm.

"Wylie, what are you doing here…?" asked Bella, still stunned.

"Don't I even get a 'hello', Arabella?" questioned Wylie, arching his brow.

"What are you doing here?" repeated Bella.

"You forgot something," answered Wylie.

He took her hand in his and gently placed something in it. Bella stared down at her hand.

"What is it?" whispered Bella, somehow needing to hear the words from him.

"Its love," replied Wylie, removing his hand from hers.

Bella looks down at the newly painted Scarlet penny and gasped.

"I left it for you."

"You put it in my pocket when you hugged me. Cathella used to give it to Fin when he left so that he would come back home to give it to her. I'll ask you again - why did you give it to me?"

"Because I wanted you to keep it."

"You're lying. I gave it to you, and still you gave it back to me."

"So what if I gave it to you? You could have posted it to me if you didn't want it."

"Is that what you really wanted, for me to post it? I came here for you…I flew here for you, Arabella," replied Wylie, like that explained everything.

"I sold the castle," stated Bella.

"I know, and I'm the one that bought it. Come home with our penny to our castle, our home," begged Wylie, hope shining in his eyes.

"What do you mean?"

"I bought the castle for us," replied Wylie, slipping his arms around her waist.

"You don't hate me for selling it?"

"I am standing here in your house, asking you to come back with me. That is the opposite of hate!"

"And if I were to say no?"

"I won't let you say no," answered Wylie drawing her closer in.

Bella smiled for the first time in a long time. She saw unshed tears beginning to brim in Wylie's eyes.

"Take me home," whispered Bella breathlessly.

Wylie let out a breath and hugged her tight. Bella laughed and let him hold her. He lifted her chin up and kissed her on the lips. They both pulled back and gazed at each other.

"Do you love me?" asked Wylie.

"Yes! I love you, Wylie McIntosh!" shouted Bella happily.

"Good, because I couldn't ask you to marry me if you weren't in love with me."

"You want to marry me when we haven't even dated yet?" asked Bella.

"Yes, Arabella McCullen - and don't you ever ask me to call you Bella again, because I fell in love with Arabella," said Wylie, leaving no room for argument.

"I wouldn't have it any other way," sighed Bella, hugging him.

Bethany walked in a while later, finding them still holding onto each other.

"Look at you two. You see Wylie, I told you it would work," Bethany said with a small smile.

Bella turned to face her mother.

"Mother, you planned this?"

"Dear, I am your mother and I know you so well. You gave him that penny to see if he would come home to you, don't even think of lying to me."

"Mom, thank you so much for knowing me better than anyone else. I was too stubborn to see what I had, and I almost lost it without even trying to fight for it," admitted Bella.

"And I was too stupid to see what I had to do to keep you," added Wylie, giving Bella another lingering kiss on the corner of her mouth.

"I expect lots of grandchildren soon and another wedding in Ireland as soon as possible," said Bethany, without a hint of irony.

"I expect you to come live with us - my mother needs a friend," replied Wylie.

"Me? No, I'm to old to move," laughed Bethany.

"Mother, you are never too old. Please come home with us," pleaded Bella.

"Alright...I'll go with you, but only so that my grandchildren will know me and see how much I love them," declared Bethany.

They laughed and watched her walk away.

Later that evening, they were lying cuddled together on the couch. They were trying to watch a cheesy romance but quickly lost track of the plot, focusing instead on just soaking in each other's presence.

"The penny has done it again," whispered Wylie.

"No, love has done it again," answered Bella lacing their fingers together.

"We will always have our love, no matter where we are in the world," said Wylie.

It was silent for a few seconds before Wylie spoke again.

"But we won't be far from each other again. We'll be in Scarlet Manor with Corkun and the rest of our family, right where we belong."